P9-CAF-476

MOLE'S PITY

books by Harold Jaffe:

MOLE'S PITY

DOS INDIOS: A NOVEL (forthcoming)

R.M. BUCKE'S "WALT WHITMAN" (A Critical Edition)

THE AMERICAN EXPERIENCE:
  A RADICAL READER (co-editor)

AFFINITIES: A SHORT STORY ANTHOLOGY (co-editor)

MOLE'S PITY

by

Harold Jaffe

FICTION COLLECTIVE, INC.　　NEW YORK

Two sections of *Mole's Pity* have appeared in *Aspect.*

Two other sections, since much altered, appeared in *One* and *Dhara.*

Grateful acknowledgement is made to *The New York Times* for permission to reproduce material originally published between 1974 and 1976.

This publication is in part made possible with support from the National Endowment for the Arts in Washington, D.C., a Federal agency, the New York State Council on the Arts, Brooklyn College, and the Teachers and Writers Collaborative.

First edition.
Copyright © 1979 by Harold Jaffe.
All rights reserved.
Library of Congress Catalog No. 78-68129
ISBN: 0-914-590-52-9 (hardcover)
ISBN: 0-914590-53-7 (paperback)
Published by FICTION COLLECTIVE, INC.
Production by Coda Press, Inc.
Distributed by: George Braziller, Inc.
            One Park Avenue
            New York, N.Y. 10016

To the alone, homage

Those who find no rest in God or in history are condemned to live for those who, like themselves, cannot live: for the humiliated.

Camus

Call me Ismal [sic]

Arthur Bremer

Some blind force has put an end to the life of F. Patrician Dix, President-elect . . .

LEAP YEAR: As always. Wrapped in the earth that is himself, Mole on his roof touches Dix with his eyes. Which cannot "see."

Dix makes his way to the dais. Takes the steps slowly. Grinning, but eyes unstill.

Lights, cameras, microphones, citizens   poised:

The dais mounted on an uranium platform beneath me.

With chalk I trace a circle in the tar, within it a smaller circle. Back up ten or twelve paces to the edge of my roof. Shake open my knife, strop the blade against my thigh, aim (I cannot keep Mole's hand from trembling), loop it . . . It lands in the wider circle, several inches to the right of the smaller circle. Fetching my knife, I back up against my books, do it again: this time the knife lands even farther to the right. I do it again: the knife lands a few inches to the left of the smaller circle. Again . . .

The smaller circle looks like this: **₿**

The Dix family "logo."

When it became clear Mole was to kill him, I was compelled to stalk him, to familiarize myself with his habits so as to assure access to the fat flinty heart.

Acceding to the counsel of the Republican kaisers, that he "promote" his recently acquired image as a virulent anti-Communist, the senior Senator from New York contrived a ten-day visit to the sub-continent so that he could shake hands with the junta leaders in Chile and Brazil, and encourage the rightists who were making their move in Guatemala, El Salvador, and Nicaragua. Dix, you see, was mistakenly considered an expert on Latin America because of his family's extensive bauxite holdings in Chile, in which country he once stumbled through an "address" in something roughly approximating the native language.

In the meantime Mole adjusted his mask, procured tourist cards, and booked his flight to Guatemala three days before Dix's own DC 8 was due to lift off.

Once in Guatemala City I took a room on the top floor of the Todos Santos, a small hotel on the main drag of Zona 1, close both to the Presidential Palace and to the Pan American Hilton, where Dix and his entourage had engaged two floors.

I observed that the local, government-influenced newspapers devoted substantial space to Dix's impending arrival, alluding to him as the *"Presidente futuro de los E.U."* In the city itself I counted eleven *"Bienvenido Senador Dix"* signs, the largest of which was plastered on top of the arcade leading to the Presidential Palace.

Mole occupied his time by walking through the city (noisy, polluted, virtually without architectural interest, having been entirely rebuilt after the 1917 earthquake)—walking, reflecting on what would have to be done come Election Day. Not once questioning why it was Mole who was elected to do it.

On the morning of the evening on which Dix was due, an awkward thing happened: Mole had gone to see Peter O'Toole as Jesus in "The Ruling Class." Not until afterwards, when I got back to my room, did I become aware of not having my eyeglasses. Thinking I left them in the theatre, I hurried back there, located my seat, but even with the aid of the usher's torch, was not able to find them. Not good! They were the only pair I had brought, and nearsighted as I was it would be damned hard to see Dix. Nor would there be time to make up another pair since the swine was moving on to El Salvador the next morning. I would have to do the best I could.

The Dix jet touched down at 5:40, Dix embraced by Garcia Valdez-Kunst, the Colonel *qua* Presidente, photos snapped; then the Senator and his party surrounded by a cordon of police and funnelled into one of the main lounges. A few hundred people forgathered there, mostly government, functionaries, reporters, and an audience of eighty or so salaried to attend such occasions. In addition, a few dozen curious travelors. Also Mole, straining his eyes to witness.

Dix, a red, white and blue 🅱 button in his right lapel, an Organization of American States seal in his left, was waving a chunky hand, grinning broadly. But under his bifocals his eyes were darting warily—suddenly he tilted to the right, slipped his tongue into the ear of a bodyguard. The bodyguard stealthily withdrew to a distant corner of the lounge, then extracted a walkie-talkie which he placed to his mouth. Mole experienced a sudden tightening in his temples. . .

Dix was speechifying, slowly, painstakingly in his execrable Spanish . . .

Afterwards four white Lincoln Continentals whisked the Dix party to the city and Mayan luxury of the Pan American Hilton.

Instead of myself góing to the city, I hopped on a bus headed for Lake Atitlán, seventy kilometers to the northwest, at which site Dix was to confer with Valdez-Kunst at 9:00 PM. Like the city busses on which I had ridden, this bus was crowded with local people, many of them Indians carrying babies and produce and livestock. Fortunately I was sitting in the only seat roomy enough for my legs, directly behind the driver.

The way to Atitlán proved steeper than I had anticipated, and the old dilapidated bus, which strained and chugged while climbing, was raced unconscionably whenever the grade was straight or down mountain. Never mind the steep 180 degree curves, the Ladino driver, cigarette in mouth, gabbing loudly with a crony who collected fares, had a fire in his vivid fool eyes which proclaimed: "Machismo Before Hesitation—No Matter The Cost!" Mole observed the driver closely. His face, with its bright brief eyes, pencil mustache, fleshy cheeks, was both child-like and capriciously brutal. Reminded Mole of a psychopathic uncle on his mother's side.

The higher we got, the narrower the road became, and when we approached a curve, the driver would swerve to the left so that he had room to turn. On these occasions it was left to his apprentice to pull on the cord that worked the klaxon, so as to warn approaching vehicles. Occasionally he wouldn't bother, and twice we nearly crashed, each time forcing the approaching car off the road against the mountain.

Mole's driver was either a democrat or received a commission on fares, because never once did he hesitate to stop on a *centavo*—and anywhere—where an Indian or Indian family materialized out of the brush or from behind a mountain to board the bus. The single seat next to Mole contained a young Mayan couple with their three children, one papoosed, and three broad wicker baskets, two containing vegetables (fruits?) I had never seen: spherical, yellow, somewhat hairy. In the other baskets were four live turkeys. Thus we proceeded: seats, aisles, narrow racks above the seats not merely filled, but filled to beyond bursting. Yet aside from the constant chatter between driver and ticket-taker, there was nearly total silence within the bus; not even the children or livestock seemed inclined to utter the slightest sound. A few of the Indians dozed; some—especially the children—glanced now and then through the window; most focused straight ahead: their black eyes still and unblinking under the colorful, involute head-wraps and *rebozos* . . .

The entire thing: becalmed Indians, their creatures, the jammed bus with its abrupt thrusts and turns—had, for Mole, the aspect of a totem. The frozen starkness of the surface, yet the dynamic within, the secret tumult. Immediately following this perception, I experienced an extraordinary feeling of deflation, as if a lifetime's accumulation of tension had instantly—without fanfare—departed. But then the bus stopped, most of the Indians aboard were streaming off. We were in Chimaltenango, evidently they were attending its weekly market.

The bus, more or less half-filled, was moving again, up mountain and Mole, feeling chilled, raised his collar, pulled his jacket tighter about him. The driver, meanwhile, had negotiated a hairpin curve, and abruptly pulled to the side of the road. A party of fifteen or twenty laden Indians were patiently squatting against the mountain. The group contained several very old women, and Mole decided to relinquish his seat and move to the back of the bus. As soon as I stood I felt a tightening in the temples and dizziness from eyestrain and, particularly, I supposed, from the altitude. I made my way to the back of the bus slowly, unsteadily—when I saw him: Dix! Dix unmistakably, sitting—wedged—between two Indians, a young woman and very old man, in the seat in front of the back bench on the right side. In the meantime more and more people were pressing into me, filing into the bus. I managed though to maintain my position above Dix and to his right. What in Styx was he doing here—and alone? Was he, like Henry V, anonymously mixing among the people to gauge their morale? But what had these *campesino* Indians to do with the senior Senator from New York? Besides, far from being disguised, Dix was wearing precisely what he wore when he disembarked, except for a ludicrous (on him) native straw sombrero. Perhaps it was fear of assassination in Guatemala City. No; in that case the Dix party would have continued on to El Salvador. Doubtless there was a motive for his incredible presence, but I had no idea what it might be.

Though Mole was scrutinizing Dix openly—taking in the dyed orangish hair under the hat, the Prussian folds at the back of the short neck, the protuberant jaws, the thin, tight-lipped Lutheran minister's mouth—in spite of Mole's brazen anatomizing, and the at once apparent fact that the two of them were the only whites on the bus, Dix refused to acknowledge me . . . Happening to glance out the window, I was astonished to see a huge emerald green circle of water shimmering several thousand feet beneath us. Lake Atitlán, it must be. Surmounting it on three sides were volcanic mountains, their opened peaks shrouded in dense white cumulus clouds. But then we were turning steeply, all the while tearing down mountain—before I could take hold I was thrown off balance—flung against Dix's seat. Actually against the Indian woman sitting to his right. I was virtually in her lap for several seconds with my head twisted towards Dix—when I saw it. He had his right hand under the woman's thigh—her dress beneath her *serape* was about her knees—he had an erection . . .

The bus straightened, as did I, muttering an apology to the woman, but with my eyes on Dix. His erection—beneath the trousers stretched tightly about his thighs—was loathsomely visible. At last he looked up at me with narrow red eyes, even as he obscured his groin with his right hand. At which point I thrust out my own right hand as if to shake hands, saying: "Senator Dix, I've always wanted to meet you."

Under the tinted bifocals the pig eyes registered surprise (perhaps contempt as well), but immediately recovered their pseudo composure; deliberately he raised his stumpy right hand (with its absurd splayed thrumb), away from his crotch, towards me. Instead of accepting it, I tightened my fingers and punched him hard in the chest—but I must have punched through him, because I didn't feel anything, and my next realization was of standing precariously in the bullrushes of Lake Atitlán, gazing intently at my distorted reflection in the green water.

What Mole understood at once, nor ever forgot, is: I need not stalk Dix to know him.

March 1: Dix gone then. Yet swelling, as ever, in the sun. Or from the reflection of the uranium. I can't tell which. On my roof it has begun to rain. I am cold. Reluctantly I collect my gear (what's perishable), go inside.

Mole works for a public service radio station. Without pay.

"H-E-L-P, hello."
"Mole? Is this Mole?"

"Yes."

"Look, I don't know whether you care or not. I'm what they call a dwarf . . ."

"Yes? Go ahead."

"Yeah—look, I can't really say it the way it should be, so I wrote it down. Do you mind? I mean it doesn't really matter, does it?"

"No," I say. "I don't mind."

"Okay. I said I was a dwarf. Big head, squat body, the whole bit . . ."

He has stopped talking.

"I'm listening. Are you still there?"

"Yeah. Look, can I read it, what I wrote, I mean?"

"Yes."

"It's a poem. A kind of poem."

He reads it. Twice his voice breaks. The next day I receive the poem in the mail.

FOR THE DWARF

> the hole in the tar of the roof
> is round as his fist—
>   he
> punches at it—on
> his hands and knees, his fat
> hair tainted with night—he
> punches at the hole in the tar
> until it is large as his
> head—head first, then, he has it
> suck him back—but only
>
> —and always this horror this—
>
> back out of Dream into
> the ice dawn black about him)

The dwarf's name was Harry. There was no way Mole could get back to him.

March 3: It's stopped raining. Only the rain has almost effaced Mole's circle. I take out a piece of white chalk from my right breast pocket and trace the circle. Within it the smaller circle: **ɸ** ,which resembles the peace sign. Or the Mercedes Benz trademark. Or a snake devouring its tail. Or the ancient mark of Cain. Or a spider's web.

The spider spins out of his abdomen. Not so the Senator's grandfather, Sylvan P. Dix, who accumulated mightily. First oil; afterwards, even more shamefully, uranium.

I withdraw my knife, open it, loop it. It turns twice in the air, landing nearly within the smaller circle, quivering in the sun. The tar is hot. Dix, beneath me, is not wearing socks. It is one of his concessions to commonality. Sockless even in Montana, in the mountain cold of his three thousand acre ranch.

New York is thought of as a "cold" city. Which is, I suppose, why I'm here. If Mole is on the roof of the Pan Am Building and pointing at Dix as the hypotenuse confronts the right angle. And within range. You work it out.

"Why do you wish to work for H-E-L-P, Mr. Mole?"
"I'm interested in helping people."
"You are aware that the position comes without a stipend."
"Yes."
"Not even carfare, as a matter of fact."
"From where I live I can walk to work."
"Have you ever had any experience in what you call helping people?"
"Yes, though not any formal experience."
"In your application you used the term 'paraclete.' What exactly did you mean by that, Mr. Mole? . . ."

Sunday, March 6: Dix breaks for church. Preceded by golf:

"That's exactly right, gentlemen, I'm sixty-six years young, and gearing for a new and, obviously, super challenge. Most would call it the greatest challenge in all of public life. And I'll tell you now, in all candor, since you have queried: Not only am I most ready to take on this great challenge, I am, figuratively speaking, licking my chops. That's correct. You inquire as to how I maintain my vigor. I'll tell you. In all candor" (winks). "I take hormone shots. At least four times a week."

Pause; uneasy stirring and avid note-taking among the Press.

"Gentlemen, I can see that you are all curious as to the nature of this hormone I mentioned. Well" (rascally glint), "I'll spell it for you" (slight pause, wide smirk): "G-O-L-F. That's right. That's the secret. And gentlemen: I recommend it heartily."

Applause . . .

March 7: I chose it today. A "Savage-Anschluss Model 170 Bolt Action." With scope-mount. 30-30 caliber. 3 shot magazine. That should be enough. Certain to receive it long before E Day.

I prefer a knife. Inaccurate as I am with it. Or a bow and arrow. Connection.

People don't know how to die. The desire to die one's *own* death will soon be as rare as living one's own life. One comes on the scene, finds the life ready-made, slips it on. And death—one dies the death that belongs to the disease.

(Mole's been reading Rilke.)

Dix? His present senescence is as far as he'll get this time around. As for Mole, he need not wait for his angina.

But why Dix? As the leftist Cambridge don writing for the *New York Review of Books* put it: "Of what use was the assassination of one more fool, powerful as he was, beastly as he was?"

A pertinent enough question. The "answer" to which

forms the basis of this narrative. Let me here cite three names, in no particular order:

Sri Sen

Abaddon

Mole's father

Marya (we live together), resembles my father. Slim, fine spun dark hair, pale skin . . . She wishes (she's often said) she knew him. Before he died.

March 8: Mole's roof? Not the Pan Am Building of course, but a tenement. A lived-in place. Corners of shadow. Begonias, moon on the grille outside your window. Outside your window, as within and throughout the tenement: the always body of the dream about to burst, because after you, another . . .

My roof has a certain winsomeness. The steep ascent. The heavy cover, like a coffin lid, though quite square. I've learned to raise it with one arm, with the other maintaining my balance on the narrow iron ladder.

Tar . . . TV aerials like pawn warriors. The sooty cityscape beneath sky.

Beneath the TV aerials, the old model Admiral. Or Stromberg-Carlson. Or Zenith with its round screen. It is the centerpiece of the living room in its mahogany cabinet and is corona'd with artificial flowers. Lofty and erect, it stands between the two windows with their venetian blinds. Facing the other blinds across the narrow gutter.

The furniture: on sale from a department store warehouse. Symmetrically positioned. Sofa, two easy chairs, coffee-table, end-tables with lamps. Two pictures, one an oil reproduction, gaudily framed, of "Venice," the gondolas gobs of Veronese green receding into the background.

Above, on the poorest tars: pigeons. Rats with wings. The male ruffling his wings, aimlessly strutting about the female. The Puerto Rican elevator operator, squatting on his hams, reaches his right arm through the grate. The bird nuzzles against his fingers.

Next morning, just after dawn, his adolescent son undoes the wire that serves for a lock, pulls open the coop door, leaping back. Then boy plunging down the fire-escape to . . . Not to school.

The clothesline is a fugue. Underwear, socks, shirts, underwear . . . Clean not new.

The chimney's black smoke. Now oil.

The used rubber. Trojan brand. Remnants of the teenage passion still palpitating in the far corner of the roof.

Expanse. Tar smelling of earth, aspiring to sky.

Here Mole has set his books. Stretched his hammock . . .

In 3f live the Metzes: Artie, Fay, Sheldon, and Irwin. Sheldon Metz one of my first and closest friends. An unusual boy, athletic, bright, virtuous beyond his years. Though not in any way extraordinary physically, there was—what to call it?— an infra-texture about Sheldon which nearly everyone who knew him felt, which Mole liked very much. It was the summer of '51, while the Metz family was summering at Kiamesha Lake in the Catskills, that Sheldon became ill. He walked to the ambulance under his own power, carrying his small portable radio tuned to the Brooklyn Dodger game. "Infantile Paralysis." That eerily abstract and forbidding title. It was rarely called Polio then.

Sheldon had contracted Infantile Paralysis, nearly dying of it, spending the next four years in and out of an iron lung. Finally returning to apartment 3f on iron crutches, the right side of his body twisted, stunted; his face long and drawn; but his eyes clear—if not trusting, at least not unforgiving. (Mole could not forgive.) After losing nearly three years of school, Sheldon returned. Went on the Brooklyn College, travelled there by subway, on his iron crutches, painstakingly making his way to the last, usually uncrowded, car.

The Metz apartment smelled good, sweet, cake-like. Safe. Sheldon and Irwin, his older brother, listened to "Stan Lomax on Sports" every weekday evening at 7 o'clock. Artie and Fay would be sipping tea with lemon, talking quietly. Fay, Sheldon's mother, was a stout woman with an open face and varicose veins in her legs, which became visibly aggravated during and after Sheldon's illness. Artie was a tall, thin, bland-faced bald man who worked in textiles. He was a self-possessed person, who remained that way—at least outwardly. Mole knew that both parents blamed themselves for their son's misfortune.

Irwin, though gentle, was the least impressive Metz. He wore spectacles and had a bad case of dandruff—this last seemed to Mole an indication somehow of Irwin's inner turbulence. He was a lazy, good-natured fellow who became a substitute teacher of General Science in a neighborhood high school.

March 9: "Can you hear me?"

"Yes—yes, I'm listening."

"Mole, listen to me, man. I ain't gonna do it jus yet. But if and when I do I'll tell you how I'm gonna do it. Can you hear me alright?"

"Yes."

"Looka here, Mole, like I said, I'm not fixin to do it jus yet and like I don't wanna hog your lines and shit. I mean there could be some rube gonna do it right now less he get through to you. You follow, Mole?"

"Yeah, I do. Don't worry about anyone else calling. Go ahead, talk. I'm listening."

"Dig it, Mole. At night. No moon. Climb out on one of them cables of the George Washington Bridge. You know how fuckin high up that is, man! Climb out on one of them. Make sure your back is to the water. Holding on. Feeling it, man. Yeah, jus when it gettin real tasty—you let go. Jus like that. Back first, slip away. Dark to dark, baby. How do that sound, Mole? Can you dig it?"

H-E-L-P comes out of a loft. Quite south. Below Houston. It has no decor to speak of. Five phones, Sklar, the engineer. Also G.J., who does this and that. Mole, who walks to work.

While others sleep, awake. East at Twelfth Street for several blocks. To Third Avenue, where the whores press their haunches against broken shop windows. Fingering the tracks on their arms.

South to the Bowery, smelling of India: its sorrow without its shadow, God's shadow. Here I sometimes pause for a coffee.

To Houston Street and east, where the Jews have died, and some few yet scratch at living. Buttons, haberdashery, hats. Small narrow shops with a single door. Wizened canals receding to darkness. Intestines clogged with accumulation, which is everything. Not anything. Since the first wanderer, hunchbacked with history. Though it wasn't yet written. At the shop's rear, under a naked bulb, mother, father, only son huddle about the radio, which, though broken, broadcasts Wagner. "Siegfried"—the golden future . . . The mother is biting her arm.

How many times have his vast lungs drawn in air, wanting to embrace them whole, invest them with blackness. Their own. Light.

Mole insists he isn't "strange."

(You have defaulted your birthright.)

At least one has known me. One of the letter writers to the station. The majority of the letters have been favorable. Among those which haven't, a handful or so have aimed for my jugular. Or my testicles. Of these, only one has been on target. A very special letter writer whom I've named Abaddon. I refer to "him" merely out of convenience. In fact on occasion he is almost female. His first note which arrived "coincidentally" on the day I hit upon Dix, was written in a literate hand in light blue ink on a small unlined index card. It read:

Congo Coons Rape Nuns

Aside from the damage he does *inside* my house,

Abaddon hadn't communicated with me in a long while. When I read the card there was the initial alarm. But then I remembered I had been expecting him, and Mole smiled— crookedly.

March 10: Though the tar is hot my body is cold here on my roof. The mind works. Peony Dix: Dix's niece, whom I tutored in Abnormal Psychology. She was preparing to transfer from Sarah Lawrence (where she had done miserably), to a college for spoiled rich girls here in the city. Blond, thin, stiff-limbed, nineteen years old. She told me once she had no recollection of anything that happened to her before age ten. I considered fucking her (infusing her with memory). It could have been done. But she inspired in me no desire whatever. All this happened some five years ago, for a period of about ten months. I used to visit her where she lived with her mother and maids. Not once did I see her mother. I was paid fifteen dollars per hour.

Currently as you know I am employed at H-E-L-P. It will be my last job. Though it pays nothing. What then do I do for money? Think of me as having toppled out of the pages of Henry James's final period. That is to say, with means. For James—though not with his elder brother's urgency—came to know. I'm speaking of the phantoms. Of John Marcher who, hurling himself onto his love's grave, had become the thumper he was waiting for.

Under Abaddon's prodding, Mole used to dream of his mailbox filled with urgent letters, parcels. But either he could not locate the box, or the key to open it. A recurrent dream.

No more . . . tossing my knife. Higher this time, so that it revolves three times before landing . . .

Mole is concerned about his books. 1500 books he is in the process of transferring from his apartment to his roof. The problem is three-fold: to smuggle them aboard; to maintain them aboard without arousing suspicion; and to protect them from inclement weather. Already there has been a casualty: a first edition of Elias Canetti's *Auto da Fé*, waterlogged from

Sunday dawn's heavy rain. After that Mole moved his books from the north to the east wall of the roof, apparently well-shielded from the weather by the tar overhang. But I will have to wait for the next rain to be certain.

March 11: The National Rifle Association (Babylon, Long Island Chapter) approved my application on a "contingency basis," according to a letter from the chapter secretary: "Denton R. Haertel (Lt. Col., Army, Ret.)". I will be using their range twice a week beginning Thursday, the 24th. I should become proficient long before November 3. No problem. Though he has lost most of his juice, Dix is a splendid target. Fat hips, thick white skin. Or if Mole happens to fire high: the preposterous head with the area around the occiput oddly pushed forward. The fetally translucent ears, long and long-lobed, but close to his head. Dyed hair. Mussolini jaws.

I caress my knife. It's a fine knife. I picked it up for a few *paise* in Benares. Sri Sen chose it for me. It is a knife with a history. Dating back to before the Mughals. Shiva, who both dreamt and did, whose lingam was infinite, who, with matted hair, sat straight-backed alone, on Mount Meru, one-pointed for eons. Shiva engraved in jade on my knife-handle.

Let me say now that I lived in India. For two years. I travelled throughout the country, from Kerala to the northernmost Himalayas. I learned two methods of meditation. One from an orthodox Shaivite Hindu in Bangalore. The other from a Tantric Buddhist in Rishikesh. This was a while ago, but I haven't stopped practicing. I continue to correspond with Sri Sen, my teacher, one of the few Buddhist Indians still living in India. He is also (oddly, you will think) quite taken with politics. That is to say, taken with what politics does to people. He knows of his student's predilections, and approves. More than approves—advises. Though usually not conventionally.

Among other skills, he has taught me to "gherao Karma," which might be loosely translated as "kicking ass."

When your natural flow (Dharma) becomes impeded by local, adventitious obstacles, dynamite first. Then analyze in the afterglow. That's Tantra. At least as taught by Sri Sen, to whom, incidentally, I just sent an international money order for twenty dollars. Holy men need money to keep them in silks, which are much more becoming than *khadi*. I'm joking. Sen spends most of his time nearly naked. He has other, more functional expenses.

How does Dix fit in? *Atcha:*

Once, late at night, in December, being summoned, Mole left Sri Sen's ashram in Rishikesh and boarded the train for Mysore in the south. I had wanted to ride third class, but it was a very long and uncomfortable ride. Something like thirty-six hours. So I decided to go first class, which meant sharing a pullman with no more than four people.

It was just before midnight when I got on the train, and I was surprised to find that I had the entire pullman to myself. I climbed on top of one of the racks, and fell asleep almost at once. I slept fitfully because we were in mountainous country and the train was jolting. Finally I was jolted awake altogether, and turned to look through the window, but could see nothing through the blackness and mist. I was about to doze again when I got the strong impression that there was someone else in my pullman. Climbing down from the rack, I edged along the wall until I found the light switch, but the light wasn't working. The corridor itself was almost entirely black but for the queer refraction of the locomotive's headlight. And I had no notion where the ticket-taker with his torch might be. But, after all, what difference would it make? Very likely there *were* one or more people in the pullman with me. One is rarely physically alone in this country. I didn't know why I experienced a vague sense of dread on this occasion. Perhaps it had to do with something I had been dreaming. In any case, the feeling, whatever its genesis, was already fading.

I edged back along the wall to my niche near the window. Taking hold of the top rack to climb back up, I touched something—releasing my hand at once. It was flesh. A naked foot. Someone somehow had gotten into my place! My first impulse was to get out of the pullman at once. But I fought it.

What was there to be frightened of? Indians were peaceable, if aggressive in certain things like getting ahead of you on line, or grabbing a place to sleep. Which is what happened now no doubt.

There was another rack on the opposite side. Was anyone in it? No, empty. I raised myself onto it and lay down on my side facing the window across from me. The car was perfectly still. The Indian man (as I assumed he was) slept soundlessly. I myself was beginning to feel drowsy again, but immediately I closed my eyes, I opened them again. The man across from me with his eyes wide open, was glaring at me.

"What is it?" I said—shouted nearly. "What do you want?" No answer. And suddenly I couldn't see his eyes. Either he had closed them. Or perhaps I had merely imagined they were open in the first place. I didn't know what to think. To do. I thought of going to the toilet in the corridor, but without lights it would be pointless. I didn't have a match. Aside from the occasional howl of a jackal or faraway yelping of a dog, there wasn't the slightest indication of any creature living. My heart was beating rapidly. In order to combat it, I began to do a breathing exercise according to Sen: inhaling through the left nostril, pausing five seconds, then exhaling though the right, lengthily. As usual, it helped. I was feeling more relaxed, and drowsy again. But before letting my eyes close, I looked hard at the rack across from me. No movement, no sign of eyes opening. And still no breathing; of course the train was making a considerable rumbling, so that it would have been hard to hear distinctly even at such a close range. My body wanted to sleep . . .

Light woke me. The ticket-taker's torch. He was making his rounds. Outside it was still dark. On the rack across from me was—nobody. I asked the ticket-taker about the man who had been on the rack. He didn't seem to understand. I said that when I fell asleep someone had been sleeping across from me. The ticket-taker said that when he entered the pullman he saw only me. I asked whether the train had stopped since Rishikesh. He said it hadn't, nor was it scheduled to stop for another two hours.

After he left, I jumped down from the rack and tried the

light switch. It worked. I examined the rack near the window.
There was no indication that anyone had slept there. But what
indication could there be? There were no pillows or blankets
in the pullman. I went out into the corridor, and into the toilet
closest to the pullman. Nobody was there. I returned to the
car, kept the lights on and read.

When a few hours later the train stopped at Agra, a
bourgeois Indian couple and child came into my pullman.
They wished to sleep; besides, the lights had gone off again of
their own accord. So we all slept. Again, my own sleep was
fitful, and the entire time, even when I was partially awake, a
curious biblical phrase kept going through my head. Awake, I
repeated it to myself, but had no recollection of ever having
read it—though I must have as a child. It was: "Put thy hand
under my thigh—Genesis." That's how it went, as though the
word Genesis was part of the quotation.

When the train stopped again it was daylight, and the
Indian couple and child got off. I continued to think about the
phrase, even repeating it aloud, wondering if it was an
anagram. In fact I had no idea what its significance was for me.

When I finally arrived in Mysore, I wrote to Sen,
detailing the entire experience from when I boarded in
Rishikesh to dreaming of the odd phrase. He wrote back at
once, and what he said was: examine your thigh. I did. Behind
my left thigh just below my buttock was a mark. About half an
inch in diameter, oval, pink, intricate. Since then more than a
few women have expressed their admiration for it. G.J. called
it a "delicious miniature mandala." Most people who have
noticed it have confused it with a birthmark. Which is not far
wrong, since in a sense it has marked a birth—or genesis.

I ought to have mentioned that the man who took my
place on the rack—his foot when I accidentally touched it was
cold, stiff. Sri Sen later informed me that the man in my rack
was dead, that he was my *"preta"* who had followed me not
merely from Rishikesh, but from the States; that he had been
with me for a very long time. That he had *bitten* me on the
back of the thigh as I slept. Abaddon, in short. The bite
looked like this:

March 12: Abaddon it was who left a stone on my roof. Excellent for blade sharpening. As I am rubbing my blade on the stone, Abaddon winks his blinds: closes, opens, closes them. Talk about resourcefulness, that boy-o is the best gumshoe going. Let him! Sri Sen is with me. I know what I have to do. My eye-glasses are soiled. I rub them with my handkerchief. It is cold. I am tired of hating.

Marya's background might be of interest to you. Her grandfather, a French Jansenist, left Lyons in the first years of the century for Cuenca in southern Ecuador, therein to impress his unremitting Jesus on the Inca. The photographs Mole has seen indicate him to have been a large, rigid and vigorous man (he reminded me of Kafka's father in his middle years), and true to his image, he impregnated several of his converts—not merely with Jesus. At least one (Marya's grandmother) was sent heavy with child to northern Minnesota, whither the Jansenist's youngest brother had emigrated some years earlier to ply at corn and cattle. Traumatized by the sudden severing from her family and the radical change of environment, Marya's grandmother delivered prematurely, herself dying in the process. The girl child (Antoinette) was reared with the brother's own four children, like them enrolling in Augustana College (where, among other distinctions, she was elected "Homecoming Queen" in her junoir year). Upon graduation she was married to her college sweetheart, a Lutheran pre-veterinarian student from Omaha. Marya, then, like Mole, spent her early years in Nebraska, the youngest (and evidently the most gifted) of the three daughters, the only one of the three with dark hair and something delicately hawklike about her face.

She left Omaha after her graduation from high school, came to New York City, where she worked alternately as a waitress and illustrator, meanwhile studying Art History in Columbia University's General Studies division. On two successive summers she travelled to Ecuador and chilly reunions with her grandmother's family (her grandfather's

Jansenism had long before been supplanted by Papists and Evangelicals); the third summer she spent in Italy and Greece, where she conceived of a series of lithographs on the theme of Orpheus. She had just completed a delicate and shadowy version of Orpheus charming Charon with his pipe (not his lyre)—when she met Mole on a Thursday afternoon in front of the frozen food counter of the A&P near Fourteenth Street. She became his *abassy*.

March 13: Though in Marya's arms, last night I dreamt again that I was pushing my frail father up Fort Washington Avenue, which turned into the steps leading to my roof. Every time I seemed to be making the least headway, his nearly inert body would slip back down. I was becoming smaller and smaller . . .

"Awake" and walking through the lower East Side streets to H-E-L-P, I came upon an old man in an oversized greatcoat and blue watch-cap pulled low over his ears. He was standing in the middle of the sidewalk looking up—as if expecting a visitation. I paused next to him and looked up also: nothing but the customary two or three smog-veiled stars. When the old man turned to me, I saw that he was very old indeed, with a wrinkled, chap-fallen face and black, disconsolate eyes. He was wearing gloves. Grey, woolen gloves.

I smiled at him.

He looked at me blankly. "I like a go back. Where I live."

"Where do you live?"

He gestured with his hand.

"Uptown?" Mole asked.

The old man looked confused. "I am eighty-one years old."

"You are? That's something." I meant it.

"Yeh."

"Are you a New Yorker?"

"Yeh. Napoli. Italy. You know?"

"I know of it. I've never been to Napoli. I've been to Italy though. Venice."

"Ah!" The old man gestured with his hand. Mole couldn't tell whether it was approving or deprecating.

"But you've lived here a long time? In New York?"

"Fifty years."

"In Manhattan all that time?"

He didn't seem to understand the question—then suddenly he did. "Yessir!"

"What are you doing down here now?"

"Ah." He withdrew a small brown paper bag from his greatcoat pocket, holding it open for me to look inside.

Three identical tins of anchovies. I removed one: it read "Rozzo and Sons, Importers, Canal Street."

"You can't buy these anchovies uptown, closer to your house?"

"I liva here fifty years." He poked with his index finger at the broken pavement beneath him, as if he had lived his fifty years in that very spot.

We were standing on the south side of Houston Street, right off Canal. To our right was a fenced-in parking lot, which though in ill-repair looked as if it had been constructed recently. I saw a few piles of rubble at the rear of the lot, probably remnants of the just-razed tenement which previously had occupied the site.

Mole was beginning to understand. "You lived in that house that was torn down?" I motioned to the parking lot.

"Fifty years! I liva here fifty years." The old man wasn't looking at me, or at the site of his destroyed house—but vaguely over my left shoulder. His eyes had become wet.

For the first time since they commenced to talk, Mole realized that he was cold. That it was growing dark and becoming colder.

"Look, why don't we go home. Where you're living now, I mean. I'll walk with you. It's getting late and your people will be concerned about you. It's too cold to stand outside like this."

"People!" The old man made a dismissive gesture with his hand. "No gotta."

"You're living alone?"

"Alone. Alone."

Mole didn't say anything for a minute. The old man was still looking over his shoulder.

"Well, you're not planning on staying here, are you?"

"Stay! Why? What's a here?"

"Okay. Let's start back. What street do you live on uptown?"

I took hold of the old man's arm, gently prompting him to walk slowly west along Houston.

"Fourteentha Street."

"You walked all the way down here from Fourteenth Street?"

"Sure. Walka."

"Where on Fourteenth Street?"

"Near the bank. You like-a?" He patted the pocket in which he had put the anchovies.

"Anchovies? Yes, I do. I'd like to get you home, though. Do you remember the name of the bank? What street it is on?"

"Big-a bank. Eighth Avenue."

Mole, who knew the area, didn't recall a bank being precisely there.

"Was it Chase Manhattan, Edison Savings, Dix Chemical? Was it any of these banks, do you remember? First National City?"

The old man didn't answer. He pulled his greatcoat collar, which had lost its button, more tightly about his neck.

"Look, do you have any identification on you? Something with your address on it? A wallet?"

The old man didn't immediately respond—but then he extracted a small change purse, which he offered to Mole.

A single dollar bill and perhaps half that amount in small change were in it. No papers. Mole handed it back to him.

"Do you know of any phone numbers? A relative? Somebody who knows your address?"

"Here no got. Napoli got."

"Are we walking in the right direction? Was this the way you came down here?"

"Houston-a Street."

"This is Houston. Do you remember it?"

The old man, who had slowed down, was looking to his left. "Vecchio," he said, as if to himself.

At the west corner of Chrystie and Houston was a minuscule winestore called Vecchio. Behind the rusted iron grate, the shelves in the window were empty.

"Was he a friend of yours—Vecchio?"

"Ah, no more," the old man moved his hand sharply away from his side. "Vecchio no more."

"Does his family still live here, do you know?"

"No. No liva."

"The best idea for us, I think, would be to take a bus. To Fourteenth Street. Then we'll look for where you live."

They walked half a block farther along Houston to a yellow line painted along the curb.

It was dark now, much colder. Mole led the old man away from the street to the shelter of a closed newspaper kiosk.

The Fourteenth Street bus came and they got on it. Mole sat on the aisle side and the old man sat stiffly by the window, his eyes fixed in front of him. They got off at Fourteenth and Seventh Avenue and commenced to walk west.

There were banks on either side near Seventh, but the old man shook his head no when Mole asked whether he recognized where he was. Nor did he register anything like recognition as they walked the long street between Seventh and Eighth Avenue.

Mole was becoming more concerned. Already he was nearly twenty minutes late for H-E-L-P.

At the corner of Eighth, they stopped. Not a bank in sight.

"It's not this street then?"

The old man shook his head.

"Maybe I ought to call a policeman." Looking around, I didn't see either a cop or a phone.

The old man was pointing north. With his other hand he tugged at my sleeve. Mole followed his finger to a store on the west side of Eighth Avenue near Fifteenth Street.

When they drew close to it I saw that it was a funeral

parlor called "Rios."

"Do they know you inside?"

But instead of stopping, the old man increased his pace—
he was listing to the left, as if he knew where he was going. At
Fifteenth Street we turned left: still another long street filled
with old tenements.

Mole's companion was breathing hard, wheezing.

"Would you like to rest?"

The old man motioned with his head, as if it was just a bit
farther west on Fifteenth Street. But at the corner of Fifteenth
and Ninth Avenue, he stopped, apparently confused.

I was about to phone the police from a public telephone,
when he was gesturing again—this time to a newly constructed
low-rent housing development on Ninth and Tenth Avenues,
between Sixteenth and Seventeenth Streets.

Again Mole took the old man's arm. "Is this it? Where
you live?"

My companion turned to me with the semblance of a
smile on his lips. His eyes still inconsolable.

Mole was led to an entrance near Seventeenth Street
which read "Community Center." A guard semi-asleep in a
chair tilted against the wall, noticed us through one eye and
reluctantly straightened.

"Do you know this gentleman?" Mole asked. "He seems
to have gotten lost."

"Yeah, he lives here," the guard said matter-of-factly.

"I know him," the old man said about the guard as he led
me (he was holding the fingers of my hand) into a rectangular
common room. Several other old people were spaced about
this room, sitting in hard-backed folding chairs, watching TV,
dozing.

A few raised their heads as we entered. But with
something less than curiosity.

"My friend!" the old man announced, meaning Mole,
still gripping my fingers.

One very old lady with an artificial yellow daisy pinned in
her thinning white hair, smiled.

"Watcha television," the old man said, not wanting me to
leave just yet.

I sat next to him in the underfurnished, overheated, rectangular room, and gazed at Channel 4 . . .

March 14: Dix went to Brown, where, as a demonstration of *égalité*, he volunteered to work in the student union for five hours a week—despite his family's billions, despite his father's purchasing his admission to Brown in the first place. (According to the Senator's admission, much later: while at Choate he preferred "joshing around to hitting the books.") In any case, Dix's offer to work was refused, the jobs being essential for those scholarship students who needed the money.

Young Dix, whose double major was Economics and Political Science, married Dorothea Hedwig, out of Philadelphia and Vassar, in the Brown College chapel on Commencement Day.

Presently the Senator is campaigning. Thrusting out his hand. Eating pizza. Knishes. Winking broadly. Calling people "fella".

I try holding the knife differently—by the blade. Also I try a lower trajectory . . . no good. It lands beyond the inner circle.

Thirty-four years old. Marya; Sklar, the station engineer; his wife Zelda—and Mole, dining out to celebrate my birthday.

Sklar, who's a vegetarian and follower of the evangelical nutritionist Jethro Kloss, is also an obsessive icon-smasher.

"That one," he points with his broad thumb, as we enter the restaurant—"That one, Mole. I can see it in her walk. The schvantzy way she moves her hips. My prediction is kaput unless she gets to you before the end of the week. No shit. Except I'm not so sure she's worth it, Mole. Worth saving."

We are in one of my favorite restaurants, Makyo: quaint and Japanese, and near my apartment, where I can hear the river.

Marya presses her thigh against mine under the table.

Sklar has ordered double portions of *sushi*, which he scoops into his mouth with chopsticks. An occasional departure from fundamental vegetarianism is condoned by the master (Sklar informs, mouth full), provided it is followed by a high enema composed of equal portions of catnip, fenugreek, and rosemary.

Each time Sklar opens his mouth to scoop, he closes his eyes, breathing thickly through his short broad nose as he chews. He resembles an athletic, mildly retarded H.L. Mencken. Women seem to find him attractive.

As evidenced by his wife Zelda, who, though Jewish, merited the accolade "Gorgeous Gal" from the New York *Daily News* a year ago, when she was photographed sunbathing in Riis Park. Zelda has long thin fingers, and the chopsticks, which she doesn't know how to use, look like chaotic knitting needles in her hands.

"Where are you going to have your high enema, Sklar?"

"Huh? At home. After this orgy," he says, not looking up from his eating, "I'm going to have me another. Guess who's going to give it to me—the enema?" He waves his chopsticks around as if I have the choice of anyone in the restaurant.

"Not Kloss himself?"

"No. He's deceased, Mole. Zelda." He rivets his right chopstick so that it's pointing at Zelda's left nipple, not quite touching it. "Zelda's going to administer the enema." Sklar turns his large head to his wife and smirks, showing lots of small beige teeth.

"I see you're looking at my teeth, Mole."

"Yes. They're nice and straight."

"Calamus and black cohosh, chum. Three enemas a week with these two babies will take care of any foulness you got lodging in your lower tubes."

The waitress delivers more plates to our table.

"Happy birthday, Mole," Zelda says.

Marya turns and kisses me on the mouth.

"How come you didn't do that on my birthday, Marya?" From Sklar.

"When was *your* birthday?"

"I thought you knew. August 7. With the friggin lions. Also some famous people. June Allyson and Patrician Dix, to name two. Now can I have that kiss?"

Marya stretches across the table and kisses him briefly on the lips.

Watching Marya stretch gets Mole hard. I like backs, and hers is lovely.

Marya orders the *sukiyaki* dinner. She is not an adventurous eater.

Zelda, who has no idea what she is doing, has selected three à la carte dishes according to her principles of euphony, though she has difficulty pronouncing even the simplest Japanese word. She is already somewhat tipsy from the *saki*.

Mole has ordered cold spinach salad with sesame seeds, *tanuki udon*, and a bottle of Kirin beer.

"How do you do it, Mole?" Zelda asks in her breathless starlet's voice, a look of semi-drunken earnestness in her lovely eyes. "I've never asked you that before. I mean it's even hard for me to understand how Sklar does it, and he gets paid for doing it. Besides, he doesn't have to speak to any of them. I mean doesn't it depress you?"

"No, Zelda, it doesn't depress me."

"It gives him satisfaction," Marya says.

"Satisfaction and a hardon," Sklar says.

Zelda makes a rasping laughing sound.

"It's called necro-feel-her," Sklar says with deep fried shrimp in his mouth.

"But they're mostly males, aren't they? I mean these people who call and stuff?" Zelda's voice has suddenly become drunkenly seductive, and she thrusts her Tempest Storm tits at Mole as she asks this.

"No, not really. Males and females call more or less equally. But the station has been going for only three months, so it's hard to see any real patterns yet."

Zelda, who stopped listening about half-way through my explanation, is tapping her fingernails on the table waiting for me to stop.

"But can you actually *feel* them over the phone?"

"Here come de *teri-yaki*," Sklar announces.

When the diminutive, middle-aged Japanese waitress turns to go back to the kitchen, Sklar points a chopstick at her. "That one, Mole. Kaput! I can see it in her eyes."

"In her eyes!" Zelda giggles, catching (she thinks) the echo of that persistent silliness about "slanty eyes, slanty snatches."

March 15: Yesterday I was thirty-four years old. Paying out the rope. The kind you hang clothing from. Fixing my hammock between a TV aerial and the flue . . .

Swaddled, looking up. The scrap of yellow moon. Pascal had no smog to contend with. (The image of my dead father comes to mind.)

I've always been partial to hammocks. The spider spins from his abdomen. When he bags his prey he swaddles it, before eating it. Just so, I seem to have always attracted smothering women, after the image of my mother (*requiescat*, etc.), which is why I've not married. Marya is an exception.

Mole turns to his books, handsomely tiered against the east wall, removes a copy of Sliespsova:

> If the priest dreams of his *abassy* and has sexual relations with her, he wakes feeling well, certain that he will be summoned and no less certain that he will be successful. If, on the contrary, he dreams that he sees his *abassy* full of blood and swallowing the sick person's soul, he knows that he will not succeed even if summoned. Finally, if he is summoned without having had any dream, he is disconcerted and does not know what to do.

March 16: Tonight I witnessed violence. On my way to H-E-L-P, walking east on Eleventh Street, I saw at the corner of Eleventh and Third Avenue two men squaring off. A lean, sullen, tattooed man, and a stocky, broad-chested Italian, each with his fists up, circling the other. The tattooed man moved suddenly, lunging with both fists at the other's chest and neck. It was as hard as he could hit, yet the broad-chested Italian received both blows full, scarcely flinching. That was it. The lean one had nothing left. I heard a collective, anticipatory, joyful shudder from the woebegone crowd that had silently gathered. I turned away.

Violence. The furious pleasure Mole's people took in watching it . . .

Yet by the time I arrived at the station, the brawling, the bystanders murdering in their brains—all of it—had faded into something like dance.

Despite Abaddon.

"This is H-E-L-P, your community-minded station on FM. My name is Mole. If you're feeling pain and would like someone to talk about it with, or merely someone to listen while you talk, try me. That's what I'm here for.

"Every call will be broadcast as is on the air. No taping, no censoring. If you want to talk with me, but not on the air, tell me that, and I'll transfer to a private line.

"The reason we are on the air is that there are lots of people in this city—in this world, really—who are having a hard time making it. It is important to realize that far from being alone, you are part of a vast network of suffering brothers and sisters.

"Why is this realization necessary? Listen to us—listen to each other—and maybe you'll discover why."

Dix says to Ronald, his bodyguard: "Get me my clubs, fella."

When Ronald returns, Dix says: "Set them under the Utrillo. I want to practice my putting. Oh, I see you're wearing a wrist-band. Real hep, fella. You remind me of Gilbert Roland."

Dix, whose knowledge of "high" art is well-known, prides himself in his knowledge of the popular arts. Among popular "artists," he is partial to Joe Dallesandro, who, Dix

says, "reminds me of early Brando. Like Brando, he has that
special something, that *je ne sais quoi.*"

This is taking place in Vermont, in Dix's "chalet," which
contains seven bathrooms, each with a bidet. (Dix, who has
circled the globe a dozen times, has bleeding hemorrhoids and
a prolapsed anus.)

10:30 P.M., the Senator at his sitz, phones Ronald:
"Ronnie, get me Senator Vorst."

"Heinie, Pat here. I didn't get you out of the sack, did I?"

"Hell no."

"Good. Well, how does it look, fella?"

"Real good, Pat. Couldn't look any better at this point in
the campaign. Just don't go and get yourself knocked off or
nothin. We've got too much on the line to lose you now—
where are you phoning me from?"

"The chalet. Don't sweat it, fella."

"I'm not, Pat. Don't worry about me. Like I said, I'm
feeling real good about the input I've been getting. Things
seem to be moving real good. Couldn't be better."

Usually Mole returns from the station between 3:15 and
4:00 A.M. Commencing with his return from his very first
evening at H-E-L-P, Mole's phone has been ringing at about
4:00 A.M., four or five times a week. When I say hello into the
receiver, Abaddon merely attends, not responding, not
hanging up. Twice I heard him breathe, slowly, rhythmically—
unless it was the echo of Mole's own breathing. After a minute
I hang up. He won't phone until the next night, or the night
after next.

Initially Marya was unnerved by these calls—until Mole
explained that they were an unfortunate but necessary
component of what he was trying to accomplish at H-E-L-P.
Marya, feeling his feeling, accepted this.

I've said that Dix is a Republican. Formerly he was
considered a "liberal" Republican, but in the last three or four

years he has moved markedly to the right in order to appease the clubhouse fathers. He commenced to concentrate his scorn on crime-in-the-streets, "welfare-chiselers," "reverse racism" in the UN General Assembly . . . all the while shuttling about the country, inserting his tongue into the ears of local honchos.

Almost imperceptibly (at first), his hips became broader. His occiput receded, finessing the mass of his head forward. His face, between eyes and chin, began to converge. He neglected to snip his nose-hairs. Acquaintances found themselves referring to him in private as "Cockamamie." Too, his prolapsed anus flared noticeably, so that nude he resembled some peculiar species of baboon.

Meanwhile, Dorothea, his wife out of Vassar, went bats.

March 17: Gwendolyn Stephens, Dix's gal-friday, received a bizarre piece of mail at Dix's Rockefeller Center offices today. Addressed to Senator Forrest Patrician Dix, it contained a polaroid photograph of a detumescent penis. Nothing else.

It inspired in Gwendolyn a sardonic guffaw. Immediately she phoned Ronald, the bodyguard, who was in an office on another floor. Together they shared a laugh at the photo, after which Ronald, unleashing his own truncheon, rummaged Gwen on the carpet.

When Mole returned from the station he was surprised to find Marya in her studio—she usually worked in the daytime exclusively. The windows were wide open, the floor was covered with newspaper, and Marya, on one knee, was intently studying a canvas on the floor.

Mole gently kissed her.

"You're working."

"Yes."

"Orpheus?"

"Yes. Daylight isn't important here. Somehow I just found that out."

"Which one is this going to be, Marya?"

"Descending. This dark grey here—kind of cylindrical-shaped—is the opening. Euridice is already gone from him."

"Hmm."

Marya picked up a wad of cotton from the floor and smudged the green in a corner of the canvas.

"It's going well?"

"Yes," Marya smiled, stood, wiped her hands on a cloth, kissed Mole on the cheek.

"How was it tonight at the station?—"

The phone rang . . .

March 18: A policeman near the entrance to my tenement.

(Why now?)

I examine him. A young, spunky Irish cop. His uniform spic and span. Shoes spit-shined. Four citations above his shield.

I veer towards the adjoining building, angle in through the side entrance. Up the stairs two at a time . . . The roof is locked.

Down again. The cop still there. I'll tell him I'm Mole from H-E-L-P. Maybe he'll let me up.

When I get close to him, though, I see that he isn't a cop at all, but a Con Edison worker, a meter-reader with his flashlight in his pocket.

the roof is cold

My father was a meter-reader. The children used to mistake him for a policeman because of his uniform.

The roof is cold tonight.

March 19: Dix at prayer in his Georgetown snuggery. DuVal Stett, Democrat from Tennessee and Minority Whip in the Senate, the prayer leader. Stett it was who was responsible for the group's name: "Life's Sacred Duty: Jesus," available on buttons and bumper-stickers as "LSD— Jesus." It was widely (at least in Tennessee) considered a master-stroke in combating the damnifying influence of dope on our youth.

Après prayer: Dix at his sitz with DuVal Stett, who promises him Memphis.

"Which should mean Tennessee. Am I right, Val?"

"You couldn't be rahter." Stett shows teeth.

Mole's father liked opera. Every Saturday afternoon. The radio dial slightly off the band. My father scratching his head. Seeming to ruminate.

He had lovely distances. He was a weak man.

The roof . . .

I loved him

. . .is cold

On his gravestone I had inscribed: "More sinned against than sinning."

I was thinking of both of us. Of Mole's people.

Yesterday I dreamt I lost my knife.

Not at all. I'm holding it in my hand at this minute. Looking up. It's dark but for a sliver of yellow moon. My birthright. Cold enforcer of the heart's privileges.

This is not the first roof.

—Listen to me!

Before roof it was cliff. Or sand space confronting sea. Or frozen hovering between moon and . . . you.

Which is what this is about. Fire that must be retrieved. But also water, that we regain motility, play, our birthright.

I say I felt this, what I'm doing, since my first darkness.

My father died too early.

No matter. He joined—he joined the Dance. My roof no longer strange. Mole wills that it be no longer strange)

The knife in my hands is my fountain.

(Abaddon recedes . . .

Stett gone, Dix elects to bend forward, head on the *prie-dieu,* flaccid cheeks facing heaven. In this wise, Gwendolyn loops his smallish pig between his thighs, so that with the prolapsed anus, it appears that he has not one but two rudimentary tails. Both of which Gwen adroitly laps.

Fay-Louella, Dix's current wife, is "out."

Dix, tuckered, retires.

Ronald, not without his truncheon, taps three times on Gwendolyn's door.

Dix sleeps fitfully—dreams of the color purple, fractured . . .

Stillness. My father walking quietly through the dawning streets. In his uniform, his tidy ledger under his arm. Descend into the cellar. Read the meter. Linger in the damp darkness, half-wondering, mute. Then up to light again.

No dogs barked.

Sunday, March 20:   "Do I sound young?"
"Yes," Mole says.
"I'm bleeding."

"A critic of the then Senator once wrote in a major British newspaper (he was not an American) that Dix was a man 'innocent of conviction.' In fact nothing could be further from the truth. It is never easy to sum up a man's—and especially a great man's—philosophy in a phrase, let alone a word. But in the case of the 38th President it is possible. The word might very well be . . .

"Mole, I'm bleeding."
"Where are you?"
"I'm eighteen, Mother Mary's the devil without nuts."

Silence.

"Did you blip that, Mole?"

"No. Where are you?"

"It's starting to hurt good now. I'm feeling a little stoned. One wrist has almost stopped dripping for some reason. But the left one is going real good. Have you ever seen a young girl's blood, Mole? I'll tell you a secret: it's kinda watery—"

"Tell me where you are."

"Yeah. Well what happens if one of those death-freaks listening to your program comes instead of you? I don't want to get fucked half dead—"

"I'll blip it. Nobody'll know where you are but me."

Silence.

"Will you do it?" Mole asks. "Please tell me where you are."

"Hold it—hold it for a second. I need time to think . . ."

". . . pus. The suppurating multitude. Greek mythology tells us of the giant Antaeus, who drew his strength from the earth. He could not be defeated until an enemy lifted him above the ground, thus cutting off his source of power. Patrician Dix was such a one. He drew his strength from the masses. Nor was the lowest of the low excluded."

March 21: Mail. The photo Mole sent to Dix headquarters—returned. Only with the tip of the penis cut off. No message.

Did I say that Sklar and G.J. (who does this and that at H-E-L-P) were lovers? Why Zelda's munificence wasn't sufficient for Sklar, even with his exceptional vigor, is anyone's guess. As for G.J., she prefers Mole, but Sklar—whose energy surrounds him like scud, who always smells vaguely of sperm—is naturally more casual about his potency.

Sklar is built rather like a younger (less patrician) version of Dix. Somewhat slimmer in the hips of course. Thicker on top. Similar heads: Sklar's more muscular, more occiput, his jaws not quite so prominent. Both have those Mississippi Deputy Sheriff folds on the back of the neck. Sweat and dirt accumulate there.

Whereas Dix resembles a flaccid baboon, Sklar, knees bent, buoyant-soled, is prime Mesolithic. Sklar's hands are uncommonly wide and his fingernails are always dirty. He wears blue and white suspenders, which make him look like a monster in temporary restraint. His pockets are usually a-bulge with herbs and roots, which he buys at Kiehl's Natural Pharmacy on Third Avenue and Thirteenth Street, in the heart of hooker territory. Often Sklar will contrive to fit in a fugitive blow-job either before or after he makes his purchases. I said that women find his brazen somatic energy attractive.

Some women.

Others, more phantasmal, farther on the continuum to radical innocence—these few prefer Lee Harvey Oswald, whose emanations, though pitched as high as a siren, penetrate through the bowels.

G.J. is nice. She can feel Mole.

Women are attracted to Sklar's bluffness—how he "fills up a room."

Dix too has a bluff aura about him. But it's inauthentic. Also it is smarmy. One can hear it in his voice, which is nasal and abrasive.

Sklar is not oily, but canny. He manages to respect me and laugh at me. That is because he appreciates (though he but dimly recognizes this) the risks I am taking, yet makes light of them to protect his own fearfulness.

G.J. is British, blondish, thirty, with a ravaged, intelligent and sensual face. More than a few times has conjured Mole while beasting with Sklar.

Dolores Licht lives in 4g; Leo Schmuckler in the adjoining apartment of 4e. Each is a three-room affair: a narrow corridor connecting to an eat-in kitchen, living room, and bedroom. Virtually identical flats, so that Schmuckler abed or at his desk in his bedroom might smell, if he had any sort of nose, Miss

Licht's porridge in the morning, her boiled chicken at evening. Leo Schmuckler's nose, though large and broad, has become moribund from disuse. His nose isn't necessary for his work, and his work is his life. Or appears to be. He is an ornithologist for the Museum of Natural History, and is duly recognized (within his circle) as the only birder in the last fifteen years to have spotted the extremely rare ivory-billed woodpecker not once, but twice, in Central Park: the first time on top of the obelisk just after dawn, and more recently astride a branch atop a tall red cedar quite near the reservoir—in mid-afternoon! Whence his nickname: "Woody." The second sighting came even as Schmuckler had been preparing a paper for "Natural History" on his first sighting. His paper naturally had to be revised in the light of the recent sighting—and it occupied most of Schmuckler's home-spent hours, which were few enough, given his dedication to his work. He is fifty-three, unmarried.

Miss Licht is a year older, an art teacher at Grace Dodge Vocational High School for Girls. She cares particularly for Matisse, and framed reproductions of the master hang in every room but the bathroom, which is clean and white and antiseptic. Unlike her neighbor, she spends a good many hours in her apartment, usually reading, or cleaning. Though she has learned to tell the difference between, say, Bach and Liszt, she does not much care for music. She is a quite small woman, almost demure in a petrified way. She likes a bit of color on her clothes, which is usually supplied by a pin, perhaps jade, or amethyst, appended to the chest of whatever high-necked blouse or dress she happens to wear.

Aside from recorded bird songs and calls, Mr. Schmuckler listens only to the news—and this rarely. He has occupied his apartment for the last twenty-one years. Miss Licht has lived in hers for fourteen. It is inevitable that the neighbors have heard each other cough (Miss Licht has problems with her lungs), or sneeze (Schmuckler, who birds in every weather, and always at dawn, is given to colds); yet any more specific acknowledgement of each other's existence has been sorely lacking.

Some of the young boys in the building enjoy (when they are feeling restless) reciting the bawdy home-made mini-

limerick to the effect that "Dolores licht Leo's Schmuckler."
There is no truth in it whatever—Mole can testify to that.

March 22: While lying in my hammock I dozed, dreamt
that Dix and I were swaddled in the same hammock, which
resembled a shroud. Strung up between an Egyptian-appear-
ing obelisk and a TV antenna. Dix was partially on top of me
("young scorpions ride their mothers' backs"). We were both
on our stomachs looking at the waning moon. Dix was
preparing to suffer Mole. I could hear him accumulating
saliva. My mouth was open—when I awoke.

A stone landing hard on the roof near my books
awakened me. It looked like the same stone Abaddon had left
for Mole a week before. Evidently he didn't approve of my
dream.

Mole sighs . . .

Dix, fastened to the animal that is his putrescent body,
sighs repeatedly. Fen-mouthed, rising at 10:30 on arthritic
legs, he totters to his sitz, phones Fay, his drugged second
wife, abed in another room. She picks up the phone on the
seventh ring.

"Look, we're due at Vorst's for brunch. Try to put on
a normal, if not a happy, face, will you? And lay off the poison
until it's over, will you? Do you hear me? I feel like I'm talking
to a damned zombie."

Dix hangs up, sighs.

Fay-Louella Dix, *née* Bell, forty-four, blonde, blue-eyed,
wrinkled. Top-dollar Carolina stock. Dropped out of Chapel
Hill in her sophomore year. Addicted to codeine and Valium.
Sucked off Ronald the bodyguard twice, the last time nearly
nodding asleep at his pig.

"And what in hell will I do with her if I get in?" Dix sighs,
as he gets into his flannels. He has a golf date after brunch
(nine holes) with Jock Zurco, his chum and coach and
General Manager of the Washington Redskins.

March 23: I can tell by the feel (I have my hand in my mail-box) what it is. A letter from Sri Sen. The evelope is contrived out of a sheet of newspaper, the back page, which is usually partially empty. Today it is from the *Hindu*. Last time it was from the *Hindustani Times*. The flap is secured with a small safety pin.

Sen would like some money. A "modest contribution" to his ashram. His teachings go well. A few stiff-legged western-ers taking it in, as well as half a dozen Indians and one sexy Nagaland girl whom Sen has named Durga.

In the second paragraph, alongside which he has drawn an Om sign, Sri Sen asks whether I have "definitely selected" my roof-top. The hammock (which I had mentioned in my previous letter) he approves of, but he strongly suggests that I continue my practice of *Asanas* and *Pranayamas*, either while lying in my hammock, or, better, on a flat hard surface of the roof. "You shall see then how much better it will be." I do not know whether here Sen is referring to my state in general, or to the job I have to do. About the latter, Sen wants me to write immediately the rifle has arrived.

And about Abaddon, whom we had called by a different name in India, Sen says merely: "He must remain."

In the meantime his prayers are with me.

I burn the letter, as per Sri Sen's wishes.

March 24: First day at the rifle range, Babylon, Long Island. Interviewed by Theron Loggin in his carrel office behind the target area.

"Here y'are, Mr., uh, Mole, is it?"

"Right."

"Right. Put these shere in your ears. Else it too damned loud to hear ourselfs talk in yere."

He hands me two small cotton balls.

"Go haid, stick em in. Ain't gonna do no harm. I got to ask you some questions, see."

Loggin, lean, straw-haired, with a raw face and acne pits

on his neck, examines Mole's application.

"Okay. Now we approved of your appication here on a contingency basis, by which it means you ain't in tough here till you show you're serious and dedicated. Do you understand what I'm saying, Mr. Mole?"

"Dedicated to what?"

"What's that?"

"You said I'm not approved until I show that I'm serious and dedicated. Dedicated to what?"

"Dedicated to the ideals of the NRA, is what it means," Loggin explains. "To give you a example: was a guy in yere six, eight months back, also with one of them goatee type beards, who dropped his fetus. It was his first day. He dint know beans from firin. I was talkin to him like I'm talkin to you. Rightchere. Explainin him. And he made out like he was cool, like there weren't anythin to it. Okay, we go to the line, I slip the clip in, hand him the weapon. He's in position, everthin's okay. He fires, and the weapon recoils a little because the jerk-off wasn't holdin it tight enough against his shoulder. It kinda knocks him back a little. The next thang I know I smell shit. The sombitch done dropped his fetus." Theron Loggin, who was avoiding my eyes, now looks at me squarely, his small light grey eyes hard. "You don't chew, do you?"

"What's that?"

"Tobacca," Loggin says, holding up a tin. "I take it you don't chew."

"No."

"Mind if I do?"

"No. Go ahead."

"Well, needless to say, he dint make it. Not after that. Now, I don't mean to say that you look like a chump. But neither did he, is what I'm drivin at. Can you shoot without them glasses, Mr., uh" (he glances at my application), "Mole?"

"No."

"They're pretty damn thick. Actually, let me tell you somethin." Loggin bends towards me conspiratorially, his mouth a few inches from my glasses. "I could care less. You understand what I'm sayin? I jes work here. You chump out, it ain't no skin offa my bun. You understand what I'm tellin you?"

"I think I do. Yes."

"Right. Let's roll out. Alley number five, right there."

Wiping the mist and tobacco flecks from my glasses, Mole follows Loggin . . .

March 25: It rained hard this morning. Mole's books, tiered against the east wall, withstood the rain. Mole looks at his fingers under the misted-over moon: long, slender, though clubbed at the tips. He removes a copy of Schram from one of the lower shelves.

After a night of incantations they deliver the neophyte to a room shut off by curtains. And there

> they cut his head open, take out his brains, wash and restore them, to give him a clear mind to penetrate into the mysteries of evil spirits, and the intricacies of malaise. They insert gold dust into his eyes to give him keenness and strength of sight powerful enough to see the soul wherever it may have wandered. They plant barbed hooks on the tips of his fingers to enable him to seize the soul and hold it fast. And finally they pierce his heart with an arrow to make him tender-hearted and full of sympathy with the sick and suffering.

Mole has become allies with a cat that frequents his roof to sleep or eat. A beleaguered alley-cat. Black, with a white and black muzzle and a soiled nose. I call him the Jewish Cat. No petting. We acknowledge each other silently, each going about his business. His: sleeping, scrounging for food, hanging out. Mine, well . . .

A right-winged columnist, who had gone to Yale, recently described Dix's head as "Olmec." Don't believe it. At his "best" angle, which is front-left profile, he resembles an impotent Mussolini. Possibly Dix noted the remote resemblance, since according to his niece, Peony, he admired *il Duce* in certain particulars, which she however could not enumerate.

I thought of this resemblance the other dawn as I was making love with Marya. More than thought—I managed virtually to merge with Dix-Mussolini. Dix's billions centered in my head, swelling my temples; Mussolini's massive potency in my loins.

I turned Marya onto her stomach, and without greasing my prick entered flush into her ass in one fluid motion. We both came rapidly, I fiercely; after which Marya turned her lovely head to me and smiling whispered: "Hitler."

I have not, you see, been unfortunate in love. Psychoanalysts are fond of citing Lee Harvey Oswald (who was supposed to have said, "My penis made me do it") as the paradigmatic assassin. It is a neat formulation. Too neat.

Gandhi, whom I love, evidently raised his hand and sighed *"Ram,"* before falling.

Sri Sen told me this. Dix, he prophesied, would topple at once, beshitting himself. His myriad-petaled uranium lotus contracting hell-wards.

I know this is true, though I won't live to verify it.

(Marya would like more. She wishes to "go" with Mole. She has not been happy; yet the work on Orpheus continues, improves.)

March 26: A problem: I couldn't dive. The janitor, still juiced from his nightly binge, demanded who I was, where I was going. I looked at him closely. I told him to listen intently to my voice. Then I said certain things to him. Do you recognize me now? I asked.

Mole. You sound like Mole from that radio station. His eyes cleared, he became respectful. I told him it was important for me to get to the roof. He nodded. "I think you'll be able to see Paddy Dix from there later when he comes."

"Much later," I said.

Conn, the janitor's name. We shook hands.

My father, I said, was lost. And in me, since I was a child, was a mountain. Barren, bruised smooth by *yugas* of devastation. Not impermeable, but mystic, beyond absorption.

This was the heart's meadow. I needed it, though when I entered it, I would sleep merely.

Sen helped me to do while sleeping.

I'm on my back in *Halasana*, looking at my books, fingering my knife, which is in my left side pocket. Previously I had kept it in my right, but somehow it found its way into my left. I like the feel of it there.

"When the cities kneel to the Monster, there are left the mountains."

March 27: Though Dix let people know that he was an aficionado of the popular arts, in his head he knew that this was slumming, not to be taken seriously. The Senator's interest in organized sport, and especially in professional football, was another thing. Here he was in deadly earnest; and often as not his mood for the next few days would ride on the outcome of the Redskins' game. The Washington Redskins is Dix's team. And John (Jock) Zurco, that master of boldness and sanctimony (who resembles Richard Nixon as filtered through Central Casting), is Dix's hombre, an intimate at Dix's dinner table (where he usually manages to sit next to Ronald). An occasional partaker of God (after golf) at the Senator's prayer meetings. And most of all, an *ad hoc* counsel to Dix in times of crisis. Indeed Dix has tended (to the dismay of his aides), to consult Jock before, or instead of, his staff to such an extent in the last several days (since the Redskins locked up the Eastern Division), that these same aides have taken to referring to the Senator as "Jock's Strap." Not a good pun perhaps, but bear in mind: these aides are lawyers, not comics; and it is surely vivid enough to illustrate their private feelings about the senior Senator from New York.

Meanwhile, as the political stakes became ever higher, Dix commenced to assert himself with more authority (not to be confused with the subtle patrician authority always implicit in his behavior), and drew upon the tropes of his mentor Zurco more and more unabashedly. The fact that Bette Andiron was being bandied about as a possible running-mate of Sanderson, his chief democratic opponent, evoked this from Dix: "We're just going to have to change our game-plan. Hell, if their quarterback starts favoring our weak side, we'll just have to move our free safety into the line of fire. I mean it's a question of anticipating, wouldn't you agree, Jock?" (The question proffered following "Evening Prayer.")

"Yes sir, I would."

"You bet. Look, Jock, my butt is bothering me. I'm going to have me a little whirlpool in the library. Come on in with me. I want you to hear what Gwen's taken down. This Andiron broad is making her pitch to Women's Lib and all that. And to the third stringers who feel guilty and so forth. I had my staff work out this multi-pronged broadside addressed to the so-called particular needs of women. I'd like to hear your input on it, Jock."

"Will Ronnie be there, Pat?"

"Sure he will, fella. Why do you ask?"

"He has a cousin, a sophomore in high school down there in Georgia, you know? Well, I understand the kid's a super prospect. He's already 6-5, goes 235, 240. Super prospect from what I hear."

Dix at his sitz. His aides (four lawyers, one media-man); his press secretary, Nubile; Gwendolyn; Sally the stenographer; Ronald and Sven, bodyguards; and Jock Zurco: variously positioned among the Utrillos, first editions, morocco bindings, and uncut pages.

Dix: "All right, we all know that Sanderson is mulling over that spinster Andiron. Now what we don't know is whether he'll follow through and actually grab her. But we're not going to take any chances. I mean there's a great deal of output about this thing this year, this Women's Lib. And then with this thing happening in Houston, that broad undressing in the window at the guy's orders, then him shooting her anyway. As if she couldn't have gotten away if she really wanted to. In any case, it's hep, it's in the air, and we're going to move just in case it happens to stay in the air come November. Comprende? Okay, we're changing our game-plan. Never mind that the other side accuses us of inconsistency. It's the zig-zaggers who make the touchdowns. If this lib stuff happens to blow away, as I personally think it will, so what! We've lost nothing. Rather, we've gained. Because we've anticipated, which is a very good habit to get into.

"Okay, then, this is what we're thinking of putting out. It's called 'Safety Tips for Women.' If any of you want to input, or clarify, whatever, do it now. We want this thing in the media day after tomorrow at the latest."

(Mole cites but a selection of representative items from the Senator's broadside, which is divided into "At Home," "Driving," and Walking"):

AT HOME

Women who must live alone should list only their surnames and initials in phone directories and on their mailboxes.

Never open the door automatically after the bell rings. Instruct delivery boys to leave packages at the door. Make sure not to overtip because of misguided notions of liberality.

Do not enter the elevator with a stranger. If an individual whose presence makes you uneasy for whatever reason gets on after you, get off at the next floor. Stand near the control panel. If attacked, hit the alarm button and as many others as you can. As a last resort (repeat: *as a last resort*): hit him in the crotch with your purse—or use your knee.

Never undress in front of an open window.

DRIVING

Travel on well-lighted streets and thoroughfares. You have no business on ill-lit streets. Keep windows and doors of automobile locked at all times.

Keep your car in gear while halted at traffic lights and stop signs. If your safety is threatened, honk, honk on the horn to beat the band. Someone will come to your aid.

Never leave car keys in the ignition, even if you park for only a short time. If you are not carrying your purse, and have no pockets in your dress or skirt, secrete the keys on your person *securely!*

WALKING

As you walk, keep looking behind you, even if there is no visible indication that you are being followed. If for some reason you happen to be out in the evening alone, in addition to looking behind you, cross the street, crisscrossing back and forth. For this purpose it is a good idea to keep a pair of light-weight flat-heeled shoes (sneakers, whatever) in your purse in the event a quick change should become necessary.

If a car starts to follow you, run in the *opposite direction*, and scream, or, better, blow your whistle (sent to you free as a public service from Dix Headquarters, Washington, D.C. 10010).

If you do get into trouble, scream FIRE! Or, even better, scream RAPE! It will bring more people to the street quicker.

Dix: "All right, that's it. Let's kick it around. What do you think, Jock?"

"Sounds fine to me. Real good. I'd like to mull it over some."

"Righto. What about the rest of you? We got to get the show on the road. The timing thing's very important here."

"Mr. Senator," Holstein, an aide, with his finger in the air. "Mr. Senator, that next-to-the-last item in the 'At Home' category: 'Hit him in the crotch with your purse—or use your knee.' I wonder whether 'groin' might not be, uh, you know, more suitable, while conveying the same force as the other."

Silence.

"Well, all of you, what do you think? Holstein's raised a point. We can't stay up half the night with this thing."

"Well—well, I question whether 'groin' *does* convey the same force as the other input, 'crotch.' I frankly don't think it does." This from Dochmeier.

Rebus, the media-man, with two fingers in the air: recognized. "I hold with Lance Dochmeier, Mr. Senator. 'Crotch' may or may not sound proper, or suitable, and so forth, but it's definitely the better input. And frankly I don't think we should pussyfoot in this area."

"All right, 'crotch' stays," Dix says. "Yes, Jock?"

"Right. Now, like I said earlier, I think it's fine. The entire program sounds real fine to me. I'm just a mite troubled by a word in the last item under 'Driving.' That 'secrete.' The girl should 'secrete' the keys on her person, I believe it says. Now, I may be wrong, but I was under the impression that that word, secretion and so forth, was a medical term. A biological term is what I mean to say. My own personal opinion is that 'conceal' would work a lot better in that place there . . ."

March 28: "Limited by the world I oppose, jagged by it, I shall be all the more handsome and sparkling as the angles which wound me and give me shape are more acute and the pricking more cruel."

Genet wrote that.

Consider the elegance of Mole's dream. The circle within the circle. Contamination at the hub tentacling outwards. Dix. Prolapsed anus beneath the broad hips. Also brief grey eyes, as if pinched by the glare of uranium, yet ever shifting. Dix in the circle.

The austerity of his roof. Lean dark-haired man alone, looking down (through glass). Then up. No sanction.

Mole was born in Omaha in 1941, the younger of two sons. I remember that there was always a lot of hollering in the

house. My brother died in 1946, of asphyxiation. After which
my mother (who did the hollering) divorced my father, kept
me, moved with me back to New York. Then to Delaware.
Then to New Jersey. Finally back to New York. She
waitressed mostly. Died in '52. One less Gladys.

My father had also moved to New York on his own, to be
close to Mole. He worked for Con Edison there. He didn't
marry again. We lived together in Washington Heights from
'52 to '59. His name was Walter.

He comes to me now, bent as I am, on my roof. In
Bhujangasana.

And walking through the whores to get to work, he
comes to me. Raining lightly. I don't know whether I feel sad
or nearly jubilant.

Pausing at the park on Chrystie Street, I spot one standing
alone under the lee of the park toilet. I go to her. Smiling
mildly, I point to the fly on my trousers. I say the zipper broke,
ask whether she might have a safety pin. The ingrained
suspicion on her face gives way to a partially distracted,
modified concern. She removes a small pin from her bodice,
gives it to me. I thank her. She turns away. Soon though she
can see that I am having trouble pinning my fly (which I have
attempted to do on the spot). With gruff (yet immemorial)
affection, she pushes my hand away, pins my pants in a trice. I
thank her. She briefly smiles. I don't have an erection.

By the time I get to the station, I am feeling good.

Sklar notices.

"This'll make you even happier," Sklar says, his eyes
pesky as he hands me a message. "I talked to this one on the
blip line. He says if you don't get back to him immediately,
kaput."

The message was

I am a 28 year old college-educated bachelor who works for Dix
Chemical, in the Accounting Dept. I was born with a 'strawberry' birthmark on nearly half my face. It is not exactly
hideous, but it is noticeable, and I was very self-conscious of it as
a child. About a year ago a skin specialist recommended that I

cover the mark with pancake makeup. It helped a lot, and gave my cheek such a smooth, velvety look that I started using the makeup on my entire face. Then I started using just a hint of rouge. Next I applied a very faint bit of orchid eye shadow, and now I use a touch of mascara to darken my brows and lashes.

Last week I was called into the boss's office and given an ultimatum. Either I see the Company shrink or find another job.

Mole, I don't want to see this psychiatrist person. There is nothing wrong with me. If women can improve themselves with beauty aids, why can't men! But I know nobody agrees with me, and I don't know what to do.

"Think you can handle it?" Sklar, mockingly.

"I don't know. This came in the mail, right?"

"Right. He phoned to confirm. Think you can handle it, Mole?"

"Where's his phone number?"

"On the back. It's the same prefix as yours. I guess he must live in Greenwich Village also. You know what I would do, don't you?"

"Don't tell me. You'd prescribe high enemas made up of wolfsbane and poison sumac—twice a day."

"Not wolfsbane, Mole; mandrake root. He sounds like a pretty fellow. My guess is that that Dix Chemical shrink would be glad to enemate this pretty fellow."

March 30: Dix's broadside: "Safety Tips for Women" greeted with nearly unanimous approbation.

Meanwhile, Congresswoman Andiron was mugged and molested in Pittsburgh, and as a result has faded from the list of possible Sanderson running mates.

The Redskins, who made the division playoffs for the third year in succession, lost their first playoff game by two touchdowns. Dix constipated and irritable.

Asked by the Press to comment on Governor Sanderson's statement that Recession, not Inflation, is "Public Enemy Number 1," Dix answered: "If you fellas expect me to do a 180 degree turn from Inflation tackling to Recession pump-priming, simply because it's the more popular course these days—you're in the wrong ball park."

Gwendolyn, preparing the Senator's sitz, is surprised by Ronald, not without his truncheon.

"Is he going to make you do him?" Ron hisses the question into Gwen's right ear.

"Oh, Ron! You startled me. I don't know. I hope not."

"Don't do him." Ronald grabs both breasts with one large hand.

"Don't, Ronnie. You'll get me hot. I'll ring your room when I'm through with him. You'd better go now."

"Don't do it, Gwen, because I've got me a fat surprise for you."

"Please, Ron. If the old man picks up that I'm oozing, he's sure to want head."

"Yeah. Okay. But finish up soon."

Ronald walks toward the door, then—suddenly—wheels around. Clutching his crotch with both hands, he Mick-Jagger-lips the word, "Sazeech! That's right, baby. And I ain't gonna wait long."

Dix enters in his maxi-length taupe-colored terrycloth robe. His collar is askew. As usual his nostril hairs need clipping. He is too depressed to pick up Gwendolyn's scent. Nonetheless he asks to be lapped. Fore and aft.

"Oughtn't you to wait for tomorrow, Senator, when you are feeling a bit more, uh, energetic?"

"Never mind. I'll just rinse off a bit. You get on your knees . . ."

"She led me to a room, locked it, turned the lights out & lit incest all with her back towards me."

(This from Arthur Bremer's *Assassin's Diary*. Also):

"I took off my vested business suit and layed on my stomach on the massage table, nude. She didn't see my organ yet. I started some talk about a burglar alarm that was ringing & was ringing for the last two days. She wanted to talk about the wether . . ."

Bremer couldn't spell. Nor could Oswald. Nor Sirhan
Sirhan. (Edgar Holster-Teufel, M.D., Ph.D., disciple of
Reik, offices in New York, Beverly Hills, and Vienna, flares a
nostril, licks his pencil.)

Once, years ago, my brother (much older than I) and a
friend of his dragged another boy who was too frightened to
scream, through the sand, and flung him into the ocean.
That was the start of Mole.
The Jewish cat licking himself—at a respectful distance.
Mole reminiscing in *Halasana*.

March 31: Marya is right for me. Five feet seven, slender,
with long straight dark hair. Large luminous green eyes. The
components of her face delicately askew, so that she looks
beautiful and plain by turn. A lithe and articulate pelvis.
Slightly, charmingly pigeon-toed. (She is preparing tonight to
work on Orpheus, long gone, deep gone). She is behind me at
this moment, sitting on the toilet, peeing, her slender knees
touching like a young girl's. I am watching her in the mirror as
I brush my teeth. She seems preoccupied. She is an inquisitive
person; still she generally restrains her curiosity about Mole
out of deference to Mole, instinctively understanding, more
or less, Mole's silent imperatives. Yet periodically she needs
to ask "why?" Tonight is such a time. Why is Mole Mussolini-
loined for days on end—then suddenly recessive? Where does
he go when he recedes? Why isn't it possible for her who loves
him sometimes to "go" with him?
Marya's questions are not asked demandingly, but rather
tentatively, quietly, feelingly, as is her way. Mole either has
tried to "answer" these or similar questions before; or he has
said nothing. Tonight he unlocks his word-hoard.
"I see you sitting on the toilet, Marya. Through the
mirror. I like it. If this mirror were smaller, say a hand-mirror,
and you were farther away, across the street, for example, and
your bathroom were dimly lit, and I were partially blind in one
eye, and you were Marya, but someone else as well, someone
who didn't 'know' me; if I had but a minute and a half to

watch you before you flushed and went about your lemony business, and Mole, already blind in one eye, was going rapidly blind in the other, so that your distant ferny cunthair blended with your skirt or with the tile of the bowl—if all of this were so, Mole would love you more than now—but have to die.

"To see you the way you seem to be now, is to love you less, and go on. Because there is a receding center in our life, baby, and for Mole especially who feels certain vast obligations. Being riveted is to be astonished, like the person nearly hit by the car in the middle of the street: the car screechingly stops, the man covers his face with one hand, the other hand out in front of him, saying: 'No! Not now!' He is not hit; the driver and he exchange difficult-to-analyze glares, the pedestrian composes himself as best he can and walks haltingly from the middle of the street to the sidewalk. For those seven or eight steps he is stripped, cleansed, riveted to what must be life. Love. But for twenty seconds only.

"For most of us, there are only a few of those 'twenty-second' spaces in our adult lives. Which is how it is, though the world is infinite . . . open to us. This echo-less place, this gash between us as the world and apart from it, Mole feels it his responsibility to bridge. At whatever expense. Thus he recedes. Those times he is with you, Mussolini-loined, are when, for one reason or another, he has temporarily withdrawn from his responsibility."

Mole in Babylon, at the range. Firing a Mossberg 640 K Chukster.

Theron Loggin at my side.

"That first clip weren't bad," he says, "'cept you wasn't gentlin the trigger enough. Gotta be real soft there, easin it steady all the time lookin at your target. But like I say, not bad. Some of them that come here—like that one that dropped his friggin fetus—I told you about him, didn't I?"

"Yeah."

"Right. He was firin, right? Ony his non-firin eye was lookin way the hell off to the left acrost the alley. No good.

Both eyes gotta be right there. But you can understand that, I reckon. But then you was in the service from what I recall in your appication. You was a officer there, right?"

"Right."

"Well, I could tell you had some experience right off. You fire much there?"

"No, not much."

"Too bad. Well, try this shere clip. I thank I can hep you."

April 1: 10:15 A.M. Marya out. The doorbell rings. Zelda Sklar, and breathless. She sits on the tip of the sofa. Tosses away her brief orange jacket. Her magic tits as usual un-bra'd, reverberant under her "Porno-Star" tee-shirt.

She informs me that she's been plagued by an itch which travels from the back of her neck to the backs of her thighs—and up again.

"It feels real creepy, like teeny tiny feet doing some weirdo tap dance all over me and stuff."

"Oh?"

"Yeah. And I know you know a lot about that stuff, Mole. Getting rid of demons and stuff."

"These teeny tiny feet doing their things on you are demons, Zelda?"

"Shit, I wish I knew." She twists and untwists her torso to underline her discomfort. Her tits are a nearly perfect right angle to her head.

"And Sklar didn't prescribe anything for you—out of the Jethro Kloss bible?"

"Oh. Yeah, we tried some poultices and stuff. Penny-royal and smartweed. But it didn't work."

"Uh-huh."

"Well, can you look at it or something?" Zelda's tongue caresses her top front teeth.

"You want me to look at it?"

"At them. And talk to them or something. Just to make them stop."

"Well, you know, Zelda, these demons are generally

quite uncompromising. If they agree to leave now, it's likely
they'll exact some pledge from you for later."
    "Like what?"
    "I couldn't say."
    "Yeah, well it couldn't be worse than this itching. You
don't know how uncomfortable it is, Mole. Also I think it's
been spreading to my front. Which I don't want."
    "No."
    "Will you take a look, then?"
    "All right."
    Zelda removes her shirt in one fluid motion. Then
lissomely wriggles out of her jeans. Leaving the fragrant pile
on the floor, she circles towards me.
    "Do you want me to lay down, sit down, or what?"
    "Lie on your stomach, Zelda. On the carpet here."
    "Like this?"
    "Yes, but with your hands at your sides. Palms facing
upward."
    "Like this?"
    "Like that."
    Kneeling on one knee, I place both hands about Zelda's
neck.
    "Close your eyes," I say. "Try not to think of anything.
Not even my hands about your neck."
    "Okay."
    "Don't talk either."
    For a few minutes Mole remains silent. Almost imper-
ceptibly my fingers have commenced to knead her neck.
    "Zelda, listen to me," Mole says softly. "That spilt mass
of cream and slops that is your body is not your body. You are a
girl on a golden pig—"
    The phone rings.
    "Hello."
    "Hey, Mole, is that you?"
    "Yes, Reverend Kloss."
    "Right. I been looking all over for Zelda. Gotta tell her
something. She don't happen to be at your pad, does she?"
    "Yes, she's here. Shall I put her on?"
    "I'd appreciate that, buddy-boy."

I hand Zelda, still prone, the receiver.

"I can't talk now," she whispers languidly into the phone. "Yeah, I know, but can't it wait? Look, not now . . . All right, I will. Here," she hands Mole the receiver. "He wants you."

"Hey, buddy-boy," Sklar says. "Whatcha doin? I mean, like you ain't up to no good or nothin, are you? Cause I don't expect there's anyone got balls enough to put horns on Sklar's head. Dudes have come on to Cuntie before, you understand. It didn't fucking work, Mole. Not even close. In case I never told you before, one thing I know is my cock's ocean, baby. And it ain't no faggot dribble, you can bet. What I'm saying is you spritzed her tubes, your ass gonna be in a sling . . ."

Three or four minutes more of this, until Sklar roars "April Fool!" into the receiver, and hangs up.

As it turned out, though, Zelda was serious (as serious as her capacity allowed): she didn't leave until I was finished with her.

What can Mole say about Nicaragua? It was unconscionably hot. The indigenous people had been killed off, and those who remained: mestizos, blacks . . . looked broken. Yet the sun was too hot to care.

Managua, whither Mole flew from Guatemala, was still rubble two years after the earthquake. It was said that the problem of how to reconstruct the city without traversing the major fault was under consideration by Nicaragua's best scientific minds. Their work-week was doubtless curtailed by the heat.

Mole's plane set down at ten minutes past high noon, some three hours behind schedule. After a perfunctory customs check by a sleepy and tetchy customs officer, Mole inquired about Granada. He was told that no busses were running between Managua and Granada.

"Since when?"

"Since yesterday."

"Until when?"

"*Quién sabe?*"

Granada was the country's third largest city, allegedly the oldest city in the hemisphere, and the gateway to the volcanic islands scattered through huge Lake Nicaragua.

"Why are the busses not running?"

A shrug of the shoulders.

Taxis were running. Twenty-five dollars one way. Mole had no choice but to enlist one.

The ride was speedy and dusty. Once away from the congested outskirts of Managua, where thousands of refugees from the earthquake had set up camps, the country looked empty, sere, yet impressive, with purple buttes and volcanos yoking the horizon. More birds than people: flycatchers, magpie jays, warblers, swallows. About fifteen miles out of Managua I saw a surprisingly small yet strikingly feral butcherbird crouched on an electric wire—and promptly remembered what Mole was compelled to do . . .

Granada itself was hot, white, spread out. Cobblestoned streets, the usual contingent of colonial churches; an admonition on a chaste old building which read: "Granada Patriot's Club: God, Order, Justice"; the grassy city square filled with commemorative statues, stone benches. No sign of the lake. The taxi drew up to Hotel Alhambra, a *muchacho* took Mole's suitcase, and I checked into a second floor room with a terrace that looked out at the square. It was 2:20. Mole's instructions were to be at Punta del Oriente at dusk.

In the meantime I was tired, wanted to lie down. The narrow bed was lumpy, the white ceiling was cracked, fugitive voices drifted in out of the sun—Mole was suddenly feeling India. Sen had told him it would happen, assured him it was good, the vast white loneliness was good—but only if you didn't rush to fill it, let it yawn, let it suck at you. The restorative void. Mole assumed the corpse position, slept.

Awoke at ten past four, still tired, wanting to shower. The water was off. As were the lights. Mole dressed, remembered to take both his prescribed sun-glasses and his ordinary glasses. Secured his papers and wallet in his suitcase, after separating all the *córdobas* he had, about twelve dollars' worth. As he was closing the door, a little groggy from his doze and the heat, he remembered that he hadn't taken paper and pen. He did this, then left.

The horse-drawn cabs were parked in tandem on the opposite, or north, side of the square. Mole explained to the wizened mestizo driver of the foremost cab that he wished to go to the place on the lake shore from where he could take a boat to the *isleta* called Punta del Oriente. The driver looked at me quizzically. Did I not, he asked, mean Piedra Sagrada? Piedra Sagrada is the principal *isleta*. No, I mean Punta del Oriente. The driver conferred with another driver, then a third. Yes, he now knew where it was, one of the smaller islands in the eastern part of the lake.

Once in the cab, the driver asked whether I knew that that part of the lake was full of *tiburones*.

No. I had read that the lake contained sharks, several species that had adapted, and even thrived, since the lake was cut off from the Pacific a century ago. But I didn't know that they were concentrated in any one part of the lake.

They were, he assured me, in the vicinity of my island. Wouldn't I prefer to go to another? To Piedra Sagrada, for example. There was a restaurant on Piedra Sagrada. Possibly other *turistas* as well. There wouldn't be anything on my island—but natives. And then there were the *tiburones*. There were accomodations for swimming on Piedra Sagrada. No need to worry about *tiburones* there. Was the Señor planning to swim?

No. I had an appointment with someone.

The driver nodded. Ah, that was another matter.

The driver whispered and whistled softly to his horse, an old pony-size, off-white mare. We were approaching the lake, emerald green, shimmering in the reflection of the sun setting in the mountains. The cab turned right onto the lake-side *paseo*.

"*Lago,*" the driver said over his right ear. "*Muy grande.*"

"Yes. And very pretty."

"*Claro. Muy bonita.*"

Mole's driver extracted a blue baseball cap which he put on and adjusted with one hand so that it was rakishly tilted on

the right side of his head. Where his neck joined his small
bony head were two deep indentations, one on either side. It
was a thin old neck, vulnerable. Mole flashed to his father,
whose neck was thin, who wore his Con Edison cap on the
right side of his head. One of his few small vanities.

The lake shore area both on the sand and off was
inhabited by small grass huts, impoverished Nicaraguans,
their chickens, pigs, wasted dogs. Occasionally a cow. Several
small native girls spotted the odd-looking *turista* in the cab and
ran behind it with their hands outstretched in front of them.
Mole handed one of them a *córdoba*, saying *"para todas."*
But the others continued running behind the cab until the
driver shooed them away over his right ear. It was India again:
Kerala, near the Arabian Sea: cow-dung, wood burning,
coconut palms wafting in the watery breeze, persistent
beggar-children . . . Sen had cautioned Mole against thinking.
The driver was saying something.

"De dónde viene?"

"Los Estados Unidos," Mole said.

"Ah, *Los Estados Unidos."*

Mole wondered where exactly the boat left from. He was
anxious to get there. To get it over with.

"Fría?" the driver asked. *"Los Estados Unidos es fría,
verdad?"*

"Yes, it is cold there."

"Ah, here it is very hot."

The *paseo* was becoming less inhabited, more wooded.
The waves were breaking roughly on the rocks. Yellow-
breasted swallows were circling and diving, skimming the
water. Mole spotted a boat-billed kiskadee pecking at the surf
among a horde of noisy grackles—as if it were one of them.

Mole was about to ask: where? when the driver pointed
ahead to the left.

"The boat?"

"Claro."

A few hundred meters in front of them Mole (who had
put on his untinted glasses), saw a small dock—but no boat.
The driver removed a cigarette butt from an inside

pocket and lit it dexterously with one hand. Then he took out a packet of cigarettes, held it behind him, motioning with his head.

"*No fumo,*" Mole said.

"Ah."

As they approached the dock, three small boys accosted the taxi, demanding of Mole whether he wanted to go to the *isletas.*

"Yes. *Claro.*"

"*Isletas, isletas.* Piedra Sagrada?"

"Punta del Oriente."

"Piedra Sagrada," one of them repeated. "*Muy bonita.*"

"No. I want to go to Punta del Oriente. Do you go there?"

"Punta del Oriente?"

"Yes. Do you go there?"

"Yes, go . . .

Mole in the bow of the leaky outboard weaving between tiny wooded islands. I hadn't realized there were so many of them. The small boy at the helm was both steering and bailing water with a rusted Shell Oil can. Once he pointed with the can to Mole's left, though when I turned I didn't see anything. A few minutes later he pointed again—this time I made out a plashing, silver . . .

"*Tiburón?*"

"*Claro.*"

"How far is it yet—to the island?"

The boy didn't understand. I asked again.

"Punta del Oriente, *verdad?*"

"Yes. Punta del Oriente."

"No good swim there. Sharks."

"I'm not going to." The sun was setting rapidly. "Is it far from here?"

"No far. You are from United States?"

"Yes."

In spite of his underlying anxiety, Mole was beginning to feel agreeably light-headed. As he usually did at sunset. He wondered where exactly the meeting would take place. The

instructions were: come to Punta del Oriente. Nothing else.
Mole thought of his roof, his people. Turning to the setting
sun, he closed his eyes.

The motor stopped. The boy was steering the boat
between some rocks towards an island.

"Punta del Oriente? This is it?"

"Is it. You wish I wait?"

"No."

"No other *lancha* going back."

"No, it's all right. I'll get back." Mole paid the boy. Then
climbed out, onto his island.

The docking area was separated from the interior of the
isleta by a rocky rise. Mole had supposed that he would be
met, but once over the rise he saw—nothing. Nothing but lush
greenery, rocks, crested magpie jays, grackles, swallows. The
magpie jay is a noisy bird, with the heavy bill and aggressive
posture of a bluejay, but with white underparts, an exceptionally long tail, and regal black crest. It was dusk. Where
was Abaddon?

Not knowing where to walk, Mole walked straight ahead
through the high grass. He remembered reading in a travel
brochure that all the islands were inhabited. Or was it "most"
that were inhabited? In any case, as far as Mole could tell, and
he had virtually traversed the island's width, this one wasn't.
Neither hut nor human—at that moment he saw something
scoot across his path several meters in front of him. Almost in
the same instant he heard a magpie jay squawking irritably in a
tamarind tree above him. When Mole looked up he saw the
beginnings of the sickle moon . . .

I had reached the other side of the island. Sun gone. The
water lashed at the rocks. Several stars out, including the faint
tracing of Triangulum. Mole turned left along the water.
When it was not possible to walk farther, he turned left again
into the island. He should have told the small boy in the
broken outboard to return in the morning. Fortunately it was
still warm and likely to remain so through the night. As he
walked Mole kept an eye open for a spot where he might
spend the night. Snakes and scorpions could be a problem in
the wooded areas. Near the shore would be safer, though

colder. The birds were already nesting—but for a few noisy jays feeding on the rocks near the water. When Mole turned towards them, he sighted something beyond them: a building of some kind on the shore, at about a forty-five degree angle from where he was. Pivoting, I began running along the rocks, needing to get to the building before it became too dark to make my way . . .

It is a church. A small ruin of a church, in design part Churrigueresque, part Colonial, with both Corinthian pillars and elaborate figures from the Passion ornamenting the brief exterior. (These observations made afterwards.) What I did at once was push open the ancient wooden door into a dimly lit narthex. I heard something. Music . . .

Worshippers, perhaps half a dozen, were kneeling, spaced about the nave. Mole directed himself to a pew—but there was no bench to sit on. None of the pews, so far as he could make out, had benches. He moved to the side of the church, leaned against the wall. Tired, very tired, and now a little dizzy from the scent of copal which was being burned at the altar. A tiny altar—Mole could scarcely see it through his soiled glasses. What he could see, imperfectly, were the old— they were all old but for a frail dark child—worshippers. Several weeping silently. It was the music. What Mole had assumed was on record, was live. A harp coming from somewhere in the church. Mole listened. He recognized the tune, a popular song he had heard first in the Managua airport, then in the street next to the square in Granada. Somewhere else as well—he couldn't remember. Here on the harp the tune sounded gentler, wistful; yet somehow necessary, or integral, like . . . breathing.

Quietly, Mole moved towards the music. In the farthest aisle, near the wall, closer to the narthex than to the altar, I saw it: an old man bent over a broken harp. Like (the image took hold) an innocent girl brushing her hair, stroking lingeringly, as though the harp were animal, caged, untame, and somewhere in its stomach's stomach, sacred. Moving still closer, Mole saw that the artist was a wizened mestizo with protruding ears on a hairless, bony head. He was bleeding from an open wound on his right temple. The blood, very

dark, had formed a stream down his face to his torn white
shirt, and onto the broken strings of the harp . . .

April 2: I remove the knife from my left trouser pocket,
lay it on the hammock. No, not yet: first I hold it in my hand,
my left hand this time, back up to the roof's edge, toss it into
the air in the direction of the circle within the circle . . . It
doesn't work. Doesn't hit it. But close, closer than I've gotten
before. At least in a while.

With my left hand I place the knife in the hammock,
Shiva side facing the Sisters. I haven't seen the Jewish cat all
day. I lie on my back on the tar. In *Savasana.* In order to relax
totally I conjure up my teacher's face: Sri Sen . . . No!
Abaddon intervenes (evidently stepping up his virulence for
the Lenten season . . .

This call at the station:

"I wish to speak to Mr. Mole." The intonation vaguely
Germanic.

"This is Mole."

"Yes, then. I wish to make an offer which will be heard by
thousands."

"An offer?"

"I have two good kidneys. I am in good health. I would
like to help someone by selling one of my kidneys. I think
there must be some wealthy people who would give a fortune
to save or extend their way of life. As I say, I myself have a
pair. Of kidneys."

"I see."

"We are being broadcast on the air, are we not?"

"Yes. Go ahead. But quickly, because H-E-L-P isn't on
the air to service these kinds of requests."

"I don't understand," the man says. "This is a straight-
forward business deal whereby I personally undergo some
risk."

"Yes, but the risk is worth the fortune you hope to make."

"What's that you say?"

"You would like to make a fortune by selling your

kidney. Is that right?"

"Well, I don't think that's any of your affair," Abaddon responds testily.

After which I hang up.

Sunday, April 3: The western veranda of Dix's George-town manse. A news conference after church. Jock Zurco at the Senator's side. Also Smegma, Congressman from Washington State, and Dix's running mate. The three broad faces are distinctly solemn. It was discovered in a "routine medical examination" (Dix parses out the words), that the Senator's wife, Fay-Louella, was suffering from a rare blood cancer. "She was transferred at once to the world-famous Mayo Clinic for further, more exacting, observation. It is impossible now to determine the length of her hospitalization, or to speculate on her prognosis. But knowing, as I have been privileged to know, the extraordinary courage of Mrs. Dix, my wife, I remain, under the circumstances, rather hopeful."

Smegma, Zurco sitting on the dais on Dix's either side. On the uranium platform beneath me. Smegma, stocky, barrel-chested, with bristly grey semi crew-cut (grudgingly permitting his hair to grow out a bit in accord with Fashion, and for the campaign). A military man, currently Major General in the Army Reserves. Lt. Colonel in the Second War; Tank Corps, 1943−45, European theatre. Affectionately called "Smokey" by his men.

Coasted to wins in his first two terms on the strength of his military reputation, and his twin political schticks: apples and Nato. According to Smegma (whose aides thoroughly researched the subject), the "so-called food experts have tragically underestimated the nutritional potential of the homely and tasty apple. I'd go even further and say that the quality of your apple crop is a good index of the quality of your character. This may sound oddball to some of you, but you can check it in the history books. Take a look at your perennial winners: the U.S., Germany, France, Great Britain; and the up-and-coming countries like Canada. Look at the quality of their apples. And the variety too. Draw your own conclusions. Now don't get me wrong, I don't say the apple is the only index, but it is very definitely one of them."

In addition to his more visible assets, Henry Smegma's brother Marion is president of Parsons College in Fairfield, Iowa. Hence Smegma would supply a pipe-line not only to the military but to the intellectual communities, both vitally important to the man who occupies the highest position in the public trust.

April 4: Sklar seemed upset. As soon as I came into the station he handed me a clipping from the NY *Times*. "TV Talk Show Hostess Shoots Herself on the Air," the bold type read.

"You see this thing?"

"No."

Just then G.J. came in. Sklar asked the same question of her.

She had seen it on TV, she said. On the news.

Sarasota, Fla., Apr. 3 (AP)—"In keeping with Channel 40's policy of bringing you the latest in blood and guts and in living color, you are going to see another first—attempted suicide."

With that announcement, Chris Chubbuck, 30 years old, shot herself in the head today during her morning talk show on WXLT-TV. She died instantly.

According to station officials and witnesses, Miss Chubbuck, hostess of "Suncoast Digest," was reading a news report about a shootout at a bar when mechanical trouble developed with a film clip.

After a few seconds, Miss Chubbuck came back on and read a statement announcing her planned suicide. She reached into a shopping bag behind her desk, pulled out a snub-nosed 38 revolver, fired one shot, and slumped forward.

HISTORY OF DEPRESSION

Sheriff Jesse Bunch said that Miss Chubbuck's family told the police that she had talked of suicide last weekend.

"They say she's been depressed. But why she did what she did or the way she did it, nobody knows," Sheriff Bunch noted.

"Everyone's in a state of shock." said Ted Monad, the station's sales manager.

Viewers who witnessed the attempt flooded the sheriff's department with telephone calls. Some asked whether it was a joke. Others wanted to know whether it was simulated, a "dramatization."

Meanwhile the police took possession of a video-tape of the show and said they were "waging a full investigation."

"Well, Mole, how do you like them apples? Think you could have jived her out of it? Phone-spieled her out of it?"

"How should Mole know?" G.J. said. "He never met the woman."

"Yeah. Kaput. Right on the fucking screen. You know, she looks a little like Marya, wouldn't you say, Mole?"

I looked closely at Chris Chubbuck's photo. "No, I don't think she does."

"Yeah, well I do. Do you think you could've bailed her out, Mole? Talked her into shooting herself in the leg or something?"

"Why are *you* so up-tight about it, mate?"

"Look, I'm not up-tight. I mean it don't make no dif to me. We get them all the time here, don't we? I just wish I knew what she wanted to prove, is all. I mean, like why couldn't she blow her head off in her bed? Or the toilet, or something?"

"What exactly is it that's upsetting you?" G.J. put it to him. "That she did it on company time?"

"Yeah, right. Why didn't she do it on her own time? It's goddamn selfish to lay her shit on other people—people she couldn't possibly know—like that."

"That would seem to be her point, wouldn't you say, Mole?"

I nodded.

"It was shamanistic," G.J. said.

"So's my coccyx. What the shit does that mean, G.J.?"

"Look, mate, people here in this country of yours can't stop trivializing reality. They've been bred to it. One evening the 6:00 news reports an uprising in Cyprus, or an earthquake in Peru, between the commercial for Coke and the commercial for Revlon. The next evening it shows a Hollywood premiere in the same time slot."

"So fucking what?"

"Well, if Coke and Revlon and Chase Manhattan and Dix Chemical goose-step no matter what the weather, never missing a beat, then horror is equated with celebration, with fictions like 'Kojak' or 'Mod Squad'. How convenient to equate the gravity of Telly Savalas with the gravity of John Chancellor on NBC news."

"Yeah, well I like Savalas a lot better than that faggoty Chancellor. But that's beside the point. What I want to know is how does all this make that broad a witch-doctor?"

"I said shaman. She—Chris Chubbuck embodied this, this value distortion in her act. This illusion that we continue onward and upward, providing you buy our latest cars and things. We've been made into addicts with our mouths open. Didn't you admit yourself to being addicted to Johnny Carson, mate?"

"Shit. What do you think of this bird's exegesis, Mole?"

"She's right."

"It's a shocking reminder, though, isn't it, Mole?" G.J. said.

"Yes. Seeing it is," I agreed.

"You bet your ass," Sklar said. "Like seeing Ruby shoot Oswald on TV. History unfolding while you eat your granola. Fucking eerie."

"Haven't you noticed that that's what happens here?" Mole said. "On our radio station?"

"I've sometimes wondered why you came to this station in the first place, mate. It doesn't really seem your dish."

"I'll be honest witchoo, G.J. It's the bread. This Kloss shit costs. You try getting wahoo, or skullcap or pilewort these days. You'll see what I mean." Sklar pulled something out of his trouser pocket, a small paper bag, lumpy. "You see this?" He poured a yellow pebbly substance into his hand. "This here's wahoo. Terrific for burns, piles, all kinds of women trouble. Four ounces, it cost me 3.50 at Kiehls. Then there's the equipment. That was no street-whore's douche I plugged you with, G.J. Top dollar shit. That's why I work here, to answer your question. Besides, I sometimes get off on it. On the calls. Listening to Mole."

April 5: Dix is taking a brief vacation at his Palm Springs estate to "recover from the shock of Mrs. Dix's sudden illness." This from Nubile, Dix's Press Secretary.

In respone to a question from a correspondent from the Hearst Syndicate, Nubile denies "categorically" that Dix has in fact gone to Beverly Hills for a face-lift as a first step in his campaign to "inject new blood into this great old office."

In response to a question from Julia Saphire (*née* Slotkin) of WPIX, about "whether Senator Dix's deteriorating, uh, posterior condition necessitated immediate surgery in Los Angeles," a flushed Nubile dismisses the question as "impertinent," which he amends to "inappropriate," which he further amends to: "The Senator's physical condition is super. He is in absolutely excellent shape for a man of his years."

"Is it true," McVey from the Chicago *Sun-Times*, wants to know, "that the Senator is considering dumping Smegma and substituting Coach Zurco, who at this very minute is with him in Palm Springs?"

Nubile vouchsafes a smile. "Whoever put that idea in your head, Pete, is off his own noggin. Probably some gung-ho Dallas Cowboy fan who sure as heck would like to see Jock Zurco anyplace but in the National Football League. But to answer your question succinctly: no. Jock is a great friend of the Senator's. And he's a winner. But Harry Smegma is also the Senator's close friend. And speaking of winners, I'm sure you recall how Smokey ate up the yardage in Germany and France when the going was tougher than tough.

"The truth is, as I said, in all candor, that Senator Dix is taking a short vacation—a busman's holiday, you can call it—in Palm Springs because of the quite reasonable anxiety brought on by Mrs. Dix's illness . . .

April 6: Dix gone, now might be the time to speak of my roof. I feel fortunate that it is both convenient and handsome. It is true that the building is a "tenement," and that there has been talk of razing it and constructing a high-rent condominium. I doubt that the plan will be realized—at least not for several years. The tenants, several of whom have lived here for twenty years or more, would not allow themselves to be thrown to the wolves without waging a battle. Plucky folk. I went to two tenant meetings where it was unanimously agreed that at the least sign of coercion, they would withhold their monthly rents. And if the coercion continued, more drastic (though unnamed) steps would be considered.

I said my building was handsome. It dates from 1888, according to the partially effaced inscription of the Greek-Revival pediment directly below me. It is a corner building, and it has always reminded me of an elegant baker's "peel," shaped as it is like an ellipse balanced on its side. Though it appears quite shallow, it is in fact extremely well-constructed, almost entirely of steel and concrete. It has windows on each of its sides, so that it looks a bit like a lanky paranoid Antaeus.

The fire-escapes, appended to front and back, containing all manner of goods, from plants and salamis, to phonographs and gold-fish—are, for Mole, spider-webs: convolute, ancient, and innocent because in accord with the Wheel, the *Chakra,* the *adagio,* round and slowly round and . . .

Nonetheless, the building is considered an anomaly, an embarrassment. Surrounded—oppressed—as we are by all species of high-rise "cooperatives" and condominiums; by classy hotels and consulates. In fact we are close to that bastion of international amity: the United Nations. Dix's twenty-eight room triplex (the top three floors of a forty-two floor "cooperative") is within eye-shot. And his platform (and dais) is, as you know, beneath me.

Tonight is also a convenient night for chores. First, my hammock, which was partially upset by yesterday's sudden rainstorm, must be re-tied. Also wind-swept debris, some of which has accumulated near my spot, I sweep into a pile in the far corner.

The books, some 70% of which are now here on my roof,

again have weathered the assault without a casualty—except for a few rainspots on Madame Blavatsky who will not complain.

The liver (sliced finely) for the Jewish cat.

Finally, the circle, almost entirely effaced by the rain, must be re-traced. In white and gules.

Thursday, April 7: A letter from Savage-Anschluss, the gun people out of Winston-Salem. They are, they write, processing my letter, and they need to know the following:

1: Do I want a "German walnut stock" or a "checkered American walnut stock."

2: Do I want the "Redfield Olympic sights and scope-blocks," which will cost 29.95.

3: Do I want the "222 Remington Magnum cartridges" or the "22 caliber Mossberg cartridges."

Mole should receive his "weapon and accessories" between eight and twelve weeks.

That afternoon I decided to go uptown to consult some gun manuals in the New York Public Library. Thought for a second that I left my knife behind. No, it's there, under my handkerchief, in my left trouser pocket. For some reason Mole feeling more than usually tense today.

Though it was only 3:30, the subway platform was already crowded. Just as I unfolded my *Times*, my eye caught him to my left: Dix, with a rejuvenated face. Those rumors were right. But I couldn't imagine what he was doing *here* on the Fourteenth Street East Side IRT subway platform. It was Dix though unmistakably, the bags under his eyes stretched tight, bi-focals jettisoned, the hair thicker, bourbon-colored, with only modish traces of grey about his temples and sideburns. And of course the displaced occiput, and Prussian folds at the back of the neck. One curious elaboration was the hearing device behind his left ear, which, however, seemed in accord with the rough shoes, denim trousers and tan windbreaker he was wearing.

An effective disguise, Mole had to concede. But what was he up to? Could he have felt compelled to blend with the *canaille* in just this way: observe them, sound them out, so as to wage a more expedient campaign? The wily fucker was even carrying a copy of that blue-collar standard-bearer, the *Daily News.*

Seemingly anxious, Dix was now pacing back and forth on the platform, as if looking for the right spot. When the Express stopped and the doors opened, he deftly maneuvered himself into the center of a crush of young Puerto Rican factory women who had just gotten off work. Mole squeezed in behind him.

Once inside the car, we massed against one of the poles, Mole behind and slightly to Dix's left. Close as I was (privy as I am to his innermost cess), I was wholly unprepared for this next observation. He was holding his *News* so as to obscure what he was about, but I saw clearly that he had thrust his broad pelvis against the pole so that his genitals came in contact with several of the women's hands, wrists, elbows. At the same time he feigned a look of exasperation, as if to say: I'm sorry I'm in this awkward position, it is uncomfortable for me, but there are just too many people leaning on me for me to move even a few inches.

Soon the hand with which Dix held his newspaper was in the vicinity of a woman's breast, while his left leg was making contact with another taller woman's flank.

At once I felt a rush of anger, but looking around I saw that the other passengers were impervious, reading their newspapers, making peripheral contacts with their own fantasies. I glowered at Dix, and he must have been aware of my presence—yet he gave no outward sign of acknowledgement. With some difficulty Mole maneuvered even closer until I could see beneath the newspaper the revolting erection—curiously low-down in his trousers—rubbing and pushing against the hands and torsos in simulated response to the stops and starts of the train. His victims, for their part, were keeping up a steady giggling clatter which apparently had nothing to do with him.

Suddenly—before I could catch myself—I swatted my newspaper with as much force as I could muster against the top of the pole above all the hands. The noise was loud enough to be distinctly heard and eveyone in the vicinity turned to the sound, including Dix. I caught his pokey little eyes, stared at him hard, dramatically moved my own eyes in a scanning motion to the women beside him, then rapidly back to him. I uncurled my lips derisively . . .

Dix gave no indication that he was dismayed at being discovered. At first Mole saw only intensity in his returning stare, then I discerned something ironic, perhaps even contemptuous, in his eyes, in the thrust of his jaws. The swine!

I tapped a passenger next to me who looked up at me over his newspaper. I whispered to him that the man with the hearing-aid was molesting the women around him. He glanced at Dix, then at Mole, then at the people in our vicinity, some of whom had finally noticed that something was going on. Then he looked at Mole again with annoyance, testily turned his shoulder away from me, smoothed his newspaper, and continued reading.

By this time we had arrived at a central stop, and most of the car emptied out, including nearly all of the factory women. Masher Dix exited also.

Pausing on the platform, he studied the passengers who were waiting for the train from the opposite direction. As the train veered in, screaming to a halt, Dix moved several feet to the left and positioned himself behind a group of junior high school girls. But the train was sparsely occupied, which meant enough seats for everyone. Abruptly Dix turned away and started up the stairs. He walked towards the long arcade that led to a distant exit. He must have known I was behind him though he did not once turn his head.

Outside it had evidently just stopped raining, there weren't many people on the streets. He was walking briskly now, due west. His head and upper body nearly rigid, only his wide hips, arms and legs moving in the familiar Dix shuffle. He appeared to be making for the large museum that fronted the park, or perhaps for the park itself, though that seemed

unlikely, since few people would be out in this weather. It was
the museum: Dix turned right at the top of the steps and
entered the art library.

A good many people, most of them college students,
were reading at the desks. Dix paused briefly to reconnoiter,
then walked deliberately up a side aisle, stopping once to have
a close (covert) look at a young college girl. He walked back
down the center aisle, pausing again near a table filled with
young girls examining colored plates; then continued walking.
Finally he selected a chair which he adjusted to face a girl who,
engrossed in a catalogue, had crossed her legs so that the
upper portion of one of her thighs was more visible than she
realized. Dix nervously arranged the newspaper on his lap,
crossed his own legs (Mole observed that under his brogans
the loutish feet were sockless), and tilted his head in the girl's
direction. He placed his right hand on the desk (the ugly
splayed thumb wholly visible), and his left under the newspaper; remaining precisely in that position for ten minutes or
so, until the girl got up to whisper to a friend. When she sat
down again she rearranged her legs under the desk. Now Dix
began to fidget and crane his neck in other directions. He
stood and nervously scanned the reading room. Mole stood up
also. We locked eyes for an instant, then he pivoted and made
for the side exit. The door opened into a long narrow corridor
which led to the galleries.

We were in the Medieval and Early Renaissance Gallery.
It was poorly lit, nearly empty: I was able to make out only
three other people in the entire hall. I paused before a
painting of the Annunciation. Mary's gown was vermilion and
the Angel Gabriel wore a sky blue robe. Neither of them
smiled. To the right of this canvas was a large gothic
representation of the Deposition. Jesus looked like a shrivelled monkey. They were all pawing at him. Mole reached into
my left pocket and withdrew his knife which I shook open. I
made a slash about five inches long in the area of Jesus' loin-
cloth. I was about to slash again, crosswise, when something
heavy stopped my arm, twisting it behind my back. I heard the
knife hit the parqueted floor.

"Son of a bitch!" I felt the violent hiss in my ear, and as I tried to twist my body free, he dropped his newspaper and exerted more pressure on my arm. Then someone else—a guard—also held me, hard across the chest.

Naturally he got off. And without much ado. Revealed himself as the senior Senator from New York. Pointed out that there was absolutely no injury done to the canvas ("I happen to be a collector myself, as you may know.") As for the knife, he had meant merely to pare his fingernails.

The Dix team smoke-screened with consummate skill. Not even the rabidly anti-Dix tabloid, the NY *Post*, made mention of the incident.

The *Post*, however, did headline Dix's face-lifting in this wise: "DIX PULLS A PROXMIRE."

Senator Proxmire from Wisconsin, you may recall, was the first and most notable major politician to admit to getting a face-lift.

(Orpheus' head is severed; but now Marya is stuck . . .

April 9: The soulful hour, 3 A.M. Mole in his hammock thinking of connections. "The sleepers are very beautiful as they lie unclothed, / They flow hand in hand over the whole earth from east to west as they lie unclothed."

Whitman, who knew that when we wake we sleep; that when we sleep (truly)   we unfurl:

The Jewish cat folding and unfolding on the tar beneath me. I think of my people.

Moishe, with numbers on his arm, a peddler of old clothes, phoned Mole at the station. He said that he felt endangered by young thugs, gentiles, who followed him as he pushed his cart through the gutters. Taunted him. He took himself to the cemetery finally, seeking rest—but found his

people's gravestones overturned, the sacred inscriptions
defaced. He didn't know what to do. He asked Mole to "heal"
him.

Sklar was listening. When Mole got off the phone he said:
"Too late, Mole. You can't help that joker. Kaput."

"You're wrong, Sklar," I said. "You're dead wrong."

Tuesday, April 12: Fay-Louella Bell Dix dies peacefully
in her sleep at the Mayo Clinic in Minnesota, the Senator at
her side. Interment, which will take place in Bellmont, North
Carolina, limited to family.

Jock Zurco on Cancer: a prepared statement he read
before a Press Conference in his offices at Washington
Stadium following Mrs. Dix's passing:

"In the alphabet world of pro football, you might think a
defensive lineman's nightmare would be having an O.J.
coming right at him. Or a D.D., or a Y.A., or an R.C.

"But the most important stop one of my best kids,
defensive tackle Doug Witecki, ever made was on the Big C.
He stopped it right on the goal line. A few seconds more with
the ball and it would have scored. Doug would have lost the
ball game.

"The doctors' word for Big C is Carcinoma. A deva-
stating ball-carrier right out of the University of Hell. Number
1 draft choice. Franco Harris is a pantywaist compared to Big
C who has 20,000-yard seasons all the time and goes into every
game the overwhelming favorite.

"Big C ran over Witecki's position in the summer of 1976.
It put such a good juke on Doug, he was almost mouse-
trapped. It might have scored, except Doug got a lucky
break—his appendix burst.

"It happened on a handball court in Pittsburgh. Some of
the guys wanted to go out for a few beers afterwards, but
Doug was having these stomach cramps. He thought maybe
he'd go home and lay down. Now when you're 6 feet 8 inches
and weigh 270 pounds, you don't let a belly-ache stop you. I

mean, if you did, and gave into a little stomach hurt, you'd never be able to stand up to Gino Mastucci all afternoon.

"But this belly-ache was double-teaming him. And Doug went to the hospital. They knew the appendix was rupturing when they opened him up. But that was the good news. What they found in him, knees and cleets and shoulder-pads, was the old number zero-zero. Big C himself. And he had the ball.

"The doc told Doug that if it hadn't been for the appendix, the cancer would have gone undetected. It might have been five weeks. It might have been five years, even. But if they didn't catch it then, it was going to win the game.

"Cancer cannot be played one-on-one, so the doctors resected part of Doug's bowel and hoped that Big C had finally fumbled one.

"That was four years ago, and a couple of hundred quarterback sacks ago. Witecki still goes in for periodic checkups and, in fact, he underwent one only last week. You never give a quick whistle to Big C. You make sure he's down.

"The season after his operation Witecki led our club in tackles. And this season, as most of you probably know, he led the league in quarterback sacks and made All-Pro. You see, nothing carrying a football and wearing a number can ever scare Doug Witecki. As far as Douglas Joseph Witecki is concerned, his Super Bowl was won four summers ago—with less than a minute to play and the other guy having the ball. That's one opponent he never wants to see on his schedule again.

"Senator Dix's beloved Fay-Louella was not so lucky. The docs didn't find out until it was too late. I'd like to request from all of you a minute of silence on behalf of her memory."

April 13: Mole withdraws Maxim Gorky from his place on the roof. Consider this passage from his *Life of a Useless Man:*

Inside the entrance to the church hung a picture representing a saint who had caught the devil and was beating him. The saint was a tall, dark, sinewy man with long hands, the devil a reddish, lean, embryonic creature who had the appearance of a small goat. At first Yevsey did not even glance at the devil—he even wanted to spit at him; but then he began to be sorry for the unfortunate little figure, and when nobody was around he gently stroked the goat-like chin disfigured in the picture by dread and pain. For the first time compassion was born in the boy's heart.

In our instance it is the wounded Dix with his refurbished skin who is "embryonic," and (according to the hundreds of phone calls which have been coming in to his Washington offices since his wife's untimely death), "saintly." Or so reported Nubile in a candid interview with the Washington *Star.*

Mole it is, long and lean and dark, with thick spectacles over deep-set eyes, with fingers like Zelda Sklar (though clubbed at the tips), who will be Lucifer—until disinterred by Sartre, or some such, who will proceed to broadcast the rediscovered truth: that Mole was a fallen (which is to say, only possible) angel, traduced by bourgeois interpolators of history.

Think of Mole then as a martyr to soulful scholarship. To the feeler-thinkers. And to the mutants, who already know, but are enfeebled. The stertorous "vast majority" will have to wait until the ichor filters down; until the coke-and-molasses lyrics of John Denver (or some such) jackal it across the airwaves on CBS.

Tough.

Yet that's the way it seems to be in this time of Kali. I mean the desecration of the just.

Nonetheless, call Mole Arjuna, the roof his chariot. I have my work . . .

Of the thirty-two families living in my building, six are black. Mole wishes there were more. The Simmons live just below me, in 6a. Jesse, his wife Gloria, and two daughters, Eleanor, seventeen, and Delores Jean, eleven. Eleanor is an unusual, even extraordinary, girl. Already in her second year at Cooper Union on a scholarship, majoring in something called Mathematical Design, she is both ruminative and uncommonly curious. On a sunny autumn Saturday afternoon you might find her in her room quietly strumming on her guitar for hours without pause. Or she might be walking (in her long-legged preoccupied way) from an African bookshop on 125th Street, to the Lincoln Center music library, to the Museum of Primitive Art on 54th Street, and finally to the central branch of the New York Public Library: therein to the third floor reference room where she will check out obscure 19th century periodicals or compendiums of design or collections of poetry: Cesar Vallejo, say, or Anne Spencer; read, ruminate until well beyond dinner time . . .

Eleanor is a tall, slender, esthetic-looking girl, with a delicate horsey face, large pensive eyes, and long tapered fingers. Though manifestly proud of their daughter, Jesse and Gloria are concerned about her. Her absentness, her dreaminess, troubles them. Her responses to them, though rarely disrespectful, often seem somehow askew, as if (like a record) she is on a different "speed."

Among the things about their daughter the Simmons don't know, is that she has recently fallen in love with Herbert Cohn, a forty-six year old divorcee, and her professor of "The History of Design" at Cooper Union. They have passed several very happy afternoons together at the professor's apartment off Washington Square Park.

Jesse Simmons, an assistant manager of a textile factory on West 26th Street, has for the last five years been going to Baruch College in the evenings, and will receive his long-deferred Bachelor of Science degree at the end of the summer. He is a thoughtful and sometimes moody man. Gloria, who is surely justified in being moody, having recently undergone a mastectomy, is a vibrant, consistently genial, and efficient woman, who is both a senior secretary at Dix Chemical (the sole Negro on the fourth floor), and an assiduous housewife.

Delores Jean is attractive, popular, an average student, as yet without any of her older sister's unsettling proclivities.

April 14: This call:

"You Mole?"

"Yes."

"Look, I need your help. I need a woman real bad. For twenty-seven years I lived without a woman and I'm still a virgin. Like I'll settle for almost anybody and do anything she says. Any fucking thing. Only stop me from beating my meat three times a day before I go blind."

I slipped the call to blip.

"I'm talking to you now on a private line," Mole told him. "Nobody can hear us. Do you want to tell me your name?"

"Yeah, yeah. It's Dan."

"Okay, Dan. I've got somebody for you."

"You do! No shit! Oh, great—when can I see her? Like what's her name?"

"Do you live in the city?"

"Yeah. 90th and Columbus."

"I'm sure that she can see you tonight then. Her name is Zelda."

. . . and Gwendolyn kneeling over a supine Dix, fresh from his sitz. Gwen's paper towel on the carpet beside her.

"I want you to swallow it, Gwen. Forget about those paper towels of yours for once."

Gwen recoils, her lips unfasten, her irises arch in dismay. "But—"

"Put your mouth back there. What are you worried about? You've done it before. And for lots less than you're getting here also. Besides, it's supposed to taste pretty good. Though I wouldn't know."

"The swine," she thinks, her mouth full of stiffer than usual fool. "Since Fay's death, and his own preposterous renovation, he wants this, he wants that—"

"You're not concentrating, Gwendolyn. Your mouth has lost its wetness. I'd like a little wetness. And pay attention, will you?"

April 15: Since April Fool's Day Sklar has been notice-ably less voluble with Mole. G.J. has noticed it.

"All right, mate, let's have it. Why so darksome of late?"

"Darksome? That must be a limey word. I'm not familiar with it."

"You've been on the rag, is what I mean. Have you noticed it, Mole?"

"I have, yes."

"Talk about darksome, Mole here is darksomeness in fucking panavision. Am I right, buddy?"

"Why are you getting on Mole's case, mate?"

"Mole's case! Because Mole gets on every fucking body else's case, is why. He's made a convert of my wife, you know."

G.J. looks at Mole with interest.

"What has he converted her to?"

"Ask him. What've you converted her to, Mole?"

Mole says nothing.

"It's what he does with all of them," Sklar says. "That undefinable fucking X. Rasputinism—or whatever the shit it is."

"He raised her consciousness, you mean," G.J. says.

"Yeah, right. Only Zelda's consciousness was between her legs, which is where I liked it."

Peony, Dix's ice blonde niece, whom I tutored some years back (she it was who informed me of her uncle's distaste for socks). I said we never swived. That was a partial truth. Mole tried to once but was impotent, came almost immedi-ately. After that I stopped giving her lessons . . .

This "confession" given on my roof, while in *Sirshasana,* which Sri Sen calls the truth *Asana.*

I wonder whether Dix can see my long muscular legs, now spread into a wide V.

The Jewish cat, my compeer, who I assumed was male, is in heat. Tomorrow I'll bring her some cottage cheese.

April 17: Full moon. Mole here, high, under it. Beneath me, Dix. I can make him out clearly, bathed in his pseudo light.

Sri Sen was right. The yoga *Asanas* are helping. As for *Pranayama*, I can't breathe as forcefully as Sen would wish, for fear of someone hearing me. Indeed I thought that Dix himself recognized me earlier when I was standing close to the edge in *Sirshasana*. He was kneeling on one knee on the dais, whispering something to Ronald, when, unexpectedly, he swiveled in my direction. Mole thought surely he must have recognized me from the subway caper. But nothing. No response.

At the moment I'm comfortably bent backwards in *Halasana*. My hamstrings feel nice and limber. And the moon.

"Yet poetry makes nothing happen," according to the man who worshipped boys.

Mole answers: When being begins "no-thing" matters . .

Sen says we do as we must, once we find the must-place. Which is in one's tunnel.

My knife. Caressing Shiva in my left pocket with the fingers of my left hand is impious, according to weak-lunged Hindus—to which Sen, with his monkey's tail for a cock, laughs, displaying betel-coated teeth.

Weird John Brown. Twisting slowly, slowly in the wind. Yet the Dream's *telos* cannot be wrong. Though it may be misapprehended: the tunnel having many turnings, and Fear it is (the most sapient one), who whispers: "This one, take this one in the semi-light."

My father, I feel, heard Abaddon.

For Mole it is the real dark. No false dawn. No more turnings until the *turning*.

"As for Orpheus's head, it was laid to rest in a cave at Antissa, sacred to Dionysus. There it prophesied day and night . . ."

Mole discovered this quotation in the bathroom, on a torn piece of paper bag, on the floor, in Marya's hand.

Easter Sunday, April 18: A telegram (unsigned) delivered to Mole's place in the early morning. These words:

Commie Rosenbergs / Christ Killers

According to Nubile the "heady mission" began on Easter Sunday, 1898, when St. Paul himself appeared to Sylvan P. Dix aboard his private clipper as he was being transported to Hamburg on business. The first great renegade, citing his own example, succeeded in "commissioning the illustrious magnate away from Bauxite and into the area where he might do the greatest good, namely Public Service. As the venerable old octogenarian himself vividly phrased it many years afterward while accepting a meritorious award from President Coolidge: 'Providence had made me a trustee of his fortune for the benefit of man.' "

This revelation bestowed in semi-hushed tones at a Press-Briefing-Easter-Brunch. Nubile said he did not suppose there were any questions, but Brafman, a Capitol Hill regular from the Miami *Herald*, insisted on being recognized.

"I had heard about this—this great experience of old man Dix—from another source, who went on to say that the great man—the apostle, I mean—looked a lot like Karl Malden. Could've been taken for his double even."

Nubile, who had chummed with Ziegler, Nixon's tool, at USC, glared at Brafman—but remained mute.

The great old tycoon's grandson, Forrest Patrician Dix, senior Senator from New York: still abed in his southern Vermont rancho, his renovated phiz unlovely in the gloaming of the master bedroom. The stained-glass mirror on the ceiling above the king-sized oval bed (specially designed by Alexander Calder at a cost of $65,000), misty from the Senator's open-mouthed sighs and labored breathing. A copy of "Sporting News," four Sunday newspapers, two Danish porn magazines, and Dix's custom-made truss lie helter-skelter on the Afghani rug beside the night table.

Ronald, after a night of venery, yet fresh as calamus, and not without his truncheon, enters quietly with a tall glass of papaya juice and the Senator's hormone drops.

When the factotum taps him, the Senator snorts awake.

"Hmnfff . . . Ronald."

"It's nearly 10:30, Senator."

"Oh, shit, I feel like death. You have the drops?"

"Right here."

"Mix them then, fella. Let's see how it is with four this time. The juice is not too cold, is it?"

"Nope. Everything's as usual. Except that lots of people are in and around the chapel. Things supposed to start about 11:15."

"Yeah. Right. Where did Rebus leave the sermon?"

"It's on your desk in the library. Bound. All set."

"Did he triple-space it this time like I told him?"

"I don't know. I didn't notice."

"Yeah. Well it's his ass if he didn't. This is an important thing today, this Easter thing. This speech. Okay, let's have the juice, fella."

"From worrier to warrior": that would be Mole's transformation, according to Sri Sen.

Meanwhile Mole awake and worrying.

Before Dix, the crossbar of the crucifix had been navel-high. Dix raised the bar, mentalized the energy, estranged the body. Thus the Pope and his nasty prostate.

Gone the deific hardon.

What did Jesus, the Essene, wear beneath his seamless robe?

At nine, Mole awake and dreaming in the sanctum of Marya. Except for roughly 30% of him, which is in the tunnel, his roof.

Where as always it is cold. His hammock wet from the night's rain. TV aerials angled against the moon. Chimney oozing black fire. His books sooty. The (still warm) condom in the far corner. The Jewish cat gone, her cheese gone. Shiva alone. Knife in his left side pocket . . .

Jesus may or may not have been a ganymede, but Shiva's *lingam* is infinite. Back straight, lotused alone on Mount Meru.

For the lesson of Prometheus is not so much his courage, as his "long stubbornness."

The truth is that Mole was feeling guilty at having finally fucked G.J. It occurred in the studio during an extended lull. It was very nice. Afterwards they discovered that something had gone wrong with the phones. In fact several people had been trying to get through. This deathly Easter.

Sklar had taken the night off to attend a Jethro Kloss memorial in Teaneck, New Jersey.

Mole had finally yielded to G.J. and, as I said, liked it. Yet afterwards he felt bad because he had swived while his people died a little trying to get through to him. G.J. smelled good. Mole had not even sensed that his people were wanting him. He fucked her from behind while standing on the floor facing the dead phones. She was on her knees on the sofa. She felt his cock and balls with both hands as he went in and out of her. Spreading her fine ass with his hands, he fingered the pretty brown eye with his right forefinger, though poetry makes nothing happen; and "even the dreadful martyrdom must run its course / anyhow in a corner."

And Mole, afterwards, sidling over to the edge of the wall to scratch his back, is worried—despite what he knows.

Easter, Miss.—In the southeast corner of this small delta town, whose proud motto is: "We Move Heavenward, not Forward," Snitt's Poultry stands where it has stood. And today, like every other day, it is open for workers. Bessie Frazer, black, 38, widowed with four children, is one of them. She splits chicken gizzards with a pair of "poultry shears." That's all. She never cuts the liver, or pulls out the craw, or picks out the pin-feathers, or cuts the throat to spill the living blood.

She does not even clean the gizzard. She merely cuts it open and passes it on. Some days she splits more than 4000 gizzards.

"The shears be so dull sometime you cain't hardly cut," she said. "And your hand get sore too." She held up her right palm which had a raw orange-red welt in its center.

"The craw-pullers, now, they hands gets messed up pretty bad. Also the gut pullers."

Mrs. Frazer goes to work at 5:30 A.M. Usually she does not get home until after twilight.

About 400 persons, most of them women, most of them black, work in the two poultry plants in Easter. There are hundreds of such plants across the South. Some are owned locally, but most are owned by large national corporations, including several Dix Chemical affiliates. All offer the same rewards to their workers: their wages are near the bottom of the industrial scale. They provide few fringe benefits, and virtually no job security.

"We not satisfied at it," Mrs. Frazer said. "But I guess we just have to put up with it. They ain't nothing else to do . . ."

Enough! Enough!
Somehow I have been stunned. Stand back!
Give me a little time beyond my cuffed head,
  slumbers, dreams, gaping . . .

INTERMEZZO

Inward. Huge accumulations of "matter" pressing inward would "produce objects approaching infinite density within an infinitely small radius." However, the gravitational field of such an "object" would not merely attract light—but emit light.

Thus Mole, his tunnel and thirteen years old when I left my house late at night in snow. Rode the subway to Harlem. Walked from 103rd Street to 125th along Madison, the wind blowing hard, I saw no one. Crossing west to Fifth Avenue, I headed downtown again. She was in a doorway of a burned-out store-front church at 112th. Yes, I said, following her. She dragged slowly through the snow because the walking was hard, and her left leg was in an iron brace. She saw me looking at it, said she hurt it recently in a car accident. But I knew that it must have been that way a long time because it was much thinner than the other leg. Her name, she said, was Butter. It was freezing outside. She wasn't wearing gloves. She crossed the street at 109th, led me to a tenement off Madison. Down steep cement stairs to the cellar. She tapped on the door twice, then looked back at me, smiled. The pimp, thin and very dark, came outside quickly. He wore a beret pulled low over his head. Also woolen gloves. He scarcely looked at me. He told Butter: hurry up, it's colder than shit outside. We went inside.

A single square grey room, dirty. A narrow cot by the barred window. Butter looked at me, smiled. She told me not to be nervous. I told her I wasn't, which was true. She excused herself, went over to a tin basin in a corner of the room, hiked her long coat and skirt, squatted and pissed, ping-ping-ping against the metal in the cold room.

Then she dragged over to me, took my face in both her hands, asked whether I would mind if she didn't take off her clothes, it was so cold. I didn't mind. I put my arms around her shoulders. She said before we started I had to give her the five, this was the custom. I did. She slipped the bill under the part of her brace that was near her thigh. Then she touched my penis. I was hard. She made to unzip my pants, but I told her no.

I took her hand and led her to the cot. She settled down on her back and spread her legs, but instead of lying on top of her, I got on my knees on the floor and put my head into her. She said Ah, in surprise, holding my head with both hands gently as I pushed. I remember it was only a little wet and smelling of nothing really, and I pushed with my tongue and my chin, my eyes open, not thinking. I don't know for how long . . .

Stopping, I got up quickly. Said I had to go. Opened the door. The pimp was outside with his arms crossed, shivering. I wasn't at all cold.

I walked all the way home, which wasn't as far as I had thought. Feeling light.

(Marya wants to know how long. The grey-haired technician tugs at an ear-lobe . . .)

"Matter entering this universe from other universes carries with it the physical 'constants' characteristic of those universes."

Mole, wafer-thin at sixteen, enters the subway at 86th Street, going down. Hectic & money ether over raw nerves' cold sweat: the Xmas-shopping equation. Except one man near where Mole enters, drunk and old and curled muttering asleep on a seat. Mole stands facing him, against the door, as if on guard. From—though—his blind side, something: a man, angles, kicking the other. Kicking, abusing the drunk, old. Mole shouts No! but unheard, moves. The long Christian moves back, eyes frozen white-grey as if iced fire. Sputum hard at his mouth's corners. Yet the drunk old man sleeps. Passengers full of packages "sleep." My father (who wouldn't drink) curled child-small, tense asleep. Yet the two of us. Large but angles, long feet, lank brown hair on a large head, hearing device, thrice me in age, eyes me hard, wary.

"No!" I say it again. "Don't kick him!" And down, beneath Times Square the train hurtles.

Hating each other without sound, going down, he seeking my fear, which borne of strangeness and the truth of my dream, is just beneath my hating him. Glimpsing it, he widens his mouth: his taunt less than the rictus wide Mole knows just how mad—only on the side of Christ who killed him in us. "Jew!" he says at my eyes, hating my father with his eyes.

28th Street: we're out, station deserted. Grappling, pulling at my hair, my teeth all over him, falling, his lips at me, and mine   plummeting the tracks are black are—gone

The brief and vivid union
of a tempestuous heart united to the tempest

Mole (child) had a flying machine flew under water. Under laughter. In class a child shit his pants, the others giggled, pinched their noses, giggling. The teacher scanned the room, stopped at Mole, who alone was not laughing, no reason to. Pointing: it was you, she said. Mole, it was you . . .

At first in the silence before sleep, Mole's machine: domed, glass, musty, still: a library, open yet impenetrable, where you read or played or simply sat (under water). After, in angry laughter anywhere, Mole would enter his steel-white meadow, at the wood round table sit, sleep, gazing out:

At the mongoloid child who with her old visibly shamed parents lived around the corner, dressed in white socks, draggled behind: she would enter.

At the two twin Negro boys, silent pariahs in the second grade in the platinum school—they would enter.

At his very friend, his age, out of nowhere (laughter) struck, paralyzed, iron-lunged for two years. Back at school now, gone permanently. Gone. Sheldon. He had the run of the place, Mole's.

As did others, though when they joined, lied, laughing, joined . . . young Mole: implacable.

Meadow then become austere, to the feebled ever open, to the others by petition. Election. Eyes closed, true need, dark.

Meanwhile other (Mole still) outside changed: louder, leader, classroom cut-up, esteemed. Moulted, leaving the horny, stabbed-at, segmented shell naked in the steel-white

meadow. Emerged laughing as everyman beneath Moloch.
Magical, in angry waves the machine growing for his people
yet not ice. Mole as Lucifer, as much as he knew needing to
know &

     Random   Zero   Sunlight)

    (Marya said: No, don't touch his head. Won't let
you . . .)

*He likened the situation to the "oft-cited representation of
the universe in terms of galaxies sprinkled over the surface of an
expanding balloon. The balloon represents the four-dimen-
sional curvature of space and time. As it swells the galaxies
draw farther apart. However, there is a matching universe on
the inner surface of this 'balloon,' linked to the outer one by
'white hole-black hole' connections. Matter falling through a
black hole from this universe comes out as anti-matter in the
white hole of its brother universe, whose anti-matter composi-
tion balances the domination of our own universe by matter."*

    Thus the furnaces. Leaving the blood of his skin behind,
Mole university'd in the "best," learned Psychology. Excelled.
    On the train after four strange years. Rectilinear. Mole
took a wrong turn, though into the old place: found it . . .
gone. The sea there, derision—yet his meadow gone. Instead
of (bloodless) breaking up, he pushed farther, farther . . .
    When they "saw," classmates, professors couldn't see
why; though of course strain and excellence might distend
(verily). Yes it would be temporary. Bottom out. Balance.
    Mole meanwhile joined the circus. Into the cannon's
belly. Black. And full of light—zagging.

    Yet out again—for that's the way it goes. Tugged out of
the white hole of nature into the black hole of history—
untransfigured. The way it's always been.

Mole goes to work in a "half-way house" on 47th Street between Ninth and Tenth. Psychotics forgather there. Told to talk, Assistant Director Mole out of Harvard out of . . . listens. Not to words merely. One only, Storn: angular, near deaf, brutal grey-ice eyes, long feet—likes not Mole, a piece of him.

Others though do, or at least, don't not. Lila, twenty-three, never without her ratty floor-length coat, yet lovely, touches Mole under the table at every "conference." Her fingers knowing, move Mole, though her expression never wavers from schizophrenic "calm."

All Hallow E'en: the half-ways ironically plan a party. The motif: Sanity. Each will masquerade as a "sane" person who figured in his file. Except for mother and father who (even at this remove) emit too much energy. Admitted: there will be little or no recognition among patients, none having known each other before; whereas the sane mask will be strained out of the individual's past. Solipsistic masquerade.

And Mole? They want Mole to do the reverse, become for the time insane. Not however someone from my past, but from here, here, the half-way house. Mask myself as someone here. When I recover from the unexpectedness—the queer-ness—of the proposal, I naturally object on therapeutic grounds: it might inspire rancor, or jealousy among them; it might—they won't hear of it! Twenty-three of them and I (the director out of town, attending a symposium), in the common room. To the person, they approve the idea—never before had I seen such unanimity on any matter. All right, I say, I'll do it.

Making up a problem at first. Which is good, since in spite of the consensus, I am not keen on too visibly parodying any half-way. But then surprisingly, it begins to work. Though Mole had not worn makeup since acting in *Wozzek* at college, I didn't forget how to apply it. And like then, I find myself getting caught up in it—in spite of conscious reservations.

Since "recovering," I had forgotten that my fondest wish was to be immaterial, so that I might fuse my spirit's body with others. Masquerading as someone was next best to masquerading as no one. And particularly this "someone." The only (minor) difficulty turned out to be the hearing device.

The party was scheduled to begin at 9:00. I arrived at 8:45 feeling at once embarrassed and vain about how convincingly I was disguised. Mole expected to be among the first to arrive, but no, most or all of them seemed to be there. I could see their silhouettes in the ground floor window as I pulled my car to the curb. They didn't seem to be making much party noise.

When I entered they turned to me: most of them grinned, evidently recognizing whom I impersonated, appreciating the skillfulness of it. But their response didn't register on me right away. What I noticed immediately was that none of *them* were disguised. They looked quite as usual. Was Mole the butt of some strange joke? Or had they all concurrently, without consulting each other, decided that they themselves—science, society notwithstanding—were truly sane? Before Mole had a chance to clarify this, one of them, a confidant of Lila, told me she was waiting for me in the basement, near her locker.

At once Mole walked out into the narrow corridor and to the basement door, wondering whether Lila had decided finally to remove her long brown coat, and wished to demonstrate it to me. The wooden stairs were steep (the director and Mole had been complaining about this health-hazard for several months—to no avail). For a few seconds Mole forgot where precisely the lockers were, having been in the basement but twice in the five months I was employed. But then I heard something—either a sigh or a laugh—which sounded like Lila's tremulous soprano . . .

Mole walked on the rough cement for a few more meters, then turned the corner: —Sprawled on the floor, spread wider than he would have imagined was Lila yellow and pink on her rat brown coat. Mole himself between her thrusting sleekly then out, her frail legs crossed about his back, his cock very long, black—his ice grey eyes glaring sidelong at me, the hearing aid catching light from the naked bulb)

Dr. Sianni prophesied that the "first indication of the existence of 'black holes' would come from the detection of a massive, yet invisible object circling a visible star. Such an object would manifest its presence through energy emissions and its gravitational influence on the visible companion. The companion's debilitated energy, drawn in by the irresistible gravity of the black hole, would, after being modified by its contact with the 'gas' on the hole's outer fringes, be expelled in a regenerated form."

Mole then, *Bodhisattva* of Washington Heights, constrained to return, collared outside Carnegie Hall after Schubert's kindred winter. Her name was Faith, having just seen *Yellow Submarine*, she pulled up in front of me, with her hands on her hips, grinning teeth and agate eyes in a golden head. She saw my light, she said, about my head. So powerful—she had to stop. Who was I? For her part, she was a sooth-sayer. Astrology, Entrails, Tarot . . . the whole gig. How about some coffee?

Jeaned, golden, "laid back": Southern Cal entire she seemed but for those agate pin-wheels, eyes. Also her spiel, dotted with beyonds. Straight white teeth flashed through her coffee (black). She liked (she said) me, because of me. As would others "feel from this time on your power." We went back to her place.

88th, Central Park West: posters, incense. Mystical effects. (She had "studied" in Burma and northeast India.) Now she lived in a "brotherhood," six others, none there presently, all dedicated to help. "Help what?" People, she grinned. (Poe's Berenice only gold.)

"But who *are* you?" she grinned.

As I talked a bit, she grinning (distracted I at first thought), heard between me. Which powered me.

"Yes," she grinned, "let's do it. Only mouth only. Which is our way in the brotherhood."

She at me first. When I at her, she said: "Don't be so careful, I'm not made of glass."

At each other. Good, though her teeth refracted her eyes, as if glass, as she bit me wanting me . . .

In India finally. Nothing went right. The train outside
Rishikesh stopped unaccountably. For more than two hours it
didn't move. Not a word.

Mole through the window watching an untouchable
"sweeper" squat on the edge of the trestle where the tracks
fronted space, nearly 11,000 feet up. Black-skinned peasant
wearing grey-striped, boxer-style undershorts—multi-patched
—for trousers. No shirt on his wiry top. Shoeless. Smoking a
"bidi" through his cupped hand, squatting, back straight,
centimeters from the edge, His vivid black eyes facing me,
though not looking at me. Looking, it seemed, at nothing.

When the train stopped in the thin air I saw him. All the
time it remained (as it got colder) he was there, not having
budged, except, rarely, to pull deeply at his bidi, though never
(as far as Mole could see) exhaling smoke. Squatting, his
toughened prehensile feet as if locked into the mountain
earth. Yet beyond, about him: clouds, sky. Locked too into
his *dharma*, a rung above the mangy brown bitch discon-
solately skulking near the train for something to nourish her
sapless teats. A rung or so above the starving pig Mole saw
nudge the defecating children squatting near the tracks
around dawn.

I wanted to give him something. Not so much because he
needed it, though of course he did; but because of his
nakedness—his naked autonomy. I motioned to a small boy,
and when he came to the window, I handed him two *rupees* in
paise, telling him to keep fifty *paise* for himself, give the rest to
the sweeper. Instead he clutched the money and disappeared
around the train. I would have to do it myself. Wrapping my
scarf about my neck, I walked through the nearly empty car to
a door in the corridor, and then out. The thin air bit, but felt
good. As I walked towards the squatting sweeper, I realized
that he was farther away from me than I thought when I was
staring at him through the (evidently distorting) glass. Indeed,
after fifteen or twenty meters, he was still at least that much
beyond me. I walked more rapidly, got to him and extended
my hand with a five *rupee* bill in it.

He turned to me without surprise in his eyes, but instead
of taking the money, he gently took hold of my wrist. Mole

heard something—the lurch of the train. It was starting. Yet he didn't let go of my wrist, nor did I pull away from him.

"Rishikesh," I said, not knowing how far it was from here, and concerned about my luggage. "I need to go to Sri Sen's ashram in Rishikesh."

Still holding my wrist, he looked at Mole with just the slightest glimmer of—what? Approval? Recognition? At the same time he made a magnanimously dismissive gesture with his other, cupped hand, as if to say: "Ah, Sri Sen, Rishikesh. That is not a problem."

Without withdrawing my hand, but planting my feet (not wishing to get any closer to the edge), I turned to the train which was chugging slowly on the narrow gauge—away from me. When I turned back, the sweeper was standing, the bidi was in his mouth, and he had a large straw basket on his back and fastened across his forehead. He let go of my hand, with the same gesture taking the five *rupee* bill, and waving his own hand broadly as he commenced to trudge in the direction of the train. Evidently Mole was to follow him.

Focusing alternately on the sweeper's basket on his strong bent back, and on his sinewy legs and thick splayed feet, Mole walked behind him at an even pace alongside the tracks for several hundred meters. Then he turned off to the right onto a barely visible trail which seemed to be going up grade, higher into the mountains. I was about to protest when he motioned with one arm without turning. I was to continue to follow.

The weeds and sparse growth of evergreen ceased; it became noticeably colder. It was getting towards dusk, and the clouds ahead of us were turning faintly orange under the mist. Mole heard bird cries, but all I could see were turkey vultures, a few above us, many more circling the lower cliffs beneath us to our left. Meanwhile the rocky path was becoming narrower as we continued to turn up the mountain.

Though I was feeling light-headed and uncharacteristically pliable, Mole did anxiously shout "Sri Sen!" once, as the sweeper seemed to be pulling away from me, turning up around a steep curve, and out of eye-shot. When seconds later, along a straighter grade, I saw him again, his head was

turned to me and he was smiling—so openly, so radiantly, that
bewildered as I was, I found myself spontaneously smiling
back.

This went on: into the muted, magical sunset (cliff
swallows cutting, diving between the circling vultures); but
also into the ever thinning and icy air of wherever it was we
were going. By my reckoning Rishikesh was in another
direction—and down mountain. Yet, oddly, I wasn't feeling
especially tense about my luggage which no doubt already had
arrived without me and was misplaced or stolen.

I glanced at my watch, but it had stopped. We must have
been trekking for at least two hours, the sweeper trudging
upward at a steady pace irrespective of the grade, apparently
not the least bit tired despite his load. What was his load?
Mole had not even noticed what he was carrying in the large
straw basket.

Venus and the three-quarter moon suddenly visible as
the spent sun sank lower towards the horizon. I was tired. I
must have been feeling tired for a good while.

"Look, when do—"

Before I could finish, the sweeper gestured with his hand,
indicating that "it" was just ahead. At this juncture I wasn't so
much concerned about where we were going, so long as I
could sit when we got there.

But "it" wasn't just ahead. A good forty-five minutes
after he gestured we were still pushing up mountain. Orion,
Pleiades, the blade of Taurus at Mole's throat (through
Mole's misted-over spectacles). What else? A piece of the
Great Bear. The moon like a cat in the mist. Mole felt himself
being pulled closer, closer to delirium—when all at once they
were "there." The flat bald summit of a mountain. The
sweeper, grinning at me, was unburdening himself, then
sitting against a rock, motioning Mole to do likewise. I did,
wanting to talk, to find out where in the world we were.
Instead I slept . . .

I dreamt of my place, my tenement, which stood upside
down like a great inverted tree, its roots like Medusa's hair,
facing heaven . . .

When I woke it was dawn. Not at all cold. I was covered

with a section of old brown tarpaulin. I had no idea how long I had slept, but I felt replenished. I was alone. My eye-glasses were gone. Immediately I stood, but before I could panic, I saw that one side of the mountain wasn't especially steep, and it seemed to lead along a wide trail to a township which must be Rishikesh . . .

(Marya smiled

I remember: I resume the overstaid fraction,
The corpses rise . . . the gashes heal . . .the
    fastenings roll away.
I troop forth replenished . . . one of an average
    unending procession;

Aug. 31: My eye-glasses weren't gone. Nor was my knife. No change.

Mole wangled a list of his tenants from the renting agent. They were all there.

The Coiros in 2f occupy the largest apartment in the building. Vincent (called "Junior") Coiro bats fourth and catches for the Seward Park High School baseball team. He has a quick temper and the biggest hands in the neighborhood. John, his oldest brother, was killed in the Pacific in the Second World War. His mother, Maria, a blockish, thick-legged old woman, has worn black since 1944. She doesn't speak English. Nor does her husband, Vincent senior, who smokes "guinea stinkers," is well over six feet tall, and repairs everything from toilets to brick walls, though his specialty is cementing side-walks.

Carmine, the oldest surviving son, works with his father. Two or three times a week Mole will see him wheeling his barrow to or from some injured sidewalk somewhere. Another son, Dominick, recently returned from Naples with a Neapol-itan wife. They look like brother and sister: both olive-complexioned, small-featured, clear-eyed. The wife is preg-nant. Dominick is a construction worker.

There are two daughters, both unfortunate: Katherine (called Tubbo by the neighborhood kids), the largest member of the family, having the disposition of an angel, with though an unalterable sadness beneath. The other daughter, whose name isn't known, must be middle-aged by now. An "idiot," she is hospitalized someplace on Long Island. Until two years ago, she was kept and tended to by the family.

Once every other week, usually on Sunday after church, Mole will witness the entire family stolidly betaking itself to the subway; thence to the Long Island Railroad for the long trip eastward to visit with their idiot child. Included in this pilgrimage is the dean, if no longer the force, of the Coiro family: Vincent senior's ancient father, Vincenzo, eighty-four years of withered libido; who otherwise is to be found sitting straight-spined at the smaller kitchen table wearing a tattered blue carpenter's apron, old grey cardigan sweater, smoking Luckies and sipping strong black coffee.

What the Coiros had done was knock down the walls that separated the dining room from the living room, and the living room from the bedroom—and transform the entire space into a kitchen. The kitchen then was the theater for their appetites— the only space nearly large enough to contain them. As for sleeping, Vincent senior and Carmine constructed two more small bedrooms in the back yard, adjoining their vegetable garden . . .

As for Mole: no change. Stiffer from lying is all. My books intact. Everything evidently intact . . .

I remove the knife from my left side pocket, shake it open, lay it in the hammock. Then I fold my purple bath towel into a square, place it within my circle, center my head on the towel:

I'm in *Sirshasana*, my legs describing a medium V among the TV aerials. Thinking of Sri Sen's brief letter (undated) waiting for me today.

According to Sen, his own intuition was verified by a *Siddhi*, namely that much of the malignant energy in Gandhi's Brahmin assassin found its way into the breast of Forrest Patrician Dix, after the assassin's own death in 1948. "The evil *apana* discovered congenial ice in the breast of the renowned Senator," as Sen put it. "A hot ice, which if you come in contact with it for longer than a few seconds, repulses you with its current."

H-E-L-P reopened. Calls all night, among them, this one:

"I heard you was away, Mole."

"Yes. I'm back now."

"Right. I know whatchoo mean, cause I'm there too. Like I'm 6-10, you dig? Also I'm black. I don mean no coffee-colored, high-yeller, that shit. True African un-fucked-over black. Which is jus the trouble. I mean like I don play basketball. That mean there something wrong with me, right?

As a matter of fak, I don play no other sports neither. You understand what I'm saying? I don bother with coppin a attitude. A brother got to have a attitude. Or else! You dig? I love the brothers, you understand, but it get me sad to see them come on like *brothers* all the time. Now I don say there anythin wrong with diggin youself. Diggin youself just what we need where we at now. But *watchin* youself—that ain't where we should be at. I get tired jus thinkin bout it. And sad. Because, like I said, I love my people. I jus wish they was natural. Jus because you stopped conkin don mean you natural. Not jus our hair, is what I'm sayin. You whites is bad fucked-up, and we hate yo ass so much we fuck ourself up badder bein *unlike* you. Thas right. Ony I cain't do it. Maybe if I could I would. But I cain't. Which make me queer, odd, ofay, dick-sucker—you name it . . ."

Coincidentally, Dix headquarters made a to-do by announcing the formation of a committee called "Blacks for a New Beginning," which is to say, for Dix-Smegma. The titular head of the committee will be the 7 feet 4 inch registered Republican, black basketball superstar and multi-millionaire, Abraham McKinley.

The committee idea engineered by Rebus, Dix's media expert, whose star until this coup had been declining rapidly. Rebus profited from his brainstorm sessions with Jock Zurco, who, as head coach of a professional football team, inevitably spent many hours with Negroes.

Sept. 1: Abaddon hasn't let up. Mole didn't expect him to. The old knife-sharpening stone appeared again, this time near the pigeon coop. Beneath the stone on a three-by-five index card was this:

Speak English / Garbage Spic

The Jewish cat, who has never paid much attention to the pigeons, is back. Reposing in Mole's hammock with her nose pointing to Emerson.

"An institution is but the lengthened shadow of one man."

An admirer of Dix's grandfather copied this Emerson quotation in gold and red with impressive flourishes, then sent it to the old billionaire—who promptly had it framed and hung behind his desk. Between his signed portraits of Teddy Roosevelt and Jay Gould.

According to *Time*, who interviewed her on her most recent birthday, Ayn Rand claimed that Senator Patrician Dix bears a striking resemblance to Marshal Pétain who, in turn, resembles "my vision of the Fisher King."

What can it mean?

According to Eliade, "primitive" people, and particularly the peoples of North Asia, "conceive the otherworld as an inverted image of this world. Everything takes place as it does here, but in reverse. When it is day on earth, it is night in the beyond (which is why festivals of the dead are held after sunset; that is when they wake and begin their day)." The summer of the "living" then corresponds to winter in the land of the "dead."

"The Beltir place the reins and a bottle of wine in the corpse's left hand, for the left hand corresponds to the right hand on earth. And everything that is inverted on earth is in its normal position among the dead."

If only, Mole thinks, it were (here) all Dix. All of it swinish, inverted, blind, without the universe's lustre. Without the seldom lustre of virtue. That would be preferable. Instead no perpetuation. No clarity. The integer fractured . . .

Sept. 2: Since Zelda's April Fool's visit, I've been leaving my flat at 3:30 in the afternoon, twice a week.

The scene is the subway. IRT, 28th Street and Seventh Avenue. It is 4:10.

She wanted to go to a street which the conductor informed her was four stops downtown on the Local. The tall pale man with the wispy red mustache happened to overhear this exchange. So did the two young army Pfc's, in on a weekend pass from Fort Dix. The man with the eye-patch listened to the brief conversation, and the weary-looking executive standing next to him must have heard it also. Each had noticed her walk down onto the platform, glancing over her shoulder, then to the left and right, in obvious confusion. But she located the conductor, and managed to consult him before any of them could offer to aid her.

She couldn't be more than twenty-one or two. Her vivid orange mini-skirt clung enticingly to her thighs, and she was bra-less (buoyant! buoyant!) beneath a translucent green jersey that fell short of her tiny convex navel. She carried a minikin green jacket in her hands. Though her face was pretty, her smallish regular features seemed as yet unformed, and a neutral semi-smile was evidently her predominant expression. Probably she was visiting the city for the first time, yet even in her bewilderment she looked oddly self-contained. That is, her face did; her body managed to luxuriate in several piquant directions—as if she were the innocent custodian of a storehouse filled floor to ceiling with fleshly (motile) uranium.

The Local pulled into the station and she entered a center door. Instead of sitting she leaned her scented, undulant rump against the pole, looking straight ahead, though not apparently focusing on anything, still blandly smiling. Her left foot in its high-heeled sandal was nonchalantly turned ninety degrees to the left in the manner of a ballerina. Her thighs were several inches apart, and the two GI's sitting opposite were trying to see between them. The other three—the pale man with the wispy red mustache, the weary executive, and the eye-patch—were also in the subway car, but were not so favorably positioned as the soldiers.

On the third stop a strapping construction worker got on, immediately noticed the girl, and took a position to her right, from where he brazenly appraised her. Her five original admirers shuddered, thinking the un-subtle son of a bitch might blow it for all of them. But she seemed unruffled, nearly insensible to anything that was going on in the train.

At one point she sneezed, and the construction worker extracted a large blue and white checkered handkerchief, which he offered her. She shook her head no, smiled vacantly, and took out a single small tissue from a minuscule opening in her skirt.

Five or six young boys were zig-zagging through the train from car to car, and when they spotted her—they stopped, glaring at each other with a wild surmise. One of them whistled through his teeth, and two others made appreciative smacking sounds with their lips. But they only paused for a minute, then went on.

Later she dropped something she was holding in her hand—a small golden clasp for her hair. But an officious old priest sitting to her left, retrieved it and handed it to her just as she was about to bend.

As the train edged into her stop, the young GI's stood. So did the pale man with the wispy red mustache. The weary executive and the man with the eye-patch were already standing. She got off first, with them discreetly in tow. Mercifully, the construction worker cast one last brutish stare and remained behind. Had he known that this particular stop had an unusually steep flight of stairs, no doubt he would have exited with the others.

Several other passengers, whose stop this really was, converged at the narrow stairway, and the original admirers found themselves jockeying for position behind the girl. Then it started: a few words were exchanged, and after a short pause they were grappling—one of the GI's and the man with the eye-patch—at the foot of the stairs.

In the meantime a remarkable thing happened: the girl stopped, let the other passengers pass her, turned around and walked down the few steps to the subway platform. Pausing in front of one of the chewing gum machines, she took a coin from her pocket and purchased a stick of gum.

By this time the stairs were almost cleared, and the soldier and the eye-patch had stopped fighting. She commenced to walk up the stairs. Her five admirers, touching in order to walk abreast, trailed her by ten feet. She walked—actually mounted, they were that steep—the steps slowly, even deliberately. And . . . and more than any of them had dared to anticipate: she was naked under her tiny skirt. For a full twenty seconds they climbed without a sound . . .

Outside, a few feet from the exit, a large red car was waiting for her. A tall dark man with thick glasses held the rear door open. As she was about to enter she turned towards her admirers, massed incredulously at the top of the stairs, and smiled at them sweetly, compassionately.

That was Zelda, on assignment. Mole himself it was who was chauffering Sklar's fire-engine red Pontiac.

Sept. 3: Mole in Babylon.
He finds Theron Loggin in his carrel, feet on his desk, riffling the pages of *Cosmopolitan*.

"Hey, where the hell *you* been?" Loggin says, catching me sidelong without looking up from his magazine.

"I had to go away. It was sudden. I'm paid up through October."

"Is that a fak? Well, I don't have your appication here. Don't thank I do."

"Here's the receipt." I place it down on the desk.

"Yeah, well—you was doing good too," Loggin says, turning the pages of *Cosmopolitan*. "But these kinda layoffs. Did you do any firin where you was?"

"No, not really. I'm sorry, Theron. It couldn't be helped. I plan to fire regularly from now on."

"Yeah, well . . ."

He removes his feet from the desk and swivels his chair so that he's facing me. "Hey, didn't I tell you once before to call me Hoss. Ain't no fruity Theron round yere that I know of." Loggin flips the magazine onto the desk. "Look at them kazooms! You ever see this shere—Cosmo-politan? I found it in the lobby. Fine piece of titty on the cover, but ain't worth a turd on the inside. These shere stories and shit bout what to do when your period is late. Hell, I already *know* what to do: haul ass, Mister! I mean get the fuck away quick. Like what you done, right? Where'd you go anyways?"

"It's a kind of archipelago," Mole says. "Not very far from here."

"Is that a fak? Well, I reckon you wanna get to firin

today."

"Is it possible?"

"No, not hardly. There but two alleys in operation, as you could see. Ain't no time to open 'nother now."

"Okay. I'll come back on Thursday then. Is Thursday all right?"

"Shit yeah. Perfek. Jus as long as you don't go back to that archi-pelago in the meantime."

Sept. 4: "Why," Marya asks, "did he turn back so close to having saved her—and himself?"

She means Orpheus.

I say finally: "It was his nature. Orpheus was not meant to rescue innocence, but to sing of its betrayal. In a place of stone."

"Stone?"

"Yes. The scene must have been prepared long before his sinking. Had he come up with her, it would have been a different song. Without resonance."

"Orpheus sang of love," Marya says.

"Of its deprivation," Mole says, "death being mother of beauty."

"But one can sing of something other than death."

"Yes . . ."

Three of Marya's Orpheus lithographs were accepted on consignment by a Madison Avenue gallery. Notification came only today, and she and Mole were celebrating by dining out.

They were sitting on low stools across a small table in the darkened interior of a vegetarian restaurant, newly opened, on Ninth Street, just east of Astor Place, called "East-West," full of plants and posters, brick walls, "ottomans" to sit on . . .

After a few minutes the salt was delivered in a lacquered bowl. I was about to ask for the menu when the waiter (in a leather jerkin) whirled and was off in another direction.

Marya tried a little sesame salt on her finger. "It's good."

Mole did the same. "What *is* this?"

"What?" Marya looked up.

"An odor." Mole raised the salt to his nose. "Dung."

"In the salt?"

"No." Mole set the bowl on the table. "Around us somewhere. You don't smell it?"

Marya sniffed about her. "Could it be on your shoe?"

"This is human dung. We might be sitting too close to the damn toilets. Are we sitting next to the toilets?"

Marya looked around. "I'm not sure. It's too dark to tell."

"Let's move. Please. Take your chopsticks." Mole stood.

"What about the sesame salt?"

"Never mind the sesame salt. It's probably tainted."

The waiter in the leather jerkin accosted them. He was carrying menus.

"It smells over there. Can you show us another table?"

"*Smells?*" Offended, he raised his nose, as if himself suddenly discerning a foulness—which could reside only in Mole. He pointed . . . "Over there. Inside, by the wall."

"Right. Thank you." Mole relieved him of the menus.

We made our way into the still darker interior, Mole very nearly stumbling over a fat executive's stockinged foot. Not ottomans here, but flat cushions next to each other on a straw mat containing two teak trays and a candle.

We examined the menu.

"What do you think the 'Samadhi Surprise' is?" Marya asked.

"Where is that—oh, I see it. 'Samadhi Surprise, $4.95.' I'd guess it was Franks and Beans."

"Hey! They serve only vegetarian food here."

"I mean soy franks. Whatever it is, I hope it doesn't smell of dung. Like whatever else it is that reeks here."

Marya looked at me. "You still smell it? The same odor you smelled on the other table?"

"The very same shit, Marya. Only ranker. You see that fat executive there—straining against his trousers?"

"You think it's him?"

"You still can't smell it?"

"I'm trying to . . . No, I don't think I do. Are you sure it's not somebody's feet. Lots of people have their shoes off."

"Shit. Not feet," Mole said irritably, closing his eyes: suddenly recalling India, the human waste odor every waking hour. "Let's leave, Marya. Do you mind?"

"No. Not if you're uncomfortable. Let's leave."

Again Mole nearly stumbled over the executive's feet.

The waiter in the leather jerkin watched them make their way out.

"I'm sorry," I said as we exited into the night air of Ninth Street.

"Don't be." Marya fitted her hand under my arm. "I want us to enjoy this meal."

"We are celebrating," Mole said, kissing her hair.

"So much for Samadhi," Marya said, laughing. "Where shall we eat?"

"How about 'Surma' on Carmine Street? Bourgeois Indian food, plastic flowers, honest lies . . ."

Sept. 5: Mole on his roof on his head smelling dung. The sensation hadn't left him since last night. He smelled other smells as well, such as Marya's skin, or the tar on his roof, or the mustiness of his books spread against the east wall—yet the shit was there. The infrastructure was shit.

Dix meanwhile off to South Korea on a "fact-finding mission." Smegma will bear the brunt of campaigning for a week.

Sanderson, Dix's Democratic opponent, who resembles Mark Hatfield, but is slighter of build, better bred, and considerably wealthier, had once been expelled from the University of Virginia Law School for cheating—but was rapidly reinstated. Presently he is Governor of Arizona, and the prime backer of a movement to boost Chicano migrant farm workers' salaries from a dollar seventy to an even two dollars per hour. In the last two years or so he has succeeded in assimilating some of the Kennedy speech patterns and gestures into his repertory. He is considered an impressive man.

Lemming, Sanderson's running mate, the junior Senator from the state of Connecticut, is six feet four and a recent convert to Roman catholicism (which may or may not hurt him at the polls). Formerly a big-game hunter-buddy of Norman Mailer, his people recently (and astutely) adjusted his image so that it read "Virile-*Ecologist*." At this very moment, in fact, Lemming and "three associates" are canoeing on the Colorado River to call attention to his cause. A well-built man, Lemming (according to his own testimony in the May issue of *Penthouse*), conquered his stammer in his junior year at Yale, and is one-eighth Jewish.

G.J., who is not, nor planning to become, a U.S. citizen, hands Mole a Sanderson-Lemming flyer. Sklar, sitting on the table and eating sesame butter from a jar, manages a scoffing grin.

"You know what the catch is, don't you, Mole? Duke Lemming spent a term at Oggsford after the war studying Limey History. So he's alright with G.J."

"It was Cambridge," G.J. says. "I like Lemming. I'd prefer him to be running for President and Sanderson, or someone else, for the lesser job. But even this way, it's a great deal better than Dix-Smegma."

"Now I don't agree," Sklar says. "To me they're all kaput, except that Dix has a cuntie secretary, that Gwendolyn Stephens."

"You like her, do you, mate?"

"I'd like to moose her."

"You're not voting for Dix-Smegma, are you, Mole?" G.J. asks.

"No."

Sept. 6: A letter from the gun people in Winston-Salem to tell me that the shipment of my "weapon with accessories" will be further delayed because of the unexpected absence of a part (not specified). They say that it will be delivered by October 1, at the latest.

That's cutting it close.

Sept. 7: Mole's father, who couldn't make it out, didn't actually know he couldn't make it out. What he knew, though it would have embarrassed him to say so, was that his cellar was snug, earth-moist—yet of a piece with what might be called "history" in the faded photographs and unwanted clothing and boxes and mirrors stored there.

Dawn with tentative pink fingers promises—each day a gloved fist)

My father in the dawn, in his dark grey uniform, with his flashlight, quietly walking through the echoing streets . . .

Once, at dawn, he was stabbed behind his left shoulder. He sank to the pavement without looking behind him. Not a very serious wound, as it turned out, though three inches lower it would have been his heart.

His attacker said afterwards that she had confused him with the insurance investigator.

When that same afternoon I visited my father in the hospital I recall that he looked up at me in a certain way, without the visible affection usually in his eyes, but with something almost like recognition.

The next day his old affectionate look back in his eyes. The other look—gone. Pushed cellar-wards.

Six days later he was back to work. Moving gently through the dawn.

Not yet light, Mole in his "cellar," smelling dung . . .

Not far from Rishikesh is Benares. Thither it was that Sri Sen led Mole, new in India, on a "pilgrimage."

When Mole asked what precisely they would be doing in Benares, his teacher touched my arm and displayed his betel-coated teeth in a smile.

"Pre-cisely," Sen repeated ironically, his eyes sparkling.

(Mole's compulsive questioning had become a joke between us.)

On the bus Sri Sen got into an animated conversation with a doughty old tribal shepherdess from the mountains around Rishikesh. Though the conversation was in Hindi, Mole recognized enough words to perceive that as Sen was explaining that he was taking his student to Benares, the old woman erupted into laughter, stamping her bare feet on the floor and spitting through her reddled teeth.

When I asked what the joke was, Sen patted my shoulder in an exaggerated way, and both of them broke out laughing again.

As the bus was sputtering into Benares, it was assaulted by dozens of beggar children selling *chapathis*, cucumbers, mangos, sweets. One young boy of nine or ten had leaped on board and anchored himself at the head of the bus near the driver. Displaying small jars of something very pink and viscous which he hurriedly unwrapped from soiled newspaper, he recited non-stop the virtues of the nostrum, holding it high in his right hand, his other hand sweeping dramatically from his head to chest to stomach to groin . . . There was evidently nothing it couldn't cure.

Several of the children running alongside the bus had their eyes particularly on Mole who was the sole foreigner aboard. One small boy, more importunate than the others, was carrying what must have been his sister: an emaciated girl-child with stumps for arms, her legs wrapped tightly about the boy's shoulders. Mole gave the child *paise*.

Next to me Sri Sen sat with eyes closed, munching on his betel like a cow, the tracings of a smile about his lips.

The terrain around Benares was generally flat, arid, treeless—and filled with people, mostly peasants trudging behind or ahead of their bullocks; the women with their long arched backs, naked and sinuous beneath their threadbare saris, bundles on their heads, piquant expressions on their beautiful dispossessed faces. Black buzzards and crows shared the sky . . . Then, before Mole was able to transpose any of this into contours familiar to him—they were there. Benares: wriggling after Sen out of the bus into what looked like some gargantuan animal's stomach laid open under a merciless sun.

Though fingers kept catching his sleeve or arm, Mole

dismissed them, as you will yourself to do in dream, so that they were both there—and not. The Ganges was there, as it was in Rishikesh, where, closer to its source, it actually resembled a "river." Here it was a huge sweltering basin of coppery liquid teeming with brown bodies and gossamer-like slivers—which were boats . . . Sri Sen, carrying his sandals, was leading me onto one of them.

"What now?" Mole asked.

"The Ganga," Sri Sen replied, motioning to the river.

Mole smiled. "Yes, I know."

Sen was remarkable for belaboring the obvious in just the way to ring Mole back to the present, away from his pernicious questioning.

As usual I persisted.

"Where are we going on the Ganga?"

"Go-ing," Sen echoed in his pesky way. "We are here, are we not?"

Deftly, gently, he placed a finger on Mole's forehead between his eyes.

"All right," Mole laughed.

The boat-*wallah* was taking Mole's wrist, leading me to the sole bench on the boat, in the bow. Sri Sen, barefooted and now barechested (having removed his shawl), was already squatting, craning his neck at the river, grinning.

We were in motion, the unusually tall, old boat-*wallah* standing in the stern, paddling . . .

Mole was watching the bathers, who were not swimming, but washing, some rubbing their teeth with the silt. Suddenly one was in our boat, grinning at us, shaking himself dry, his *lungi* hiked up like a breech-cloth. The *wallah* continued to paddle slowly, rhythmically, his deep-set rheumy eyes focused above us. I was about to question Sen, when he anticipated me and said: "Guide."

And indeed the bather had commenced to guide. Squatting on his hams in the center of the boat, the sun glistening on his wet hair, he was pointing at one of the banks. Mole could see smoke.

"Burning ghat," our guide was saying. The boat was turning in that direction.

"The corpse is placed there. Upon the bier. The eldest son will split the skull, then light the fire. It is our custom, you see."

These words were carefully, even excessively, articulated. The inflexion determinedly British. The guide was surprisingly young, perhaps nineteen or twenty, slim, high-strung beneath the smooth manner. He stopped speaking to allow us time to get closer to the "ghat."

Very near the smoke I saw young boys diving in the water. The guide answered the unspoken question. "It is for the embroidered gold of their shrouds, or for that in the teeth."

Just then Mole saw a boy emerge onto the bank waving a long piece of purple and gold material. He had a wide grin on his face.

"They are piled, these corpses, on the ghat itself. To await the proper time . . ."

Mole was nodding his head, doubtless somewhat vacantly, since he was watching with astonishment a beautiful young woman bathing in the midst of ashes and smoke and jackal-boys diving for remains. The front of her sari was open—I could see the delicate egg-shell breasts, the rich curve of hip. Gracefully, deliberately, she was wading out into the river in the direction of our boat. She was smiling. Our boat was turning away from her.

". . . it will not stop . . ."

"What you see here continues day and night," Sen explained.

Mole nodded, looking over his shoulder at the girl, the smoke spiraling behind her.

"However, the holy *Saddhus* are drowned, not burned . . ."

"Why is that?" Mole asked.

"It is our custom. They are holy, you see . . ."

The boat-*wallah* had scooped up something with his oar. A dead fish. It was adhering—somehow—to the oar. The *wallah* didn't notice it. Mole heard something. Chanting. He realized that it had been going on all the while, coming from near the burning ghat somewhere. Straining, he could make out a few of the words: " . . . *Hari Ram* . . . "

"What is the music?" I asked the guide.

"Yes. Well, you see it is the widows. Of those who have been claimed. That large structure alongside the ghat . . ."

Mole was twisting to look behind his shoulder.

" . . . They shall live there, you see. From this time on. It is only for the very wealthy . . ."

Plash!

Sri Sen had lowered himself into the water and promptly disappeared.

The *wallah*, who had laid his paddle across the stern, was standing stiffly, with his eyes closed, looking primeval.

Sen reappeared, floating on his back, rubbing his teeth with the silt from the river-bed.

Our guide blew his nose into the river, then said: "It is very good, you know. We use it as a tonic. For the entire body." He meant the river.

Sen was gesturing to me. "Come, have your bath."

"Oh . . ."

"Take it off, what you wear," the guide suggested. "You wear some garment underneath, do you not?"

"Yes . . ."

Sen, still on his back, his monkey head a-light with sun, was grinning.

Mole commenced reluctantly to remove his trousers . . . He felt the water with his hand. It was colder than he expected. He remembered his eye-glasses, which he fitted into his shoe, then lowered himself into the river, all the way, so that his feet touched the spongy bottom. It couldn't have been deeper than eight or nine feet. When I emerged into the startling sun, Sri Sen had his hand on my head. With his other hand he was holding on to the boat. He motioned for me to do the same. Then he was whispering into Mole's left ear—in Sanskrit; I recognized most of the words: ". . . *Ganga* . . . *Pooja* . . . *Rudra* . . . *Bhakti* . . . *Tantra* . . ." At certain intervals in the invocation he deposited drops of water on my head. As suddenly as it had begun, the "ceremony" ended with Sri Sen gently pushing Mole's head under the water . . .

Mole lightheaded almost naked drying in the Hindu sun in the boat slowly wending south.

Sen, who had collected some Ganges water in an old mayonnaise jar, was humming softly.

". . . From throughout India," our guide was intoning, "they come to the Ganga. To bathe . . ."

The terminus of our "tour" was a rickety bridge that crossed from west to east. We got out and I deposited a total of four *rupees* and fifty *paise* into the cupped hands of the boat-*wallah* and guide. This was less than they had asked for and a great deal more, Mole was certain, than the standard fee.

Sri Sen observed with a droll expression on his face. Money was a matter of indifference to him—so long as his pupil took care of the expenses.

Sen was leading Mole over the bridge, evidently back into Benares' underbelly. They passed mendicants, pilgrims, swamijis, an occasional flea-ridden, cataleptic hippy, bullocks, pariah dogs, buffalo, cows, a random camel . . .

Mole walked slightly behind and to the left of his teacher, who with his saffron shawl, grey matted hair and unruly beard, resembled any number of *Saddhus* in Benares—or Rishikesh, for that matter. On closer inspection, it could be seen that Sri Sen was in fact one of the comparatively few authentic "teachers." The power and steadiness about his eyes; the spontaneous infantile grin. And his body—Mole was watching the rhythmic ripples in his straight back as he walked—remarkably elastic from a lifetime of Hatha Yoga; he was sixty-six years old.

Though he was a Buddhist, Sen had a special affection for Hanuman, the divine Hindu monkey—and he himself was distinctly simian, with his small head, articulate body, and impish sense of humor. At that moment he pointed to a temple across the road—a large rhesus monkey, serenely balanced on one of the towers, was munching on a cucumber.

"Monkey," Sri Sen said, grinning.

Meanwhile the beggars had been obstructing Mole, pulling at him, brandishing their sores, stumps for arms . . . I distributed what *paise* I had, then tried to ignore them—treat them as part of the landscape: unsuccessfully. At one juncture, just outside the entrance to the bazaar, I was effectively cornered by a legless beggar on a trundle who was making high-pitched, whimpering noises . . . Before Mole had an opportunity to empty his pockets, Sen intervened, gently dispersing the beggar, leading me by the elbow into the bazaar.

My teacher gestured, a tonka, or scooter-taxi, stopped —or perhaps the tonka stopped before he gestured. In any case, we were enfolded, one on the other, in the tiny cab pocket as our driver lurched through the dusty turbulence . . . Abruptly—jarringly, we were at a standstill in a chaos of water-buffalo, bullocks, rickshaws, cows, tonkas, people . . . As in Rishikesh, there was no real distinction between the unpaved streets and unpaved walks. The way traffic moved was: suddenly a space materialized and the drivers—whatever their vehicles—would make for it. Our own driver, a broad-shouldered, white-haired Sikh, whose turban tail extended jauntily to his shoulders, was casually masterful at this gambit, and his frenetic zig-zagging; the hundred peremptory odors of animals and dung and ripe fruits and foods frying and petrol; the unceasing clamor of hawkers and yowling dogs and children; all this on the heels of a bowl of curried vegetables (which I had eaten at Sen's insistence), caused Mole's stomach to veer from nausea, to mesmerized calm—and back again.

Everything seemed a matter of centimeters here: the bullock brushes the child, the rickshaw brushes the bullock, the taxi nudges the tonka, the tonka butts the bicycle. The occasional, always battered, bus, looking like a reclaimed corpse, but the largest creature around, is sovereign, with its persistent off-key klaxon and belching anus, forcing its path through the center—immediately in its wake the mad motleyed traffic hurtling centerwards like the waters of a deranged sea.

Though I am crouched next to Sen in the tight cab interior, no hawker fails to notice me—I am beleaguered with "*Sahibs,*" and hot things on sticks, and mangos, and coconuts, and proposals to massage my head with mustard oil, and

several proposals to change my dollars into *rupees* at black
market rates, and three or four times, jeers of "heepie!"
because of my beard and longish hair . . . Sri Sen, a puckish
smile about his lips, his eyes partially closed, is imperturb-
able . . .

We are "there." The driver said something in Hindi to
Sen who said *"Atcha."* Mole gave the old Sikh a *rupee* and
climbed out.

"How do you like this place, then?" Sen inquired as he
placed his hand on Mole's elbow.

Mole looked at him: it appeared to be a perfectly serious
question.

"Do you mean Benares?"

"Yes, Benares itself. How do you like?"

After a brief pause, Mole said "very interesting."

"Very interesting, is it not?" Sen was grinning, inclining
me to the left, apparently into a small Shaivite temple.

"Now we thank Shiva for our deliverance?" Mole
quipped.

But when I looked up I saw that it wasn't the temple
proper we were entering, but a queer ramshackle wooden
extension behind it. Mole simply wanted to get out of the
fierce sun.

Someone had placed a hand on my shoulder. A slight old
man in a saffron *lungi* and torn dishcloth wrapped about his
head. He was saying something to Sen, who seemed to know
him, his hand now holding Mole's wrist. The two old *Swamijis*
were conversing in Sanskrit, very affably.

Sen said *"Atcha."* Then he said it again. Finally he and the
old Saddhu said *"Atcha"* simultaneously, and they (and
Mole) were entering, not the wooden extension, but a stall
appended to the temple on the opposite side. The stall was in
fact a small square platform with walls on three sides, and
Mole was surprised to see perhaps a dozen barefoot young
men squatting against the walls of the cramped space doing
some kind of small work in the poor light. They appeared to be
jewel-fitting with their fingers and miniature, though primi-
tive-looking, instruments.

Meanwhile the old man had taken hold of Mole's wrist

again and placed an object in his hand. It was a knife—an odd-looking pocket knife, black with an image of a dancing Shiva carved on the handle in what appeared to be jade.

"Something good," Sen said.

"Is this jade?" Mole asked.

"Yes, jade," Sen said. "Lord Shiva as Nataraj. Very powerful."

"Pow-fool," the other old man repeated grinning. Mole saw that he was toothless.

I tried to open the knife, to expose the blade . . . The two of them were giggling as they watched my efforts. Finally the old man took the knife from me and shook it open like a razor. The blade was about five inches long, very sharp. He closed it and handed it back to me.

Mole shook it open. "It's very nice."

"Very nice," Sen said. "He ask eight *rupees*."

It hadn't occurred to Mole that the old *Swamiji* was a tradesman. Eight *rupees* was just over a dollar.

"All right, I'll buy it."

The deal was closed, Sen and the old man exchanged goodbyes, each touching his right hand to his heart and bowing slightly. Mole put the knife in his pocket and followed his teacher out into the sun.

"What now?" Mole asked.

Sen, steering me into the temple proper, turned to me with a serious—even penetrating—look. Then he grinned. "Something good. I think you will like."

A diminutive old beggar-woman (Mole hadn't noticed her before), squatting in the dust under the shade of the building, had gardenias and fruit in her straw basket. Sen selected papayas, jackfruit, bananas, mangos, and a bouquet of flowers, which the old lady wrapped in newspaper and Mole paid for.

As soon as Sri Sen opened the high stone portal, I felt the cave-like coolness and smelled the incense—a very rich amber. We were in a kind of antechamber which led to another closed door. The only light came from a small stand on the left side: three candles flickering beneath a stone statue of Durga mounting Shiva.

"*Yab-yum*," Sen said.

"Yes."

They paused to look at it more closely. It was an exceedingly ornamented version of the famous theme. Shiva looked almost Tibetan in his fierceness.

Sen, placing his finger on the point of genital contact, said, "This is always. It will never change. Do you know why?"

"No, I don't."

"Because Lord Shiva is able to withdraw his ejected power back again. It never truly leaves his *lingam*."

"Oh."

"Oh-oh!" Sen mimicked. "This is *Tantra*. You wish to study?"

"Yes," Mole said vaguely. Then: "That's what I've come here for—I mean to India. To study *Tantra*, no?"

"We shall see. Come."

Sri Sen knelt in front of the closed door, touching his forehead to the stone floor. He motioned me to do the same. Then he rapped on the door with the knuckles of his left hand . . .

The events that followed can only be sketchily reproduced for two reasons: they were, though still vividly—palpably— alive in Mole's memory, unclear somehow, as if existing in another dimension. The second reason is that Sri Sen and "Kali" exacted a pledge from me not to disclose the more intimate details of the initiation (or "pilgrimage," as Sen called it).

. . . The door opened to a bridge, quite narrow. Hunched on the rope that served for a rail, was a large rapacious bird, furling and unfurling its wings. These were so extraordinary that Mole thought it must be a condor—but then it raised its head and I saw that it was a turkey buzzard of exceptional size. Sri Sen was crossing the narrow bridge . . . When he got to the other side he cautioned Mole:

"Not to look down. And slowly."

Mole took hold of the rope and promptly lost his balance—the rope was slack, almost useless as a railing; no doubt because the heavy bird had hopped from the rope to the bridge, straddling it with its back to Mole.

Mole entreated his teacher with my eyes.

"Do not think. Go!" he ordered.

Mole did. The vulture had turned to him menacingly, its great arms extended. My long legs had never been much good for balancing, and the bridge was even narrower than it appeared. I bent my knees slightly and legs askew was sliding down the banister—a razor! Gladys (beneath) my mother had her mouth open. Mole's father slept. Sri Sen's eyes steered me across.

Kali, a huge Nepali-looking woman, welcomed us without touching us. She kept a large dog. We followed her in the darkness to an altar. Sen placed the fruit and flowers there— as well as the mayonnaise jar filled with Ganges water. Then prostrated himself on the vivid Kashmiri carpet. Mole did the same. Music: the drone of a tamboura from somewhere, a voice singing or chanting. Faintly, faintly . . .

. . . Beneath Shiva's elephant son Ganesh, in stone, dancing, in an alcove to the left of the altar, Sri Sen was undressing me . . . while Kali was juggling several vari-colored balls. One of them, yellow, is tossed especially high—Mole watches it recede and disappear. This happens consecutively to the red, the blue, and the green ball . . . Two balls remain in her hand. She gestures to me without speaking, but the question conveyed it: Which of the two would I like. Instinctively I say black and it is already in the air, Mole seeing it get smaller . . . disappear. It seems that I am waiting for several minutes for the ball to fall—when it does, with a great thud. As I stretch to catch it on the first high bounce, I am pierced. Kali in purple pierced my thigh, depositing the drops of blood in the Ganges water . . . then caressing me, my lingam, with oily fingers. I smell the ghee as if from a great height, watching myself swell . . . her hitched caftan, back to me, bending, fitting the huge extension that must be Mole . . . As I slide, she has a mark there like a mandala, I reach out to hold on . . . her arms behind her latching my thighs, Mole plummeting, wings outstretched / higher, higher . . .

My face wet from my eyes, her fingers handling me, I could smell the shit on me, she was steering Mole to still another door, a corridor—I allowed the flies to lead me. The "toilet" was Indian, a hole in the ground and a bucket of brackish water. My nose locked, bending to the water to cleanse himself, Mole heard a sound like teeth—then again. To his left against the wall in a shallow ditch, a rat, bloated, evidently trapped in the accumulated shit, was clacking its teeth, swallowing flies . . .

Sept. 8: When Mole awoke this morning before dawn, next to Marya who was sleeping quietly, he didn't smell it right away. But then he did. Yet was not concerned, knowing, as he learned in Benares (perhaps without then realizing it), that it was there always, that he need not notice it, that—this was crucial—Election Day was nearing.

Sept. 9: Marya and I don't see many people, preferring, as you've observed, the everdarkening trek through our own shadows. Full of untoward glimmers. Sudden pratfalls.

Tonight is different. The Madison Avenue gallery person who took some of Marya's pictures, has underwritten a dinner in the Soho studio home of another of her protégés, a sculptor called Leonard.

A squat black crossbow, the stock and bow of black steel. The mounted silver arrow tautly poised with the crimson steel tip twisted above the bow and back—so as to point at the archer. (The watcher.) This on the lintel above the door. Within, a similar passion lined the walls: leather, fur, steel, hawks'-beaks, falconers'-gauntlets, belts studded with eyes . . . Every piece (so far as Mole could make out) wonderfully wrought.

The sculptor, Leonard, a Jew, worked almost entirely

with the left side of his body, the other side semi-paralyzed by
childhood polio. Only once during the entire evening did he
look at Mole's eyes—not seeing them. He needed women to
fuel his art. I watched him surgically denude his red-snapper
with one soiled and dexterous hand, as he examined Marya
while conversing with the two women (one the gallery owner),
on either side. He talked only of his work, and the message
was always the same: "I want to fuck you."

Towards the end of the evening Mole got to Zelda (whose
invitation had come about through a connection too circui-
tous to detail here). I assumed she had been pigged by
Leonard. I wanted to know how it was.

"*You* ought to know, Mole."

"It was good, was it?"

"Uh-huh." Zelda looked at me sideways, coyly—her
green eyes charged.

"What kind of cock did he have?"

"You know something, Mole, I never saw it. And it
didn't even matter."

"Was it here in his studio?"

"Yup. Right on the carpet."

I felt a sudden prompting. "He went up your ass, didn't
he, Zelda?"

At this her gross lovely face gave off light.

"Mole, tell me, how can I be slave to two men?" She was
smirking, her spit's honey coating her upper teeth.

I continued to look at her for a minute. Then turned away
without answering.

Sept. 10: Mole phoned Leonard the sculptor, told him I
was a representative from a polling service that wished to
make a forecast about the upcoming election. I asked whether
he was voting for Dix-Smegma or Sanderson-Lemming.

Without pause, the sculptor answered: "I'm going for
Dix."

"I thought you would," I said, and hung up.

Mole wishes it weren't so, but tenants have complained about Eartha Davis Corcoran, who is black, has a child, receives welfare, and, according to the gossip, entertains men on what appears to be a more or less regular basis.

Her husband, a "black" Irishman named Tommy Corcoran, who met Eartha in Fort Benning, Georgia, in 1972, had immediately after his marriage been transferred to Fort Dix, New Jersey. A Staff-Sergeant in the Combat Engineering Corps, Corcoran died only ten months ago under circumstances which were far from clear. The Army version was that an "A-L 5 explosive," which he had been rigging, went off prematurely. His wife, with whom he had been living in camp quarters, insists that he was murdered by the same—or by like-minded—racists who had it in for him ever since he dared make love to, father a child by, and subsequently marry a black woman in Georgia.

Eartha Davis Corcoran, who lives in 2g, a two and a half room apartment in Mole's tenement, has been living there for less than a year with her four year old child, Colleen Grace. Eartha is a small shapely woman of twenty-three, with glossy doe-shaped eyes on a delicately modeled face. Though without "education," she is quick-minded, persistent, not afraid to speak her mind. Which might mean complaining to Conn, the frequently drunk janitor, about the lack of heat; or proudly refusing to permit her daughter to accept sweets from the other tenants; or occasionally, and openly, inviting a friend of either gender up for coffee or a drink. Nor does she go out of her way to greet her neighbors; and when she does talk with one of them, it is with reserve. Thus the complaints to the renting agent, an easily intimidated, essentially lazy man, who, Mole suspects, will do nothing unless the complaints increase in number or intensity.

Sept. 11: According to US News and World Report, Dix's fact-finding five-day visit to South Korea was a "resounding success." On the way home the Senator planned to make stops at Singapore, Islamabad, New Delhi, and Teheran.

Jock Zurco will be joining Dix in New Delhi in order to "research" a football prospect, a massive Sikh corporal by the name of Hannayab Singh. According to an item in the current *Sports Illustrated*, "this Singh goes at 6-7, 280, with 4.6 speed in the 40. But there was some question about whether the NFL would lift its prohibition on face hair for the bearded Indian, who, according to an unimpeachable source, wears a beard and turban-like head-covering for 'religious reasons.'

"When asked about his giant bearded prospect, Coach Zurco replied: 'He's only a kid really, and I don't think this religion thing is all that ingrained in him. If the kid looks good and wants to play football, there won't be any problem about face hair or the rest of it, believe me.'

"Asked about the pacifism and fear of hitting that India has long been notorious for, Jock said, 'We'll cross that bridge when we get to it.' "

Sept. 12: Soon!

But what of Mole's people?

Saint Francis, hoeing his garden, was asked what he would do if he were suddenly to learn he was to die at sunset. He said, "I would finish hoeing my garden."

Yet Mole is sad walking to H-E-L-P through his night. Fall, and no sign of leaves changing to die, to merge. So few trees. And those blighted. No context for their pain.

Tenements are not trees. Though Mole may wish them to be. Nor are the defaced and boarded-up synagogues tabernacles. Redolence meaning despair mostly. Nor is the black sufferer Muslim: no matter how farsightedly he stares over his right shoulder, the tracks lead up the heart's arm of his brother.

Nor is this, Mole's journal, a jungle. The Congressman will not regain innocence as a result of it.

"It is difficult / to get the news from poems / yet men die miserably every day / for lack / of what is found there."

Which is the way it must be—crazy-toothed sky grinning beyond mercy . . .

Who then am I?

Which is what Mole asked his teacher on the bus, on the way back from their Benares "pilgrimage."

"Who am I, Sri Sen?"

Without turning towards me, Sen said, "You are *Atman.*'"

Mole, startled, thought he said "Abaddon."

Sen, turning to me, looking suddenly (in the light dying) like my father, said again: "You are *Atman.*"

Sept. 13: Mole, tightly lotused, back straight, on his roof, very near the edge, gazing through semi-closed eyes down at the platform (uranium), and at the empty dais. His knife, open, on its side, balanced on his head . . . die-a-dem)

A young man—a hydrocephalic—phoned me at the station. Said that for a long time he had been hearing a whispering through his head, a "ceaseless raining." It came intermittently, but at any time, often waking him out of a dream. Always he tried to listen, but could not get what it was, what the whispering meant. Until yesterday. "It was the sea. It wants me back. I can't not go . . ."

"Talk about your high enemas," Sklar remarks afterwards. "They don't come no higher than what that guy got. In the fucking brain, right?"

"No," Mole says. "It's the skull that's enlarged because of water in the cerebral cavities. The brain is compressed from the pressure."

"How did he sound?" G.J. asks.

"Over," Mole says softly.

"Yeah. I don't guess Kloss has anything about that—water in the head. I have to check it. But probably the guy is better off ending it. How do you think he's going to do it, Mole?"

"I don't know."

"We can't do anything, can we?" G.J. asks.

"No."

Press Secretary Nubile in southern Vermont. On the west lawn of Chalet Dix. The Senator himself within, "resting" after his sojourn in the Orient.

The big news is that Dix is to marry Virginia Badleigh Templeton, native of Williamsburg, age fifty, widowed, with three tow-headed children, two girls and a boy, ages sixteen to twenty-two. Her first husband, Sewall (Big Sam) Templeton, Republican senior Senator from North Carolina, collapsed on the floor of the Senate after filibustering for nineteen hours and thirty-eight minutes on behalf of Reynolds Tobacco. The anti-cigarette bill was subsequently defeated (out of respect for the dead Senator), but Big Sam in fact did *not* succeed in bettering the record of his friend and colleague Strom Thurmond, who three years before had filibustered for twenty-seven hours in opposition to the never revived Equal-Rights-Rest-Room bill. I cite Thurmond here because Templeton managed to gain consciousness on the way to Walter Reed Medical Center, and allegedly asked the ambulance attendant whether he had "made it," meaning the record. This was in '69.

Pat Dix first met Sam Templeton in 1943 in Fort Sill, Oklahoma, where both chanced to be training as Intelligence officers. "They liked and admired each other at once" (Nubile), and petitioned the Pentagon to allow them to work as a team. Which is what transpired. For the duration of the war the two young captains were inextricably involved in the Pacific theatre, and spent their time shuttling between Monterey, California, and Honolulu. Coincidentally, each was elected to the House in '48, so that they "enriched their acquaintance" (Nubile) in the nation's capital.

Dix, childless (his only child having drowned in his Georgetown pool), became godfather to Templeton's two youngest children (the boy baptized Raleigh Patrician Templeton.)

Since her husband's passing, Virginia (called Gigi), maintained the Georgetown house, but spent most of her time either in Williamsburg or "on the Continent." Last winter Gigi and the children joined the Senator and his late wife on the Riviera, and subsequently for "a backpacking trip through the south of France" (Nubile).

The marriage, scheduled for September 30, will be a relatively small affair limited to family and close friends. The Reverend Hillary Tallow-Dunn will conduct the ceremony in the Wildhaven Episcopal chapel. (Wildhaven is the name of Dix's Montana property.)

Sept. 14: "How many zones / in the darkness . . ."

According to the NY *Post*, which Mole is reading in his hammock, the Jewish cat dozing with eyes partially open on the tar beneath me—subway traffic on the IRT Lexington Avenue line was brought to a standstill for nearly two hours during this morning's rush hour:

After T. Kelleher, engineer of the uptown local, reported seeing "some kind of obstacle" in the tunnel between Astor Place and Fourteenth Street, he stopped his train and radioed for advice. Within ten minutes, a contingent of transit policemen and subway repairmen were in the tunnel investigating.

What they discovered was a young black Army private in full dress uniform, including his cap and "sharpshooter" medal pinned to his breast, fast asleep between the third rail and the tunnel wall. He was awakened, handcuffed, and transported to the Astor Place station, where he was questioned.

It was soon established that the black was AWOL from his post in Fort Dix, where he had been scheduled to return last night from a weekend pass. When asked what he was doing in the tunnel—and asleep, he replied that on his way back to the Fort, he discovered that he had taken the wrong train—going downtown instead of uptown. Because he did not have the price of another subway fare, having just enough to take the bus from Times Square to the Fort, he decided to cross the tracks to the uptown side.

Which is what he proceeded to do. Except that once he had climbed down onto the tracks, he remembered how tired he was from the drinking and generally torrid pace of his two nights in the city, and thought that he might take a "short nap."

Having made that decision, the next question was where? The "only logical place," the black told the police with a straight face, "was inside the tunnel where it was dark and real quiet." And once inside the tunnel, what could be more "logical" than the third rail?

"At first I laid down right on the rail—on the wood on top of the rail, you know? But that wasn't all that comfortable, so I squeezed between the rail and the wall."

Hadn't it ever entered his mind that he stood a good chance of being electrocuted?

"No, not really," the black replied. "I was real tired."

The black private was booked at the Fifth Precinct for being AWOL from his post in Fort Dix, and for willfully obstructing traffic. Immediately after his booking he was transferred to the Bellevue Medical Center for observation.

In the left margin of the *Post* "story," Mole jots:

> a butterfly
>   asleep, perched upon
>   the temple bell

Sept. 15: "This is Mole. Our station is called H-E-L-P. It's for anyone who needs it. The reason I'm talking to all of you tonight, instead of to you individually over the phone, is that I've received letters and calls asking me to do this: to tell something of myself, to talk about the station, what it is designed to do, what it has done.

"About myself, I'm not sure what to say to you. Except that I'm a person, I feel pain, I respect people. Not all people. Those who mask themselves for gain, who mock others for their own gain—I don't respect. Nor do I respect sanctimony, but when it tunnels out of its pious corner to convert what's green—it becomes hateful.

"The world is green, but I try not to confuse the world with those who pillage it. To be green is to know, or even to want to know, who you are at root. Beneath the public face. It is a process of ripening, but not to blossom. To seed. To faith, only then to flower. This ripening can begin at any time, when you want it to. To murder your longest-standing anxiety will—after a brief numbness—expose green. Mole is thirty-four years old. He is one of you.

"Unless you've kept alive, green, what you were granted at birth—very few of us have—you've grown rotten in places. If you use that rottenness consciously to taint, to maim, you've become rabid. Terrified of rain. If, though, you realize your contagion, yet resist the temptation to infest others and things—you are on the way back to becoming what you are. Which in rain is unseparate, integral, dying to grow. Mole is rain.

"When you phone here it is a step towards hearing yourself, your green self, in Mole. Feeling the tie. Not only to me, since I am only a single shadow—beyond me, to Mole, to moles and dark blind bodies burrowing to any honest food that is rain.

"Yet it has been made more complicated than this, because to seek rain is to incite the hate of the rabid, who rule the manifest world by contagion. Contagion is the assurance that the foaming on their lips is both light and rain; that as a consequence they are sanctioned to insert their tongue into the heart's ear of any living thing. Wherever it resides—even beyond our galaxy.

"Our function here at H-E-L-P is especially threatening to the manifest rulers, because the only revolution they cannot effectively simulate is the 180 degree turn back to what they are. At the same time they can see that this is what we are attempting to do—which incites them to murder, fear. Fear that our burrowing root-wards will undermine them, topple them at their source, already atrophied, weakened from disuse, head-lust. We must not look back.

"Sometimes phoning here is too small a grip, your deadness too spread. Though—listen to me!—the deadness is in the eyes of your head merely. Not seeing, it thinks it sees

ice, the frozen blood that is ice. You need only close these
eyes to collapse that icy space—flowing, flow into green.

"A savaged doe nourishes the earth, so that the dande-
lion that grows, or pokeweed, or grass becomes infused with
doe. As does the child who drinks the milk. And the desolate
old lady in the Old People's 'Home.' And the beggar squatting
outside your window licking his sores against the cold . . .

"Close your eyes. Witness. Mole is milk."

The first call Mole took after his talk was this one:
"Yes, I heard what you were saying. About rabies and all
that. Well, I'm from the South. North Carolina . . ."

She paused, as if for confirmation that it was possible,
even salutary, for someone to be from North Carolina.

"Right," Mole said. "North Carolina."

"Yes, well I've been staying here, in this city of yours, for
eight days. Why, I never saw such a place. I'm staying in a kind
of dormitory, you know? (I won't tell you where.) Well,
Saturday morning I was coming out of the shower when I
suddenly saw that nigra woman. I've talked to several people
about this. There were several shower-stalls and she was
standing there, drying herself. She had just come out herself (I
thought about that later, you know), and we were probably
showering at the same time. Anyway, my mind was racing, but
I figured out that she came out of hers just a few seconds
before I came out of mine. When I saw her I didn't know *what*
to do. It was as if I'd seen the Devil himself, or I was about to
face Judgment Day. I felt sick all over, and frightened. What I
felt—I'll never forget it—is that horrible feeling of being
caught in a horrible trap, and not knowing what to do about it.
I thought of running out of the room and screaming, or
screaming at the woman to get out, or running back to the
shower. My mind was in a terrible panic. I thought of
everything I could do at once, but I felt paralyzed. I felt like
fainting, and vomiting too. It was shock, like seasickness—it
took hold of me all over and I wondered whether I was about
to die. My sense of protocol was with me, though—"

Mole hung up: it was Abaddon.

Sept. 16: "The jaguar brushes the leaves / with his phosphorous absence." (Neruda)

Mole on his roof, in *Halasana*, touches his left pocket. When he has done it and gone, what remains will be less than it was. And other, conforming to the deathliness that governs here.

But for a glowing, a phosphorescence, his (or nearly) in the hearts of a few of his people.

Which is . . . enough.

The Jewish cat licking herself in the hammock will remember Mole's liver, his cottage cheese.

Marya will remember:

The night of his H-E-L-P talk, G.J. dreamt of Mole: "You had a wounded lawn bird—a grackle with a broken and bloodied wing—on your head. You were standing on stilts, high above everyone else. And you were having a difficult time of it, because the pavement, though it looked tidy and new, was deficient. Your stilts were sinking slowly into it. As I watched you, I was surprised to see that what looked like stilts were in fact your legs—slowly being consumed.

"Though you must have been concerned, you managed to keep your face from registering concern. Why? I wondered. I understood: you didn't want to alarm the wounded bird on your head. The pavement—it seemed to be someplace around here, around the station—was absorbing more and more of you, and when you were in it up to your very thin thighs, I saw that you had an astonishing erection."

Sept. 17: A mini brouhaha eructed: Lemming the Democrat has accused Jock Zurco of violating the constitutionally ordained separation of Church and State. Now, since Zurco was Dix's unofficial, though well-known, key adviser on both national and international matters, Lemming's charge, if substantiated, would indict the Senator by association.

Only there was more to it: Elroy Diggins, who had been a second-string running-back for Zurco's Redskins at the start of the previous season, was dropped under somewhat mysterious circumstances during the fifth week, and subsequently joined the Montreal Alouettes of the Canadian League. Ten days ago Diggins signed an affidavit at Sanserson-Lemming headquarters attesting to the following:

The Redskins were divided into two factions, the "God-Squad" and the "Goon-Squad." The God-Squad consisted of maybe eighty-five percent of the entire team, who prayed together before every practice (prayers conducted by Zurco's friend, Father Sean Laragh, who was on the Redskin payroll), and attended Mass before every home game. Though Zurco himself is a Pole and Roman Catholic, the God-Squad included Catholics, Protestants, and Weitzman, the 255 pound tight end.

The fifteen per cent or so who didn't wish to pray (the "Goon-Squad"), nevertheless were compelled to witness the kneeling and invoking in the training-room. When Elroy Diggins (who is a lapsed Jehovah's Witness) said something to the effect that he didn't think this was the way to run a football team, it got back to Zurco who summarily suspended the Negro without even granting him an interview. When Diggins threatened to "take the matter further," Zurco sent him a "registered" envelope containing a cheque covering his salary for the remainder of the season, *and* a bonus worth ten per cent of his salary. The cheque was postdated for after the Super Bowl (which, as you know, the Redskins didn't make), and though there was no message, Elroy got the message. He joined the Canadian League, where he chalked up yardage, cashed his cheque when the time came, and kept his mouth shut.

Until now! Lemming, who himself played football with the (then) Chicago Cardinals, right guard, *with* his helmet (not without, as a Republican wag recently suggested), between 1948 and '52, retained many of his contacts from the world of sports. Including Sanford Moss, a leftist Jewish lawyer who represented several Negro athletes, among them Booker Jefferson, Detroit Lion fullback and close friend of Elroy Diggins . . .

Mole need not connect the dots. The resultant picture spelled (to the Sanderson-Lemming team) implicit suborna- tion. Or if not that, at least nasty ethics. But let me get to the capstone: the cheque Diggins cashed, containing his salary plus the bonus, had this insignia above its letterhead: 𝔻 , was made out by Dix Chemical Bank, and was endorsed by Leggett P. Dix, president of Dix Chemical and the Senator's sole sibling.

This was the story that was "leaked" to the New York *Post*, to the Washington *Star-News*, and to Hunt Plotkin of NBC. Dix and his people were of course furious, but for the first few days after it broke, Nubile would only say (publicly) that the Senator was "studying the text," and that a comment would be forthcoming.

In truth, Dix-Zurco-Smegma were working around the clock on a counter-thrust, which, when it finally took shape in their collective brain, proved not to be anything rococo like an end-around-double-reverse, or even elementarily deceptive like the old statue-of-liberty. Not at all. Dix's team (especially Rebus) astutely discerned that Sanderson-Lemming were making waves precisely because they were most vulnerable at their source: up the middle. The strategy, then, was to "put it in their ear" (Zurco). Senator Forrest Patrician Dix would do the punishing over center—God himself running interfer- ence.

To wit: the following Sunday the senior Senator from New York State was abruptly substituted for the honorable Lester Tierney, segregationist trial lawyer from the state of Alabama, as principal guest on "Issues and Answers" over network TV. After two questions, the first on American aid to Bangladesh, and the next on Vice President nominee Smeg- ma's latest and perhaps overreaching statement on the virtue of apples (both of which Dix handled adroitly); the Senator was asked to comment on Lemming's accusation . . .

"Gentlemen," Dix smiled soberly, "I would be happy to . . .

Sept. 18: Mole's books look undulant and quite dead against the eastern wall in the sun rising.

Orc "beat upon the wall until God obeyed his call":

Mole falls asleep while gazing at Blake . . .

When he awakes he finds the Jewish cat in the hammock, and chalk. Four pieces of chalk tied with a rubber-band, tucked into the space to the right of Huizinga's *Homo Ludens.*

Abaddon: his baroque sense of symbolism is unmistakable.

Abaddon it must be whom Mole, upside down, sees now, winking his blinds: open, shut, open . . . in the top floor of the smaller tenement to my right, behind me—No! A woman. Naked behind the (abruptly) raised blinds. She has opened the window. Mole rights himself, rushes past the pigeon-coop to the farthermost portion of the roof.

By the time I get there, she is stepping through the window, back first: her right leg already on the fire-escape, her left knee on the window-sill.

Mole shouts.

Startled—as if awakened, she turns to the sound. When she spots Mole, she nearly smiles—but cuts it off, says: "Leave me alone."

"Wait. Let me talk to you."

"Leave me alone."

"Let me talk with you. I think I know what you're feeling."

Staring at me, she doesn't answer.

Mole—gambling—turns and runs. Carefully down the steep roof-rungs; then rapidly as he can down the broader tenement stairs—and out. For a few seconds he is turned around, isn't sure which house is hers. Then he sees it: five stories, grey-brown, to his left. He takes the steps three at a time. Out of breath on the fifth floor, Mole sees four apartments. Which door? He narrows it to 5e and 5f, each of which should face the back, and his own roof. He tries 5e—but it is locked. He tries the other, which opens. (The odor . . .) A narrow dark corridor leading to rooms. Mole turns left to a glimmer and sees her naked, face on knees, crouched beneath the open window. Pausing, he looks at her: dark hair, pale skin, slender.

"Miss, please—"

She raises her head—her eyes an astonishing violet. She is grinning. "Well?"

Mole looks at her.

"So you want to bail me out."

Mole doesn't answer, then says softly, "I'd like you to live."

They are staring at each other's eyes. Her own go dazed. She drops her head on her knees. Softly, Mole goes to the window; as he is closing it, he sees someone—the outline of a tall man—on his roof. She is touching him. She has opened his pants. Mole, hard, moves back, away from her.

She is looking at his face, not grinning. Her legs spread, soft, pale. Like petals. Her bush full and black, a wide, rich triangle. Oddly luxuriant. Though her eyes. (The odor again, from the inside rooms . . .)

"Damn you! Damn you! Fuck me!"

Mole, swollen in spite of himself, undoes his belt . . .

She is tugging at his ankle—mounting him even as he is settling onto the cold floor. Wet, on him, not facing him, hard down and up on him, Mole staring at a pink moon above the slim curve of her rump, yet moving with her, within her, his hands rotating her hips gently as if to mediate between her murder and her lust . . .

Though calmed somewhat afterwards, she won't talk. Mole, almost happy after such depth of passion, dresses quickly, leaves the H-E-L-P number, hoping she won't need to use it. Leaves.

Only on his roof, in his hammock, does he, touching his left pocket, find it gone. His knife. He is up at once—as if stung. Lurching . . .

But this time the door to her building's lobby is locked. Mole rings 5f. Then again. No answer. He rings the super's bell. Several times. 5f again. No answer. He is about to ring other bells at random, when a little boy comes into the vestibule from the street, rings a bell, and is buzzed back. Mole follows him through the door. While the child waits for the elevator, Mole races up the stairs.

The door to 5f has a small hemp floor mat in front of it— which Mole didn't notice before. He rings first, then tries the door, which is locked. Mole hears the elevator stop behind him. The small boy who opened the door for him down below, now walks up to 5f. As he does, the door is opened by a florid-faced middle-aged woman.

"Yes?" She and her son look inquiringly at Mole from opposite sides.

"Does a young woman of about twenty-four or twenty-five live here? Pale skin, slim? Dark hair?"

The woman appraises Mole somewhat severely, as if those apparently desirable physical characteristics were uttered only to call attention to her own overblown middle-aged glamorousness.

"No," she says.

"What's her name?" the small boy wants to know.

Instead of answering him, Mole looks over the matron's shoulder into the apartment. The door leads virtually into the kitchen. No long, dim corridor. No smell of grief and musty Jewish cooking.

"What's her name—this girl?" the boy asks again.

"I don't know her name," Mole says, turning to the boy, who is small, dark, slender. Violet-eyed . . .

The tenant who complained most bitterly about Eartha Davis Corcoran was Edith Stoessel, in 2a, the grey-blonde hysterical matirarch of a family of five: her ineffectual husband, Henry, with his bank clerk's air; her thin, frightened fourteen year old son, Julius (ironically called "Spike" by the kids in the building); her second son, Marvin; and her neurasthenic eleven year old daughter, Eunice, who for reasons which remain obscure, labored at the tuba three times a week with a teacher who bore an uncanny resemblance to her father.

Edith Stoessel wears her spectacles on a chain about her neck, screams at the young boys who play "stoop-ball"

*opposite her window—in fact has been known to rush outside
and wrest the ball from them. Edith Stoessel's sole concession
to amiability—which proved to be abortive—was her brief stint
as a mah jong hand with some of the neighborhood "girls."
This lasted but two months, Edith Stoessel initiating a viperous
three-sided quarrel in which she insisted that two of the women
were cheating.*

*Her evenings now, when she isn't in bed, are spent
knitting, heavy woolen things, usually white, which, though
she knits rapidly, never seem to get done; or if they do, nobody
remembers ever having seen one being worn by anyone.*

*When she isn't knitting, she is doubtless sitting in her hard-
backed kitchen chair in front of the television, though not really
paying attention, since she distrusts entertainment.*

*Edith Stoessel is a convenient monster for most of the
children and many of the adults in the tenement. And she
seldom disappoints.*

Sept. 19: It is the hour of sacrifice. The priests descend
the steep temple steps and light the aromatic wood offering
with a torch from the sanctuary. Then the pontiff emerges
from the temple. Clothed in white damask, he wears a crown
of brambles. In his left hand he carries an ebony scepter with
an ivory head, which in another light is a stiletto, sheathed.
The cloth belt he wears about his waist is studded with eyes.
This is Orpheus.

He leads a disciple, a child, by the hand. Pale, tremulous . . . enraptured, the child raises his violet eyes in antici-
pation of the inspired words . . .

On every side the priests are turning on their televisions,
circling round them, intoning the hymn of sacrifice.

Orpheus becomes solemn. The words he utters to the
child issue from the depths of his stomach:

"Withdraw deep into yourself, and yet deeper that you
may elevate yourself and others, even as flame ascends from
the wood it devours . . . "

Mole was awakened by the phone; when he lifted the

receiver it was dead.

The dream, I explain to Marya, while we are dining in our Indian restaurant, was at least partly inspired by her most recent watercolors of Orpheus.

"Most of the descriptions I've read of Orpheus have described him as fair," Mole says. "With light eyes. Your Orpheus is dark, bearded."

"That is the way I see him," Marya says.

"And the child? The child has violet eyes."

"Yes. That is his passion."

"I like them—this latest group—very much, Marya. When you first showed them to me, I wasn't sure. But why are these so much less abstract than the others?"

"In the others Orpheus is descending. His vision—my vision of him—becomes clouded."

"Ah."

"I'm happy you like them," Marya, softly. She takes my hand.

The food arrives. We eat without speaking. Until dessert, which is "firni," a custard flavored with rose-water, somewhat sweet tonight—but good.

"What is it, love?" Marya asks. "What's wrong?"

"With me?"

"Yes. You know I've always respected your privacy. The times you need to be alone. But lately you've been gone so much. Receding into yourself more—much more than before."

"Much more?"

"Yes."

"Since when? Was it since I came back? Since they unleashed Mole's head?" I smile.

"I don't know. Maybe it has been since then. Do you still feel it, darling? In your head?"

"No. I don't think so, Marya. But it is getting close to a certain time. I've had to be more attentive than usual to certain things. Details."

Marya looks at me more closely. Her eyes concerned. "Is there anything I can do? I don't want to meddle. I'm not meddling, am I?"

Someone is standing by our table. A diminutive old Hindu. I didn't hear him arrive. Marya looks at him, smiles. He is sweet-looking; large black lucid eyes in a small, nearly emaciated, face. Between his eyes is a *tilak* in the form of a sickle moon. He wears a white silk shawl about his shoulders and neck. As I am looking at him inquiringly, he withdraws a small slate and a piece of yellow chalk from within his shawl, and commences to print. Neither Marya nor I can imagine what.

Finished, he places the slate on our table—it reads: "I have textiles."

I couldn't have been more surprised. "Textiles?"

I hear an odd sound—as if of air being expelled suddenly from the lungs. Then a second time. It occurs to me that the old man is without a larynx. Which would account for the shawl about his neck. But the oddest thing is that this hollow expulsion of air has an *inflexion* to it. What it seemed to say on this occasion was: "Of course, textiles! What else would I have if not textiles?"

I am about to ask where they are—when he produces them. Raises a large round wicker basket table-high, only to place it down again between his legs. As Marya and I stretch to see for ourselves, Marya asks whether she could feel the material. The expulsion of air sounds positively delighted. In fact, he has all kinds of things in his basket, including delicately embroidered silk *saris*, bolts of *khadi* cloth, cotton *lungis*, a few wool and linen rugs which look Kashmiri . . .

Meanwhile the old man has erased his slate with a cloth and is writing something else on it—which again he places on the table. It is: "Do you like?"

"Yes," I say. "You have some lovely things in there. Are they expensive?"

The expelled air—in a higher key, and somewhat lengthier—is incredulous: "Dear Sir: do you think I would charge high prices for my wares? And especially to such people as you?"

He is writing again. "Please point what you wish."

Marya extracts a bolt of red silk damask.

His expulsion seems to compliment her exquisite taste—

but what he chalks on the slate is: "Kindly choose other."

Marya looks at me.

"Has someone already bought it?" I ask.

He shrugs his shoulders and smiles.

I put my hand in the basket and come up with a white *khadi* jerkin.

"Gandhi," I say.

Hearing this, the old many expels some extraordinarily positive sounding energy, his face breaking into a wide infant's smile.

In the meantime, he produces something from the basket, laying it on my lap. It is a translucent white silk shawl which looks identical to what the old man is wearing about his own neck and shoulders.

"I like this. It's the same as yours, isn't it?"

The extended "whoooosh" the tiny textile salesman expels in response pronounces us kinsmen. Marya recognizes it also. I am prepared to say: "I'll take it," when my thumb feels something, an abrasion in the material which will soon become a tear. I hold it up to him.

Surprised, he feels it with his fingers, though without looking at it. Then in an instant he has removed his own shawl and draped it loosely about my shoulders. As he is adjusting the frayed shawl about his own shoulders, I get a momentary glimpse of his throat which is severely distended and scarred.

Marya reaches across the table to feel his shawl about my neck and shoulders. Her fingers linger on the material . . .

"Thank you," I say to the old man. "How much is it?"

He is writing something on his slate, which he places in front of me. He has drawn a circle. A small, closed circle. I extend my hand to him, but his own right hand, lightly closed, is above his heart in a gesture of respect, amity . . .

Sept. 20: The truth is that Dix's hemi-pig has sounded Gigi Templeton's cloaca more than once. Twice: she was a lousy hump both times. No mouth-work. In fact she scarcely touched him. It was in one of the upper bedrooms in Wildhaven. Two or three minutes in the old missionary position. That was the first time.

The second time, two months later, was in Dix's George-town manse. On the third floor in a canopied bed, the shuttered (Virginia insisted) window facing the east lawn cherry trees... The Senator, however, was soft and Mrs. Templeton was dry. Dix wanted to buzz Gwen, borrow some lubricant—but Gigi wouldn't hear of it. Dix thus obliged to use what was at hand—which meant dipping his pork in noxzema, exercising it (Mrs. Templeton discreetly tilted towards the cherry-blossoms) until semi-hard, then lunging at his betrothed lest it become flaccid . . . The Senator did finally penetrate—or nearly penetrate; no point in splitting hairs.

Afterwards, alone at his sitz, he detected the same odd mummified stench as he had after the first unequivocal coupling. A noisome odor, yes, but proof positive that Patrician Dix duked Gigi Templeton.

Mole, on the other hand, has been doing some yeoman loving since the mute old Indian's untoward appearance in the restaurant. Planting himself in all of Marya's nerves. Musso-lini-loined again.

As you have observed, once within Sex's labyrinth, the senior Senator from New York was not wholly devoid of strategies in pursuit of the mini-eruption (a small-caliber hand-gun discharging in a distant room) that signaled his exiting. The strategies usually revolved about his caudal area, which, in spite of the constant benumbing sitzes, was preternaturally sensitive. That is, increasingly sensitive, even as his forward tail (such as it was), became ever more exiguous.

V.B. Templeton would of course have none of it. Dix had never proffered. In truth he found his betrothed singularly without allure. Her thickened pug nose, thin tight lips, cold blue eyes, coiffed-frozen blue-blonde hair—liked not Patrician Dix. Nor her form, which he had never actually *seen*, but imagined from his grappling, as from the clothed simulacrum, to be rectangular, unwindowed, stiff. In short, a corse. And yet . . . and yet the Senator needed her.

According to Hoss Loggin, "You really cain't say what a man's made of till he shows you a piece of what's overneath."

This confidence granted in Loggin's carrel after Mole's hour on the range.

"What do you mean, Hoss?"

"You, fer instance. You done real well today. And you been firin real good these last ten days too. And I don't mind tellin you, you surprised me. After you was away on that archi-pel-ago of yours, I thought you done blowed it. I wouldn't of been surprised if you'd of dropped your fetus like that other one—you look like him, you know. I don't mean just the goatee, neither. Sumbitch! I was wrong. I admit it."

"Thanks."

"You bet. Hey, buddy, you never said. Why you want to learn to fire anyways?"

"I want to kill someone."

"Sheet, who don't? Anybody I know?"

"I doubt it."

"Hell, I don't mind tellin you that was the reason I joined up durin the Korea thing. I won't say it was the ony reason. But it was one of 'em. Not that I had anything 'gainst gooks. But it was killin them or lynchin niggers, and I thought might as well see the world and get paid for it the same time. Got me some too. Gooks."

Sept. 21: Mole, be-sneakered, in the Elizabeth Street playground, playing basketball with the kids from the neighborhood. Once a shooter, Mole, approaching middle age, passes now. And rebounds. Contesting with strength, but mostly savvy. When the kids refer to him, it's to "the man," which under the circumstances is respectful enough. Mole enjoys mixing it up on the cement court. Especially around sunset, when, even in this denaturalized city, the desperate are stilled.

The desperate are stilled, and what is stripped away leaves instincts only. Which is the way the game is played here. Swallows at sunset: black, though white-breasted, twisting, zooming, switching gears, dunking. Ever on the wing. Wonderful to look at—though it is food they're after. Remember that.

And if Mole were black—as he has often wished himself—he too would shoot from the hip. Where his roof would be. Clarity, no rifle . . .

Mole showers at H-E-L-P, which is nearby.

When he comes out, he notices an envelope on his desk, addressed to him. Inside, on lined paper, in a spare, nearly illegible hand, this:

Mole:

Help me. I can't say when it started—this hangup of mine about placentas! Just writing the word gets me going. I—please don't wince—eat them. What I do is hang around hospitals where they are not that careful with their waste. I look pretty respectable—in spite of this thing, this impluse of mine. So that it's easy enough to pretend I'm an expectant father so that I could get in where it's all going on. Once I'm in I know what to do, where to find it. Like it's a kind of homing instinct. I carry an attaché case and that's where I put them. They're almost always wrapped in plastic. Look, I don't *want* to do it. I hate myself afterwards. I can't stop. It's like there's something in me pushing me that needs to be *fed*. It's too strong for me to even think clear, let alone fight it. It's killing me! Please stop me. I'm at the Seward Park Maternity Hospital on Broome and Rivington.

Mole looks at the clock on the wall. 6:50. Still lots of time before H-E-L-P opens. I dress rapidly and go out. Catch the bus to Canal and Broome. From there walk east through the narrow, blighted streets. Dark beneath the ineffectual street-lamps. And getting colder, the wind rattling the trash-can covers, blowing newspaper bits and debris through the streets. Scarcely any one around . . . Mole cuts left through Mott Street. Rivington just ahead, and I can make out a dark box-like structure near the corner. Walking rapidly, Mole has the distinct impression of having done this before . . .

In fact I have never been on this stretch of Rivington, nor have I seen this building: brown, square, "SPMH" on the pediment above the entrance. Oddly, nearly all of the windows unlit. I notice a narrow, unroofed alcove on the east side of the building, through which one can probably get to the rear without going around the corner. Mole does this . . . The building is longer than it appears from the front, yet all the rooms above the lobby appear dark—as if unoccupied. Which if true is surprising in this high-birth area.

But where is the letter-writer? I see an ill-lit wooden door which may just lead somewhere. Mole is walking in this direction when I hear my name called from behind. Turning I glimpse the outline of a figure leaning from one of the upper windows—Mole is knocked to the pavement! Sopping, filthy about his head, in his mouth, on his glasses, coursing down his chest and back—someone dropped something on him from one of the windows. Attempting dizzily to stand, Mole slips— nearly falls. Just then two of the windows above him are lit, so that I can make out what is all over me and underfoot. Foul-smelling . . .

The substance on his face and head is pinkish, viscous, with traces of coagulant matter. Mole bends, tries to grab hold of whatever it was he nearly stumbled on. Slippery and membranous, he examines the pinkish disc-shaped substance in my hands . . .

Sept. 22: Marya found my knife.
"Where was it, Marya?"
"In your pocket, sweet. The dark grey woolen trousers. You left them on the bed—"
"Which pocket? Do you recall?"
"One of the front ones. I think the left."
Mole shakes it open. Examines it. It hasn't been tampered with.

Retracing the circle in white and red . . . holding the knife by the blade in my left hand, Mole backs up to his books, left shoulder flush against *Isis Unveiled*. Squinting, I flip it underhand, it revolves twice, it . . . misses: to the left and behind the inner circle.

Mole tries it again . . . misses again. This time the knife doesn't even stick in the tar.

He picks it up with his left hand, closes the blade, puts it into his left pocket.

I look at Mole's fingers: long and slender like Zelda's—only thickened at the tips, clubbed.

Mole (sinister) clawing through his chest's roof's tunnel, piton fingers bite into tar. Looking for . . . lost.

It has many turnings, also wind, the closer you come to the tunnel's center, the more violently it blows. This is where Mole waits. Malingers with wet eyes. Claws for hands . . .

In Omaha once they lost him, roller-skating, his friends, older than he, that Mole, weeping, couldn't get back. Nor did: the "house" he entered different having   left)

"The world," Porphyry writes, "is obscure and black; yet through the connecting power and orderly distribution of form, it is lovely and radiant. Hence it may very properly be denominated a cave, which is obscure to him who surveys its foundation, and examines it with an intellectual eye; yet in its interior and profound parts infused with light . . . "

Sept. 23: You recall that Sklar had become angry with me after his April Fool's caper misfired. He has long since recovered his snorting normalcy.

However now he is vexed again. He is waiting for me at the station when I arrive, sweated, after an hour and a half of playground basketball.

"Hey, Mole. How's the game?"

"As good as can be expected. What are you doing here so early?"

"What do you mean 'as good as can be expected'? You mean you lost something?"

"Right. I don't have all the moves I had when I was twenty-five."

"No shit? Your energy ain't what it used to be? I got

something for you, Mole."

"Can it wait until after I shower?"

"Can it wait? Yeah, it can wait. Go ahead, take your shower."

When I come out of the shower, Sklar has two substances spread over my desk: one powdery and orange, the other root-like, jade-green.

"Hyssop, Mole. This is hyssop. The green shit is motherwort. Also called lion's tail, lion's ear, and throwwort. The proportion is two parts hyssop to one part motherwort. You gotta make a tea out of it. Four quarts of tea. Probably you think you can't get four quarts out of this. Well, you're wrong—both these herbs expand like crazy. If you toss two small ginseng roots in the brew just as it's reached a boil, it ain't a bad idea either."

"It sounds like a winner. What's it good for?"

"Up the old bung, Mole. Tell me—I never asked you this—have you ever taken an enema?"

"Yeah, on occasion."

"Fucking-A. Now this tea is for a high enema. All a high enema is is four quarts of this fine tea—or four quarts of anything. The same hole, everything else is the same as an ordinary enema except it's four quarts. And it's best from a four quart enema can, which I'll lend you. And of course the rectal tip."

"Will you lend me a rectal tip also, Sklar?"

"No, that ain't good hygiene. You could pick up your own in any drugstore. Or use Marya's douche-bag tip."

"Uh-huh. What are you uptight about, Sklar?"

"Twice a day. After breakfast and before going to sleep is good. You have enough here for a week, but I predict that after using this for four days you'll have a hard cock and a deadly jump-shot from anywhere on the court under twenty feet."

Mole wondered: Zelda again? Could she have told Sklar she was doing some work for me?

"It won't fit right off, Mole. Don't expect it to. Your colon is clogged with shit. What you do is take as much as you can hold, then expel it. Then do it again. Unless your colon is really fucked over, by the third day you should be able to hold all four quarts. Yeah. One other thing: instead of laying in like one position, move around, roll from side to side so that the water can get in, since sometimes, and I'd guess in your case, there is a kink in the colon."

"And *your* kink is my energy?"

"What's that, Mole buddy?"

"Why don't you say what you mean, Sklar?"

"Yeah, well how did it feel, Mole? I bet she was better than Marya."

"Marya again. I wonder whether you do that conscious-ly—say something unkind about Marya when you are angry with me. What's eating you?"

"Yeah, well I can't believe you don't know what I'm talking about. I'm talking about G.J. You fucked her, didn't you?"

"Yes, once, last Easter. Was I not supposed to?"

"Easter, right? The one day in the year your cock faces heaven."

G.J. was coming up the stairs. Sklar asked me to meet him in the Elizabeth Street playground tomorrow at 4:30. With sneakers.

The first call tonight was from an L. Seezshur (he insisted on spelling his name), who wanted to know whether Mole could put him in touch with a "limb-deficient young woman," whom he wanted to meet with the aim of "mutual en-joyment."

When I aked him why she must be limb-deficient, he frankly admitted to being deathly afraid of castration; a fear that could only be allayed by having a partner "who not only promised to refrain, but was in no position not to."

I told him that really I had no contacts in this area, but if I heard of any, I would get in touch with him.

He wasn't satisfied with that answer, and said that he now saw that his previous impression of me was accurate—namely that in spite of my pleas for tolerance, I was governed by my own "predilections and prejudices."

I said, maybe, but that was the best I could do.
Since he didn't wish to hang up the receiver—I had to.

Sept. 24: When Mole appears at the Elizabeth Street
playground at 4:20, Sklar is already there shooting hook-shots
at one of the unoccupied baskets. He allows Mole a nod and
continues shooting. Mole meanwhile puts on his shatter-proof
glasses and changes into his sneakers on the sideline.

Sklar is wearing maroon sweat pants and a gold and blue
tee-shirt that reads "Jock full o' Nuts" on the front and "69"
on the back. There are blotches of perspiration on the seat of
his pants.

"You've been here a while, Sklar?"

"Right."

Mole stretches his back and does some deep-knee-bends.

"Your ball?" Mole asks.

"Right."

Mole handles it. It needs a little air, but the treads are
good. Mole shoots a jump-shot from the free-throw line. Sklar
brushes by him, recovers the ball, lays it in.

"'Jock full o' Nuts!' I thought you played for the UCLA
Bruins, Sklar."

Sklar snorts without answering.

Mole takes the ball off the backboard, dribbles out to the
key with his left hand, then pivots, changes hands, moves to
the right side and shoots a jump-shot that hangs on the rim—
and drops in. The rim, which is slightly tilted, is also "dead."
But the three other courts are occupied.

"Where did this club of yours play, Sklar?"

"Ocean Beach, Fire Island. Do you wanna bullshit or
play ball?"

"Tension, but no talking, in this grudge game—it that it?'"

"Tense, shit! I'm ready, Mole."

"Uh-huh."

"One-on-one." Ten baskets win. Sklar wins the choose,
and takes the ball out. He dribbles to the right of the free-

throw line, spins left, then right again from where he throws up a hook-shot which finds the dead rim and drops in. His point and his ball again. This time he dribbles left—pivots quickly, drives to the right towards the basket, and attempts a semi-hook which, however, Mole blocks, recovers, and lays in the basket.

"Shit!" Sklar says.

Though lighter, Mole is four or five inches taller than Sklar. He dribbles towards the basket deliberately, turning his back to Sklar as he gets to the free-throw line. Sklar is guarding closely, his belly and hips flush against me, one arm up, the other poking my waist or slapping at the ball. At the free-throw line Mole fakes to the right, gets half a step on Sklar, drives to his left and lays it up with his left hand—the ball hangs on the rim and drops . . . off, but Mole, inside Sklar, tips it in. He leads 2−1.

Mole, taking the ball out, is about to turn his back to Sklar when Sklar lunges for the ball—and steals it, but only after fouling Mole in the process. Mole doesn't call the foul. Sklar, who favors the right side, again goes right, fakes a hook—but doesn't fake Mole out of position. Stymied, Sklar bangs the ball hard off Mole's knees and out of bounds.

"You want to win, don't you, big fella?"

Sklar doesn't answer. He takes the ball out from under the basket, moves to the free-throw line, then, deliberately, in again, his thick hard ass and hips nudging Mole to the right side. This time he fakes a hook, pivots to his left, and tries a fall-away jump-shot, which Mole, moving into him, blocks.

"You fouled me, Mole."

"Did I? I thought I got it cleanly."

"You fouled me."

Sklar is breathing hard through his mouth.

"All right, it's your call. Take it."

Sklar moves to the left side, pauses as if he is going to shoot—then drives hard to the basket, laying it in back-hand. The score is tied.

Mole notices that a few neighborhood kids are hanging around the sideline, cursorily watching. Also a man. White, middle aged . . .

Sklar, this time, stops about fifteen feet out and throws up a one-hander, which hits the side of the rim and the backboard.

"Foul!" someone calls.

Mole, who has recovered the ball, stops, as does Sklar. It is the man on the sideline who made the call.

"Did I foul you, Sklar?"

"What do you want me to say? An impartial observer made the call."

Mole looks at the "impartial observer." He has lank brown hair, and is wearing a tan windbreaker. Sinewy and tall, he looks vigorous, high-strung.

Sklar takes the ball out again, tries to hook from the left side with his right hand, misses. Mole with the ball moves quickly to the foul-line, turns, jumps, hits.

Mole, leading, and with the ball, fakes Sklar left, then right—then drives left all the way, laying it in with his left hand.

"Travelled," Mole hears from the sideline.

"What's that?"

"You travelled. Walked with the ball," the man says matter-of-factly.

Mole looks closely at the man's eyes: they are mackerel grey, narrow, filled with rage.

"Hey, mister," Mole says. "I'm going to beat him quick. Then you, all right?"

The man turns his head away from Mole without responding. I see that he is wearing a hearing device behind his left ear.

"Take it, Sklar. Your ball."

Sklar, moving towards the basket back first, is visibly tired, and is doing lots of sweating, which smells, to Mole, of sperm. He tries a set-shot from the outside, which misses. Mole recovers, steps back to the free-throw line, then pivoting with one long step, lays the ball in off the board.

Alternately shooting from the outside and using his height advantage over Sklar from inside the free-throw line, Mole scores six straight points without giving up the ball.

When, after it is over, Mole looks towards the sideline, the man is no longer there. Nor are the kids.

"That's it," Mole says. "Another one?"

"Naw. I'm kaput. This is the first time I've played since Fire Island. That was more than two years ago. I'm going to the station."

Sklar, sulking, walks off in his blotchy sweat pants, his ball under his arm.

Mole takes out a towel from his gym bag, then sits on the pavement and changes back into his shoes.

When he slips on his jacket, which was draped over his bag, Mole is at once aware that something is wrong. In his right pocket his billfold and every-day glasses are still intact. But his left pocket is empty. The knife again gone.

Sept. 25: A letter from Sri Sen.

My Dear M:

Your letter of 18, Sept., in hand. You must not concern yourself overmuch about your knife. You shall certainly continue to "lose" it if you continue to worry about it. A warrior must be as certain of his tools as of the arms that wield them. The worrier is never certain.

Again, you must be persistent in your practice of *Asanas,* and especially for the month of October, the *Yoga Mudra,* which should always precede *Halasana.* Such practice only will help your transformation.

You have chosen your "roof," have you not? Although the roof itself is not of primary importance, it would be good if it was in accord with the favorable aspects of your chart. To that end, kindly enclose an illustration of the roof in relation to your and your Senator's residence. Only if the apex of the resultant angle is clearly facing downward, is the omen less than good. Because you must remember that *Apana* cannot be expelled, but must be reversed. Upward, along with the positive energy. From what you have previously written to me, however, I am almost certain that your "line" is not inauspicious.

Never mind what others might think about the program you have established on your roof. It is the only way, in accord with your *Dharma*, for you to help these very others, while helping yourself.

It is all of it sleep.

Sept. 26: Every day he would disappear into his mountain, and come back speechless, his hair full of shadows, his body covered with the gentle bruises of his day's rambling.

Mole on his roof in *Halasana* thinking of Camus.

"Every man has at his disposal a certain zone of influence, which he owes as much to his defects as to his qualities."

Thus Mole, within his dream, touches gently with certain fingers. Yet within his body's mind: bruised.

Words   words   words . . . Listen. Compel yourself to listen. To my spaces:

For this journal is a murdering back, a means of overcoming despair by shaping it. By charging it, as the homeopath shakes, shakes the essence that it merge with what is most alive within itself . . .

As the fasting man in our cage displays his skeleton to the falsely fed;

Marya hands Mole the phone, then leaves the room. It is G.J.

"Hello, G.J."

"Hello, Mole. What happened between you and Sklar? You're not talking to each other?"

"No, we are. Though not very much. Sklar is upset because you and I made love last Easter. You only just told him that, didn't you?"

Pause . . . "Yes. But he has no claims on me, Mole."

"Why did you choose to tell him now?"

"I don't know—really. Though it would have been the same whenever I told him."

"Have things been going well between you and Sklar lately?"

"No, not really."

"Probably it would have been better if you had told him—if that's what you wanted to do—when they *were* going well."

G.J. doesn't respond right away. Then she says: "I want to do it again—make love with you again, Mole."

"I've felt that you do."

"Yes. Don't you? Don't you want to do it again?"

"Sometimes it is not good for one to do what he wants to do, G.J."

"Oh?"

"I'm speaking for myself."

"What do you mean, Mole? I think I understand, but I'm not sure I do. Can you tell me what you mean?"

"Not very easily. And I think not now. Now is not a good time."

"Oh. All right. I don't mean to ask you these kinds of things on the phone. And Marya. Is it Marya? Never mind. I'm sorry. I'll keep my mouth closed. But Sklar. Do you feel that this is a permanent breach between the two of you?"

"I doubt it. Not as far as I'm concerned. But we'll have to see."

"It's not pleasant—Sklar snorting and dejected all night," G.J. says.

"It's not. You're right. But it can't be helped. That's the way it happens to be."

"Yes."

After Mole hangs up the receiver, he sits on the bed and removes his trousers. Then his undershorts. He walks to the window which faces the street. Draws back the curtain. People are walking around below, outside. Mole's penis is erect. He opens the window from the bottom so that the polluted city wind blows on his legs and genitals. He stands that way, four stories above the street. Nobody looks up . . .

Late that afternoon, after an hour or so of basketball, as Mole is fitting his sneakers into his bag, one of the neighborhood kids comes up to him.

"Hey man, this yours?" He is holding Mole's knife.

"Yeah, it is."

He hands it to me—then leaves.

I examine it. It's all right. The way it was when it disappeared. I hadn't really thought much about it.

Sri Sen was right.

Sept. 27: Do you remember DuVal Stett, Democrat from Tennessee, Minority Whip in the Senate, and prayer leader of "LSD—Jesus," to which Senator Dix, Speaker Vorst, and other Capitol Hill luminaries belong? Well, according to the NY *Daily News,* Stett, who twenty-three years before was a minister in his native Memphis, has been substituted for the Reverend Hillary Tallow-Dunn, and will conduct Senator Dix's wedding ceremony Sunday in Wildhaven Chapel. Though Stett refers to himself as a "Universal Christian," the fact is that he had been a lay preacher in the Adventist sect, and (the *News* reports), Reverend Tallow-Dunn has been instructing him in the nuances of the High Episcopal liturgy for the last few weeks.

Also in the *Daily News,* in the "Reed Riley" column, it was reported that Morty Levinson, the irrepressible "gatecrasher," vowed that he would have a "bird's-eye view" of the ceremony, in spite of Dix's well-publicized intention to keep the wedding "private." When, reports Riley, Levinson's boast was conveyed to Coach Jock Zurco, Jock, forgetting himself, replied: "If I catch him in there, I'll kick his butt—personally."

And Julia Saphire, on her "Personalities in the News" show on WPIX, reported that "Pat and Gigi" were sipping champagne and "holding hands" at a party in their honor given by Montana governor Darren Quonset in his mansion.

According to Julia Saphire, Gigi, "who they say can't hold her liquor, was, if not actually bombed out of her mind, pretty darn tipsy . . ."

Smegma, meanwhile, has been girdling the country in his private jet (in his own helicopter for the hustings) on behalf of the Dix-Zurco-Smegma campaign "philosophy" which— thank Rebus!—has been dubbed "America's Peace and Prosperity Lead Everything," or "APPLE."

"Not merely the universally appreciated Delicious" (expatiates Smegma in Cheyenne, Wyoming), "the uniquely tangy McIntosh, the picture-beautiful Rome Beauty, the incomparable Jonathan, the high-spirited Golden Pippin, the always pleasing Winesap—but literally thousands of other varieties are here in our great country, under our own skies, and can be plentifully and rapidly cultivated and harvested with our own advanced technology.

"I think I have already proven to you, my fellow Americans, that in spite of what a purse-full of left-of-center denigrators and part-time fruit-titionists have noisily pro-claimed, *not* the Chinese egg-roll, nor Japanese raw-fish chunks, nor Parisian fondue, nor even so-called soul-food— *but our own apple, is the greatest single unit of concentrated goodness in the world today!*

"You notice that I emphasize 'own.' This is because some of our bleeding-hearts and ego-cologists have been empha-sizing 'other.' Well, I'm here to give you some good news, you folks who feel like we do that America's peace and prosperity should lead everything. *We have it all!* The natural resources, the technology, the scientific know-how, the strong shoulders to man the machine.

"And we maintain further, unlike our Democratic oppo-nents, that in spite of a few grumblers, we have here in our vast and great country, under our own spacious skies, the iron will, good cheer, and stick-to-itness that has made our country what it is.

"I don't recall our Founding Fathers blubbering, throw-ing in the towel when the going got a little tough, looking at other countries who in fact couldn't—*and still can't*—hold a candle to us . . ."

Asked by a listener to explain what he meant by an earlier statement in which he compared the U.S. to survivors on a lifeboat, Smegma replied:

"A great many Americans all across the country have asked about this—this lifeboat morality. I'll tell you what I meant by it. Actually it wasn't myself who originated the term 'lifeboat morality,' but an outstanding Professor of Political Theory at Parsons College by the name of Ziggy. Professor Gerhard Ziggy.

"What he said was that at this point in history, the great countries, the outstanding countries, like some of the ones I mentioned who had great apple crops: ourselves, Great Britain, Germany, and France, for example. According to Gerry Ziggy, these outstanding countries are like survivors who have evacuated ships—the ships being superb functioning democracies which have lately run into problems.

"Now in order for these lifeboats—all of which are chockfull of survivors—to make it back to port where they can begin to build and grow again, they must make good time and avoid inclement weather, because they have only so much provisions, you understand.

"Well, the have-not nations are naturally in much worse shape. Rather than being in lifeboats, they are actually floundering in the rough seas. Naturally they would like to get out of the water and into the boats, but the problem is not only there is no room for them, but there is no time to stop and pick them up. And besides, these people—Ziggy mentioned India, Bangladesh, Honduras, the African countries; you can supply your own names—besides, these people have no home ports of their own. They depend and have depended for a very long time on being *admitted* into the ports of the great have-nations.

"By 'admitted,' I mean literally, but also figuratively, through what the Liberals like to call 'Foreign Aid.' The point as I said—as Professor Ziggy put it—is that" (here, Smegma's words become deliberately spaced dum-dum bullets): *"our-own-welfare-demands-that-we-no-longer-put-up-with-free-loaders-and-hopeless-cases!*

"We, my fellow Americans, have our own great task to complete. The very same task prefigured two hundred years ago in one of the greatest documents in the history of the world—the American Constitution. And sad as it may seem to ignore the apparent needs of chronically desperate nations, it would be far sadder to let them drag us down to the watery depths with them.

"This is what I meant by 'Lifeboat Morality.' "

Conn, the super of our tenement, is still a pretty tough guy and he doesn't let you forget it. For one thing he claims to be a cousin of Billy Conn, the heavyweight contender of the forties who fought Joe Louis (and lost) a couple of times. And he himself is always ready to mix it up, especially on weekends when he has been drinking.

A few months ago Conn laid into a Hell's Angel type who evidently had been harassing Flora Trachtenberg, the ripe sixteen year old beauty who resided with her widowed mother on the fifth floor.

Two motorcycles careened up onto the sidewalk in front of the building on Monday at about midnight. After noisily revving their bikes for several minutes, they started to shout for Flora to come to her window. Instead her terrified mother rushed in her nightgown down the stairs to Conn's basement apartment. In a minute Conn was outside in his skivvy shirt and old army fatigues, a monkey wrench in his pocket. By now several tenants had been alerted, and what they saw from their windows was Conn punching, and finally knocking senseless, one of the bikers while the other skulked against the wall . . .

Ten minutes later they were gone, and in spite of the lurid tales of biker revenge, they didn't come back.

Both in his disposition and physically, Conn resembles Billy Martin, the pugnacious baseball manager: wirily muscular, with large ears, small eyes, an infectious grin. Conn is

*probably in his middle forties. The story is that his beautiful
northern Irish wife left him five or six years before for political
reasons (Conn being a Catholic from Cork), taking their two
lovely daughters with her. Now Conn has his two German
shepherds, his weekend whisky, and maybe an occasional
whore.*

*His only apparent link with his wife and girls are his John
McCormack recordings. Should one, some Saturday night,
very late, happen into the basement, he might hear as if from a
distance (yet issuing from Conn's bedroom) the ancient tinny
sweetness of "Kathleen Mavourneen"* . . .

Sept. 28: An East Indian aura about the city evening,
Mole walking downtown to H-E-L-P. Lower Bleecker Street,
filled with shoppers (dancers), the bread-shops, the small
butcher-shops, the corner candy-stores, the well-kept tenements. Like boats at anchor, buildings and people shimmering
in the early evening fog beneath the street lamps.

The Italian-Americans have remained anchored here
where they've lived and worked for generations; while their
caucasian neighbors fearfully uprooted themselves, moving
back and then farther back to the margins of their lives. (The
Italians refusing to sever the connection to their source, even
as they are loath to commit their oldest relatives to "Homes"
for the aged.)

Tonight, though, more somehow than before, Mole
feeling it: that thread through time, through the capricious
change that largely governs us here. The snugness, the
gestures of the shopkeepers in the modulated light, even the
sawdust on the floors—all pointing to connection within the
box-like shadows of windowless buildings going up, up
throughout the area.

Though many of these Italian-Americans, nurturing
the illusion that a "Republican" will protect their hard-earned
interests, will vote for Dix next month, Dix can't really
matter. Not tonight.

Crossing Sixth Avenue, Mole heads east into honky-
tonk Greenwich Village. Only a neon shadow of what

it aspired to be. An ambiance of "bohemian" pretense now; another weekend evening street-corner mask. Yet even this, without substance as it seems to be, is connection. Mole feeling it strongly tonight, even as he wishes it formed a broader linking of rooted feeling, sinew. This glib bohemian-ism legislated by an Industry that sapiently modifies the requisites (trappings), so that the current crop of arty weekenders must always commence with (buy) a new vari-ation of the old "image."

Never mind. Tonight it is Indian.

Farther east begins the familiar grief. Walking up Fourth Street into the lower East Side. Shards of history pricking the devastation. The old Jews gone. Or going. Uprooted Puerto Ricans in their dolorous tenement flats, or leaning over fire-escapes, seeking out sun. Not finding it. Nor finding the thread (or chain) yoking them to their Jewish near-gone brother. A different kind of sun, though it give a similar light. (Mole's love would be to join light to . . . light:

Mole turns left through a fringe of Chinatown, even as there are Chinese "towns" throughout the world. Secretive like the Jews, they work, work against the great void in their chest—which is the vast country they've gone from. Not, finally, much different from the desert of the Jews, nor from the Puerto Ricans' island sun. Nor from the sign of the heart between the eyes: the black American's Africa.

What can it mean? "Awake": nothing. Detritus. Sea-wrack.

Mole would strip them, have them sleep, all: the infirm, sorrowful, furious, the irreparably maimed, the quislings, the fearful, the marked . . . sleep wherever they are, that they hear the breathing in each other's breast, that they become what they've never not been: unclothed earthly spectres flowing hand-in-hand through their wondrous blighted city which (touching) is without cease . . .

Among the calls for "help" tonight was this one:

"Mr. Mole, I'm a praicher of Jaisus . . . "

"I hear you."

"I love my work, Mr. Mole. I jes love doin the work of

Jaisus. I'm located in Missoura. Near the Arkansas border?"

"Yes."

"I do tent praichin. We set up what we call Jaisus shanties. But what they really is is tents. And the people—I'm talkin bout the mountain people, Mr. Mole—they come from all over the neighborhood aree to hear the word of Jaisus. Not to hear Praicher McGee, mind you, but to hear the word of Jaisus come alive *through* Praicher McGee. I'm jes a receptacle, Mr. Mole."

"All right."

"Now I don't know whether you be a religious man. I hear that you are a smart man. A man that can understand people. I'm ony here for a coupla days. On business."

"I'm listening."

"Mr. Mole—I kealed a pig!" He paused. "Oncet, a long time back it was, Mr. Mole. But I cain't ever forgit it. I tell you the truth: I love what I'm doin, praichin like I am the word of Jaisus. There be but one problem, sir, and that is there ain't anybody can praich to *me*. Course I don't mean Jaisus—he's always there. I love him. I mean some human be-an. Why, every mother's son expek old Praicher McGee to have all the answers. But I don't. I really and truly don't. And I'm glad I don't too, it you want to know. Because this is a fallen place, Mr. Mole . . ."

"I hear you."

"I know you do, sir. You're a good man. Which is why I have called to you. It wasn't easy to admit you yoursef has problems, you understand. And this pig. What it was was several years ago, in this little town near Little Rock. I guess you know where Little Rock is. Waal, it was a bitty thing, mottled, you know? Rootin at the side of the road with its curly tail and all. Weren't no bigger than a puppy dog. People don't tend to think of pigs as bein all that lovable—but they are. Because they God's critures. More: they the lowest of the low of God's critures. I wanted—I was a very young man at this time—to pick it up and jes hold it, or pet it like you might do a puppy dog. Which is what I did. Ony it started squealin so pathetic. Squirmin around and all. It was pathetic, Mr. Mole. It was the most pathetic thang I ever saw. I still loved it—but I hated it too at the same time. Cause it was so pathetic. What I done was flang it, Mr. Mole. I flang it hard against a big old elm. And when it fell I picked it up and flang it again. I did it three or four times—till I was sure it was daid. Bleedin and pathetic. I ran from there, Mr. Mole. After it was all over I ran. And for a long time I didn't let mysef thank about what I done neither. But finally I had to—*I had to!* And I hated mysef. And as I hated mysef I felt stirrin in me a growin love for Jaisus. Which is when I started my work, Mr. Mole. My praichin the Word. And I never tole anybody bout the pig till now neither . . ."

Sept. 29: Mole slept. Mole's people . . . slept)

Sept. 30: Forrest Patrician Dix and Virginia Badleigh Templeton conjoined today at noon in the Senator's own Wildhaven Chapel in the Bitterroot Valley of Montana (the "Treasure State"). The Reverend Minority Whip DuVal Stett conducted the ceremony flawlessly.

Notable details of the wedding and reception follow:

—Morty Levinson, superbly disguised as a millionaire Venezuelan bauxite producer (in purple velveteen plus-fours), not only shook Jock Zurco's hand, but slipped him a note containing the name, age and vital statistics of a giant Incan "football prospect."

—Gigi wore a "Travers of Williamsburg" ensemble; short white gloves, an off-white, calf-length tailored worsted, beige pumps—and a tulle veil. The fact is that even at her age Gigi was susceptible to unsightly eruptions, and she developed a puss-pimple above her upper lip a few days before. This is the principal reason she chose to wear a tulle veil, which is of course associated with young, virginal brides.

—McVey from the Chicago *Sun-Times*, who carried a "Ruger Security" 38 in a shoulder holster, and a Dan Lurie hand-grip in his right pocket, reserved his most vigorous handshake for Coach Zurco, whom he accosted at the buffet counter. While they were shaking hands, a stud from Zurco's shirt was jarred loose and fell into the bouillon tureen. It was not retrieved.

—Julia Saphire of WPIX was denied admission . . .

—The Wildhaven chancel was decorated with honeysuckle and magnolia.

—Julia Saphire persisted until Nubile himself reluctantly intervened, and she was admitted.

—Speaker Vorst's wife Clara, who has kidney stones, discovered a graffito on the wall of her commode: the outline of an erect circumsized penis, and the word (or name) "Mort." Flustered, Mrs. Vorst was unable to open the door of the ladies' room, had to fiddle with it for twenty minutes before being rescued by a maid.

—Morty Levinson's date, Arlene Bernstein, who resembled Theda Bara, was conspicuously bra-less under her mauve silk (imitation) Galanos. She told Julia Saphire that she was Doña Isabel Lara Mariposa-Banzer of Caracas, Venezuela, after which Julia Saphire informed her: "Señorita Banzer, you are the most exotic woman at this reception. By far!" Later Julia Saphire repeated the same words into her miniature casette recorder.

—Gwendolyn Stephens' hair was moist. She and Ronald having just emerged from the pool-house.

—Rebus, recently "separated" and secretly queer, chatted a good deal with young Raleigh Patrician Templeton, who went to military school, and for the reception was in full cadet uniform. Once Rebus followed the youthful Christian soldier into the john—only to encounter therein Lance Dochmeier and Holstein. Almost at once an intense discussion of the campaign and especially of "input" developed.

—Among the invited was Jake Dent, designer of the "Barbie Doll" and co-inventer of the Hawk Missile.

—Also Dillard, translucent in pince-nez. Dillard, who had an "Intelligence connection" with Dix during the Second War, subsequently became our chief operative in the Philippines. Famous as a "strategist," one of his best-known gambits was having his men drain the blood from Communist Huk bodies and put marks on their necks to simulate vampire killings— this to scare the Communists out of fighting. It didn't work.

—Music was provided by Lyman Herring and his octet. Herring played the organ.

—While the Honorable Houghton ("Hoot") Blasingame, Secretary of Defense, was puffing at his pipe and dilating to a covey of admirers, his wife Louise, already tipsy from the champagne-punch, was staring in the vicinity of Ronald's truncheon.

—Leggett Patrician Dix, the Senator's "kid brother," and preserver of the Dix empire, was buttonholed by the million-aire Venezuelan bauxite producer who not only squeezed his hand, but whispered in his ear . . . (Julia Saphire straining to hear, could make out but a single word which sounded like "rag-mop.")

—There were no Negroes among the invited. Dochmeier had broached the possibility of inviting Abraham McKinley, but it received zero support from the team.

—Morty Levinson, who, according to his own testimony (as recorded in the Easter issue of "Screw"), likes "shiksa food when I can't do no better"—kept on eating even after chipping a molar on Jock Zurco's shirt stud which had somehow found its way into the devilled ham.

—Ronald fancied Arlene Bernstein, but when he made his move he was politely, though firmly, rebuffed. In what sounded like Spanish.

—Even on the altar the senior Senator and proximate bridegroom found it hard as heck to concentrate on his betrothed. When he wasn't thinking "campaign," his mind was preoccupied with Gwen's supple tongue—getting to it that evening sometime before having to bed down with Gigi.

Sept. 30: For Mole it was a matter of continuing south. Thus Colombia. Cartagena, on the Caribbean coast, and "steeped"—as the brochure put it—"in history . . ."

"Steeped" too, Mole saw soon enough, in the blood of colored people. Just after high noon, near the center of the walled city, I watch half a dozen black young men, tattered, barefoot, kicking a deflated soccer-ball against the battlements, under the bartizans ("splendid specimens, lookouts: they stood off Morgan, Sir Francis Drake . . . "). Loose-limbed, the young men move about like the Africans they were once—yet as if asleep, narcotized, not talking beneath this fiercest of suns, kicking the leather sac . . . retrieving it.

An oddly divided city, Cartagena: the ancient walled section with its battlements and churches, most of the structures dating from the 16th century; and the new jet-set section, called Bocagrande: a long strip of done-up hotels, "boutiques," and terraced restaurants confronting the sea. Perhaps a third of the tourists in Bocagrande were foreigners; the rest, it appeared, were wealthy Colombians.

The Colombian women were, to Mole, revoltingly fascinating. North American women tend to go on a good deal about the brutal insipidities of machismo, as if it were exclusively a masculine trait. Especially in Colombia, though elsewhere in Latin America as well, Mole found that machismo as often afflicted the women. Above all in the coastal areas where flesh ripened early, and the weather compelled the people to the streets at night. Mental energy suspended, or funnelled downwards, it became a matter of gratifying the body. This the men customarily did by drinking, gorging themselves on street-corner food, talking and laughing and squabbling in masculine clusters in the squares, in front of barber shops . . .

For their part, the women can be found strolling—strutting—in skin-tight slacks, or brief skirts with boldly-seamed pantyhose; their valid bosoms sconced in décolleté tops with Playboy bunny push-up bras. And on their slender feet: Carmen Miranda platform shoes. Their faces are elaborately made-up in the manner associated with whores—eyes boldly mascara'd, lips scarlet, the rest of the face whitened. Much attention given to the hair (Mole estimated that beauty parlors outnumbered cantinas by fifty per-cent), which is always coiffed, usually tinted . . .

Should a *Colombiana* dressed as Mole described, chance to pass a young or reasonably young couple of whatever nationality, the *Colombiana* will (I observed it time and again), direct her entire attention to the woman, often commencing with her shoes, then working up. The *Colombiana's* expression will never indicate approval—not at all; nearly always it will be an odd combination of pouting disapproval and icy aloofness. The male might just as well be elsewhere, because though she spends her prime hours regaling herself like a whore, the *Colombiana's* head is with *La Virgen* for all time, unless—this would seem to occur but rarely—that swollen, pampered pony betrays her . . .

Thus machisma. Through Mole's lenses. Mole chose to separate himself from it. He stayed in the old city, in a pension, which though run-down gave off on the ancient outer wall and, beyond it, on the Caribbean. It was Mole's "business" that took me more often that I would like to Bocagrande. Though my contact was doubtless already there, he preferred for his own reasons to play cat and mouse. But finally (it was on Mole's fifth day), he appeared while I was having an early dinner at an Argentine cafe called "*Parilla.*" The menu, which was on my table when I sat down, had a small piece of paper clipped to it, as if containing the "dish of the day." Neatly printed, it read in Spanish: "Lifeguard Stand, 7:45."

No moon. Blue-black but for the stars, particularly Perseus stretching resolutely away from the Sisters . . . Mole stepped onto the sand behind the Dorado Hotel at 7:40.

Stupidly, he had forgotten to take his flashlight—which wouldn't matter if the lifeguard stand in question was the one to his left by the water. He could make it out in the light of the hotel . . .

By the time I reached it, it was too dark to see whether anyone was sitting in it. Instead of calling out, Mole climbed up the ladder-like front of the stand. Nobody was there. I brushed my hand across the bench, then the floor: nothing. So he hadn't meant this stand after all. There must be a good many others spaced along Bocagrande. I would walk south along the sea, look at two more stands, if nobody was in either of them—well, that was as much as anyone could reasonably expect of Mole.

. . . trudging through the sand in the phosphorescent sheen of the surf breaking, Mole must have continued for some five hundred meters—it was difficult to judge, and I was making my way slowly so as not to bypass a stand. I reached one finally, nearly colliding with it. I felt my left trouser pocket to make certain my side of the "contract" was intact. Then, instead of immediately climbing to the top, I called out . . . No reply. Dropping my shoes on the sand, Mole thought he would climb up to be entirely sure. Moving my hand across the bench, I felt something. At the same time a voice demanded—quiveringly—in Spanish: "What do you want?"

It was the voice of a startled homosexual. There was someone sitting next to him. Mole, who had evidently stumbled on a liaison, answered, "Nothing," and went back down.

As I was picking up my shoes, I heard one of the people above me strike a match and inhale loudly on a cigarette. Then the other sucked in smoke. Clearly both of them had been frightened. Mole continued trekking south.

This time it seemed I had walked considerably farther than five hundred meters. It had become distinctly colder, the trade-winds blowing the sand hard against my face, Mole shielding my face with his hands as he pushed southward. The sea was behaving like an ocean. Then I saw one—a lifeguard stand only a few meters ahead of me. At once—for the first time since I arrived in Cartangena—Mole felt fear. Stopping, he sat on the sand facing the water, back straight: he commenced deliberately to breathe. According to Sen.

Considerably pacified after fifteen lengthy exhalations, Mole rubbed his eye-glasses with his shirt, collected his shoes, stood, approached the structure. Not expecting a response, I didn't call, but quietly began to climb. When I got to the highest rung, I swept my hand over the bench—and felt something. A packet of matches in the corner of the bench. Steadying myself, then crouching, Mole struck a match. There was a good deal of sand of the floor. His light went out. I struck two matches together: something was scrawled in the sand—a name. "*Theo Mismo*," it seemed to read . . .

Back at the pension, Mole was having tea on the communal porch, facing the sea, when someone came up behind him and sat down at his table. It was the young man from California who had checked in the day before. He and Mole had previously exchanged a few words.

"Can I sit with you?"

"Sure. I've ordered some tea. Would you like some?"

He didn't respond. Mole looked at him. Except for his eyes, he had what Mole thought of as a characteristic southern Californian face: long straight brownish blond hair, smallish symmetrical features, a defined jaw line, rich blond mustache. His eyes were dark, surprisingly deeply set, and one iris (the left) had risen fatefully, displaying much white beneath.

"I asked whether you'd care to have some tea."

"Oh. No thanks. Never drink the stuff." He suddenly extended his hand. "I'm Krishna."

Mole shook the large strong hand.

"Yeah. Tomorrow I split," Krishna said.

"Going back home?"

"Not right away. I go to Barranquilla. From there— hopefully the same day—I make it to Miami. After some business there I'll go back home."

"I see."

Biscuits were delivered to the table. Mole offered Krishna one.

"No, I can't. Gotta fast."

"Krishna fasting? You should have called yourself Shiva."

"Why's that?"

"Shiva was the abstinent one."

"It ain't abstinence. It's business." His eyes glowed a little.

"You're dealing dope."

Krishna grinned. "How did you know?"

"I guessed."

"What's your name?"

"Mole."

"Good name for a dealer. *You're* not dealing?"

"No. Not dope."

"Do you consider coke dope?" Krishna grinned again. Mole was surprised to see that his teeth were bad, discolored, visibly decaying.

"Do you?"

"Not really. It's like good balling. You want more because it's so groovy. It ain't heroin. I don't touch heroin. Just coke. On a rare occasion I'll handle weed. You ever done it—coke?"

"A few times."

"Wanna snort?"

"Now?"

"*Por supuesto.* But not here. Let's make it down to the water."

"All right."

Mole followed Krishna's rangy frame over the rocks to the water's edge.

"It's windy here," Krishna said. "I've got a good idea. Over there." He pointed to a short sandy beach about fifty meters to the north. "This is good stuff. Too good for the gulls."

As they got to where the sand commenced, Mole slipped off his shoes. Krishna was already barefoot.

"I said I was fasting, right? You know why?"

"No."

Krishna laughed. "Because I carry it in my ass. Way up in the colon. The only way they could spot it is with a sigmoidoscope—a complicated apparatus they stick up your ass. Not very practical to have at a border crossing. There's a good place." Krishna pointed to a lifeguard stand which Mole had not seen before, never having been on this beach.

While I was putting my shoes back on, Krishna mounted the stand.

Mole, climbing, observed that the rungs were spaced farther apart on this stand than on the others. In fact the entire structure was somewhat different, including the sitting area (Mole fitted in next to Krishna), which seemed deeper, more recessive.

"You on board?"

"Yeah."

Krishna handed me a carefully rolled peso. "Go ahead."

Leaning back, Mole closed his left nostril with his third finger, inserted the tip of the peso bill into his right nostril and snorted. Then he reversed the procedure—this time feeling a distinct surging through his sinuses and into his *ajna chakra*, resounding there like the echo of a gong. He handed the rolled peso back to Krishna.

"Good boost, no?"

"Yeah."

"I didn't hear you," Krishna said. He was carefully arranging more cocaine on the peso.

"I said you're right, it's a good boost."

Krishna snorted. "Um-*um*, gooood stuff! Have another, Mole. Mole—I like that name. Have another."

"All right . . ."

Mole seeing the sea, hearing it give . . . take back. He glanced at Krishna, who was looking at him. Mole could make out his left eye—the iris with the white beneath it—in the darkness. They were staring at each other, expressionless.

"You're a stange dude, you know that?" Krishna said.

"Why's that?"

"I asked you before if you liked the shit—if it gave you a good boost. You didn't even answer me."

Mole found himself listening to Krishna's voice attentively. There was a certain component in it he recognized.

"I did answer you, Krishna. You must not have heard me."

"Yeah, this ain't the first time."

"What do you mean?"

"Just what I said, fella." The evenly spaced words sounded hostile. Yet disembodied.

They were still staring at each other in the black. Mole's mind was working.

Krishna's lips were widening . . .

Mole felt a tightening in his temples—then a cold shivering about his shoulders. Silently I said the name "Sen." Repeating it, fixing my teacher in my mind's eye. This gesture was completed almost involuntarily.

"I answered you," Mole said. "Either you don't remember, or there is something wrong with your hearing." I paused. "Is there something wrong with your hearing?"

Krishna, grinning, slowly began to unbutton his shirt with his left hand. Taking Mole's left hand he held it to his chest. Mole felt something metallic, cold, connected to a wire . . . Krishna meanwhile had turned his body to me, with his other hand was gripping Mole's thigh . . .

October 1: Gun's come! Mole collected the rectangular cardboard package at the post office. From Winston-Salem.

Once home I went directly to my bedroom and opened the package, within which were several other packages, each clearly labeled: "22 Caliber Mossberg Cartridges"; "Redfield Olympic Sights"; "Savage-Anschluss Model 170 Bolt Action"; "Remington Checkered American Walnut Stock" . . .

Feeling suddenly chilled, Mole lay on his back against the wall. His eyes closed . . .

Chris Chubbuck's finger closed on the trigger driving the screen blank: shapes came out of this emptiness: the brown spoor that is the beggar dying in Benares, cornering Mole with cupped outstretched hands. Mole sees the hydrocephalic, his huge wedge-shaped head gently billowing, legs trailing smoke. Out of the screen's whiteness . . . back first the young black easing backwards from the bridge cable into unwhite space— Marya comes into the room.

"Honey—oh, I'm sorry. You were sleeping."

Wakened, Mole closes his eyes. "Hello, Marya."

"Hello." She bends to kiss me. "What's that?"

Mole opens his eyes.

"A rifle! 'Savage-Anschluss . . . Winston-Salem'; what is it for?"

Mole doesn't answer.

"Did you just get this today?"

"Yes."

"What are you going to do with it?"

Mole sits up, rubbing his eyes. "Marya, don't—if you care for me—ask me that now."

"You're going to do something—kill somebody. Mole!"

"Marya."

"You're going to kill someone."

"Do you remember what happened to Grace Kelly when she tried to get old Coop to hang them up in 'High Noon'?"

"What are you going to do? Please tell me what you're going to do."

"Right now? Right now I'm going to make love with Marya because—look! I have a splendid hardon, and in spite of what she may sometimes think, Mole loves her."

Which is what happened . . . after which Mole lied to her, having to.

Oct. 2: . . . and Mole in his hammock, not yet awake: the pigeon cooing a mongoloid child, or her mother sobbing bitterly in her sleep. The subway rumbling beneath obscures Moishe, keening, bolted to his savaged graveyard. Few can hear the wind. Wind soughs through Mole in his hammock. The black man back first plummets into   sight. A seagull dives (silently), up again: nothing. Bessie Frazer with torn hands, tears at them again in Easter, Mississippi. While the young man trapped in his skin tiptoes to light—a naked bulb in a subway toilet by a river. Mole feels a thumping on his chest: it is the Jewish cat, someone (Abaddon?) placed her on Mole's chest . . .

Mole fingers the knife, still there. Beneath his hammock the rifle package still there. The Jewish cat who generally shies away from contact—purring on my chest. It is only when my left eye begins to itch under my glasses that Mole remembers he is allergic to fur.

"If we are to serve men better, we must briefly hold them at a distance."

Mole in his office reading Han-shan's "Cold Mountain," when Sklar enters.

"Hello, Sklar."

"Yeah. How they hanging?"

"Still pissed, Sklar?"

"What? I ain't pissed. What makes you think I'm pissed?"

"Uh huh."

"Hey, you haven't spoken with Dinger, have you?"

John Dingel owns H-E-L-P.

"No, why?"

"I haven't gotten my monthly," Sklar says. "Usually I get it on the 30th or the 31st."

"Why don't you phone him?"

"Yeah, I may have to do that. You didn't hear anything about us going off the air, did you?"

"No—"

"Yeah, well I did. I got a buddy on Wall Street. He has the inside track on all this shit. Media and so on—"

"What did he say?"

"Not much, except that he had a hunch we may go off. Seems Dinger is having financial difficulties with the market the way it is. He don't make shit from us, you know."

"It's a tax write-off for him."

"Yeah, maybe. But it could be he ain't getting nearly what he put in even with the write-off. Anyways, who could blame him, right?"

"What do you mean, Sklar?"

"I mean what the fuck good is it anyways? How many crazies you think you saved, Mole?"

"I don't know that I 'saved' anyone. If you mean how many people decided against destroying themselves, or felt a little better after phoning here—I couldn't say. Some. Even one would be reason enough to keep the station going."

"Would it? Maybe from your perspective. I doubt whether Dinger sees it that way."

"I can't speak for Dingel. What about G.J.? Has she gotten paid?"

"Good question. Why don't you ask her?"

"I think she may be coming up the stairs now."

G.J. comes in.

"Hullo, gentlemen." G.J. is smiling.

"Hello, G.J.," Mole says.

Sklar makes a brief gesture with his head.

"Hullo, Sklar."

"Hello, hello. Hey, have you gotten your bread from Dinger?"

"My cheque? Yes, yesterday. You haven't?"

"No. The prick."

"Don't you think you'll get it?"

"Damn well better. I heard he's in trouble."

"Trouble?"

"That's right. Money trouble. Our ass could be in a sling if it keeps up."

"You mean the station?"

"That's what I mean," Sklar says. "Maybe it wouldn't be such a bad idea."

"What's that supposed to mean?"

"Yeah, well what would you do if you were him? What does he get out of this?"

G.J. turns away from Sklar, to Mole.

"Did you hear anything about our going off the air?"

"No. Not until Sklar brought it up."

"You got it all wrong, Mole. I didn't fucking bring it up. I just told you what I heard. I mean it's absurd to think that your perspective on this thing is the only one."

"What is *your* perspective on it, Sklar?" G.J.

"Yeah, well it seems to me it ain't really worth much. I mean, what really happens here besides Mole getting off—"

"'Getting off!' If that's what you think he's doing you're dimmer, more self-centered that I've thought. Which is saying a good deal. How can you say Mole gets off on this? Do you *get off* on it?"

"Yeah, I do. Everytime Zelda gives me a high E, that hot shit coursing through me makes me think about Moishe with the numbers on his arm. And I get a hardon."

Angered, G.J. moves into the inner office, away from Sklar—but then suddenly swings around on him: "Why are you here? I want to know. Don't you have any feeling for what this station is doing? What Mole is doing?"

Sklar, the sinews in his thick neck working, removes a small paper bag from his pocket and pours some sunflower seeds into his hand.

"You won't even answer me?"

"Yeah, I'll answer you, Cuntie. No, I don't have that much feeling for what this station is doing. And I have even less for what Mole is doing. His whole fucked-up ego trip. I'll tell you something else. I don't think you do either. You're just too fucking near-sighted to see it. You think he's something unusual. Sensitive. A Buddha with big-ass eyeglasses. It don't mean shit. The world is what it is, filled to the fucking brim with rejects, and there ain't nothing nobody short of God or the President and both shit-ass houses of congress can do about it. Pretending anything else is a fucking sanctimonious pipe-dream."

The phone rings.

Sklar, sitting on a desk in the main room, stands deliberately, walks to his engineer's cubby-hole, where he turns a few knobs and puts on his earphones.

Mole picks up the receiver.

"H-E-L-P."

The connection is dead.

"Sklar," Mole shouts. "Make sure we're on, will you!"

Sklar looks at Mole ironically, then turns another knob, adjusts a dial.

A man was talking on the other side.

"I can hear you now," Mole says. "Go ahead."

"I was saying" (the voice a resonant baritone, not local), "I don't know whether you'd be interested in *my* thing. I'm forty-two. I'm from Waterloo—that's in Iowa. I've been here in New York only since Sunday. Somebody told me about your service—your program—yesterday. I thought I'd give you a try."

"Go ahead."

"Right. Okay. If you don't mind, I won't give my name. I'm an—exhibitionist."

The last word, though nearly inaudible, quivered.

"You know what that is, don't you?"

"Yes."

"Yes. Are we on the air?"

"Yes. Do you want me to switch it to just phone?"

"No—no. It should be heard."

Mole noticed that his voice had become taut, higher-pitched.

"I should be heard," the man was saying. "I show myself. There are lots of ways, you know. In New York. I've got a dilly of a hotel room—look you're not going to tap this?"

"No, don't worry—"

"Because I'm in a public phone booth. I could disappear in a few seconds."

"We don't tap phone calls."

"Yes. Well I've got a cock. A big pair of nuts. Maybe you've heard that most exhibitionists've got small ones, which is why they need to shock people into acknowledging them. In that respect I'm different I assure you . . ."

Mole heard Sklar, who, with his mouth closed, was making gasping sounds to keep from laughing.

". . . Another thing is that I don't show it—what I've got —to males. I like girls. Young women, whatever. Also, I don't hang around parks like some of them. I have a car—I won't say the make, but it's an ordinary car. The whole point, you know, is not to call attention to yourself—except for the fifteen seconds or so you're doing it. Then you're gone, anonymous as ever . . ."

The man's voice, still taut, had taken on a pedagogical edge. Mole was beginning to wonder.

". . . One other thing is my clothing. What I wear. I've got two pairs of custom-tailored trousers, each with a flap in front that you could let down—then up, so quickly that people wonder whether they actually saw what they saw. I'm sitting in my car, at the wheel, reading the newspaper—maybe the obituary page. Or the comics. In front of the girls' trade school—there are a good many of them in New York, you know. Always park on the wheel side . . ."

G.J., noticing Sklar's exaggerated attempts to constrain himself, puts on a pair of earphones.

". . . I prefer younger girls. A lot of them have never even seen a cock—let alone what I've got. I really get a charge out of seeing them react. What you do is isolate one—or at most two—of them. Say five or six of them are walking together—well, you open the door, lower your flap, then up again, and by the time the startled little puss is telling her friends, you're out of there. It's not as easy in Waterloo, you know—people know each other there. That's why I move around a lot. Chicago, Cleveland, Pittsburgh. Los Angeles is not as good as you might think. You know why? They're too blasé. Things are too easy there. You can't get a rise out of people there. Now New York—I've only been here since Sunday, but it's the best. You know, I'll tell you something, I like the coloreds. I'm talking about their reactions—"

"Fine," Mole said. "But what is it you want us to do? From what you're saying you don't seem to have any problems—"

"I do," the man interrupted. "All right? I do." He sounded offended.

"Go ahead," Mole said.

"I'm in this hotel. I won't tell you what it's called. But it's the top floor facing back. I booked it in advance—from Waterloo, and it is a fine room. For me, I mean. Not only the room itself, but the bathroom adjoining it, faces out. And there are three buildings across from me, two lower and one to the left which is higher. These are apartment buildings. Tenements. Poor people, coloreds, and so on. Well, you know that these people hang their clothes on the roof. On clothes-lines. And sometimes, actually more often than you might think, it is the young daughter who removes the clothes from the line. This, when they are dry. It's quite a feeling, let me tell you, to be standing there, my nine-incher at three quarter mast, when this young girl wearing, say, a little Roman Catholic school outfit, the short blue top and the checkered skirt with the sweet little hem raised above her knees—when she is taking down the sheet or the towel between my window and her—and when it is down, usually as she is folding it—she sees me! I'm in my bathroom, she blushes, instinctively lowers her head, folding methodically, picking up stray clothes-pins. But she has to get at least one more look, and when she does—I'm at full-mast, profiled, seeing her through a small mirror I carry with me. Her eyes linger—which is what I want. That's why I don't face her in the first place. It's a real charge, believe me—hey, you have a pretty good audience, don't you?"

"What's that?"

"I said there are lots of folks listen to you. I would guess there are lots of moiling twats out there. Fingers in the box is what I'm saying—"

"I hear you," Mole said. "There are other people who are trying to get through. Why don't you get to it."

"I like the way you put things. You mean the crux, the cross. Don't please talk to me about crosses—I hate them..."

The man's voice had changed again: it was deeper, more assured.

"... They are among the things I hate most. Which puts them at the top of a long list. You're Mole, aren't you?"

"I am."

"Yes. I saw something happen on a roof is why I'm calling. The roof to my left. In the corner of it a thin dark man who wears these thick eye-glasses was standing on his head with his eyes closed. Next to him was a hammock, blue and black. There was a long brown package under the hammock. Gun-sized. Very interesting, you agree?

"I mean you, Mr. Mole. I'm asking you whether you think this is interesting . . . Yes, your silence indicates that you do. But what is more interesting still is that he was naked. This joker was upside down with his eyes closed and naked. He was tall too, I'd say 6-3, 6-4, but—and this is the *crux* of it, Mr. Mole—he had a tiny cock. Smaller than Napoleon's—"

Mole hung up.

Sklar tossed his earphones down, threw up his legs on his desk, and belched loudly.

G.J. gave Mole a puzzled look. "What was he? I couldn't get what it was all about."

"It wasn't about anything," Sklar said. "I could tell that after the first thirty seconds. But Mole let him go on so we could all get hardons. He did have a good spiel—I'll give him that. Why didn't you cut him off? You've hung up on other crazies who weren't any worse off."

"Have I?"

"That's right, you have."

"Maybe," Mole said. "Let's get back to it. There are people trying to get through."

Oct. 3: ". . . nail him down upon a rock,
          catch his shrieks in cups of gold."

Not gold. Uranium.

Mole in *Padmasana* worrying.

Not wanting to be on his roof alone in his swollen head with his people. Yet there.

Dix on his dais in his bloated thighs beneath me . . .

Why Mole? (*DHARMA*)

Can I change it? (*NO*)

But isn't Dix multiple? Infinite? (*DIX BREAKS UP SPACE. MORE EVERY DAY*)

I am not a warrior. I'm afraid of light. I need corroboration. I've no faith in history. Sri Sen is not enough. Disinterest is not enough. Mole's love is choking me . . .

"Infected, Mad, he danc'd upon his mountain,
high and dark as . . . heaven"

Oct. 4: An unfortunate piece of news from the Dix-Smegma-Zurco camp disclosed at a Press Briefing on Capitol Hill: Jock Zurco's wife, Lois, is to be committed to Walter Reed General Hospital for (in Nubile's words) "the surgical removal of both breasts as a cancer preventive."

"No," Nubile insists in response to a reporter's question, "She doesn't actually *have* cancer. What there is is some overactive tissue, and since this tissue is marginal, it sometimes develops into cancer and sometimes it doesn't. Lois, on the advice of her physicians, decided to undergo surgery in order to rescue any possibility of malignancy. Technically, this particular surgery is known as a 'bilateral subcutaneous mastectomy,'" Nubile explains. "It's kinda like scooping out the inside of her breasts. Mrs. Zurco is expected to be out of the hospital in less than three weeks' time."

"What about Jock?" McVey of the Chicago *Sun-Times*. "What does Jock think of this—of Lois having her breasts removed? I mean does he approve of the operation?"

"To answer your question, Pete," Nubile tugs at an earlobe, "Coach Zurco not only approves of his wife's impending surgery, but applauds it as an 'act of great womanly courage.' That's a quote, Pete."

"And let me stress again that it is not a question of Lois having her breasts *removed*. It's more, as I said earlier, like a scooping out of the inside of her breasts. Technically, even cosmetically, she won't be without breasts. This fact ought to be made clear. And we'd appreciate it if you gentlemen would report it accurately."

Oct. 5: This in the *Times* this morning:

SCHIZOPHRENIA HELD USEFUL FOR EVOLUTION

. . . Schizophrenia is a fundamental human condition that through the ages may have helped individuals and cultures adapt to stress and rapid social change, a medical anthropologist contends.

Culture change, Dr. Sianni said, is a characteristic of all human societies. But most human groups throughout history have been quite conservative and traditional in coping with change. The orientation is to the past, to conventional wisdom, to what has been tried and tested.

However, rapid changes in social and biological settings do frequently occur, which often means that entire societies will

have to rapidly restructure their ways of living. When cata-
strophic changes take place, conventional cultural adaptation
may not be adequate in meeting the challenge.

The occurrence of schizophrenia, according to Dr. Sianni,
seems nearly always to increase under conditions of cultural
and social disorganization . . . In certain traditional societies,
the schizophrenics were valued as prophets or shamans, to help
the society cope with its stresses.

Dr. Sianni cited the Seneca Indians as an example of his theory.
By the mid-18th century, because of confinement to reservations, the Seneca hunter could no longer hunt. The Seneca
warrior could no longer fight. The forest statesman was an
object of contempt and ridicule. Many Senecas fell apart
psychologically. Fear of witches increased, clans squabbled
and many turned to drink.

"Star-Nosed Mole" was a Senecan who began to have hal-
lucinations while under these stresses. He heard voices that
told him how his people should behave. A new code of
socialization was subsequently advanced that emphasized the
nuclear family over clan and lineage. Men began farming . . .

The psychological aberrances of Star-Nosed Mole apparently
provided a mechanism for cultural restructuralization which
was adopted by the Seneca people with wholly benign results.

Oct. 6: Lurching through his city's underbelly to H-E-L-P,
Mole thinking of Zelda whom he had recently seen. She
was delirious and bruised purple on her buttocks and thighs.
One of Mole's would-be suicides had worked her over. I had
sent her to him, to the Bronx where he lived.
    "What if Sklar sees them? Then what?"
    Mole didn't know how to answer.
    "Do I tell him what happened—that I've been fucking
these loonies for you? What do I tell him, Mole?"
    "Doesn't he already have a pretty good idea, Zelda?"
    "What? That I'm fucking other people—like he's been
doing? Yeah, he has a pretty good idea. But not about being
beat up. He wouldn't—I don't know what he'd do if he knew
that. If he saw these bruises."
    "If he asks you about them," Mole said, "tell him to ask

me."

"Ask you! He'll want to do the same to you. He'll want to kill you if he finds out."

"I don't think so. Try not to worry, Zelda."

"Aren't you worried, Mole?"

"No."

"Then fuck me. How come you never fuck me? . . ."

I heard something. Something beckoned to Mole from an alley on Rivington Street. From where I stood on the sidewalk, I could see only a faint bluish light, glimmering. Without hesitation, Mole turned into the alley.

Evidently someone was up ahead at the end of the passage between the two tenements. It was already dark. Mole paused, strained his eyes, but not being able to see well, he continued, moving slowly.

He could make out the murmur of voices from one of the buildings, also a muted voice on the radio. As he drew closer to the figure in the passage, the radio voice became louder.

Five or six meters from where the figure glimmered, Mole stopped. It was a woman—a large woman. Her back facing me. Mole moved still closer. He found himself straining to hear the voice on the radio, which was just outside his range . . .

The blue light came from the woman, but it was too luminous for me to see precisely what it enveloped. But then I saw: it was the woman's vast and wrinkled behind, she was wriggling out of her corset, her head was turned to me over her left shoulder and she was grinning, displaying her teeth enticingly. Mole's ears heard the voice on the radio: his own on the telephone at H-E-L-P . . .

Outside again, Mole caught his reflection in a shop window—what he saw astonished him. Gaunter—so much gaunter he could scarcely recognize himself. His cheeks bony protuberances under his eye-glasses. He removed his jacket: his arms were thinner than they had ever been, and his shoulders: two stark right angles. His ears ringing, Mole slipped on his jacket, continued walking to H-E-L-P.

A few streets south he saw a scale in the lobby of a

drugstore. Without bothering to remove his jacket, Mole stepped on to it. It read "158," which was at least fifteen pounds less than his usual weight . . .

What could it be? He was eating pretty much as always—maybe just a bit less because of the increasing time spent on the roof.

When I got to H-E-L-P, I phoned Marya. No answer. Probably she was working in her studio with the door closed.

Mole went into the bathroom, stripped completely and stepped on to the scale. It read "172." Next Mole examined his body in the shaving mirror: what he saw was the familiar Mole, nothing like the spectral semblance he witnessed in the shop window.

My ears had stopped ringing, but now they felt clogged. Mole dressed and lay on the sofa . . .

Oct. 12: Startled awake by some urgency in his dream, Mole is on the bus to Staten Island. A "Trailways" bus, two-thirds full, Mole going to the cemetery. This anniversary of his father's death. Who carried him pig-a-back from the bathroom to the bedroom . . . patting my forehead, gently, till I slept. Love is not enough.

Marya (gentle) had wanted to come. No.

Columbus Day.

Marya wanted to come. Mole needed his . . . space. Black space muff, place his hands in it, clubbed fingers touch across. His father . . .

touched Mole's belly on the bed once playing, Mole touched back his father's belly, then (five yrs old) his fingers moved to his father's "fly," opened the zipper, partially . . .

His father drew back. Got up. Hurt? No. Unprotected. His son suddenly the world pulling at him . . .

Playing after that less often & always with the stain on it. Growing to   Mole)

He loved me the only way he could. Which is not enough. Witched.

Selah.

May he rest. May he
rest.

Mole dreamt again. Of mail. The old dream. He couldn't claim it. (What was the urgency that woke him?)

It's almost over.

. . . pulling at him;

Mole who doesn't smoke would like a cigarette. A tit inside his muff / there's not one.

Marya wanted to come.

Mole got his bus in the Port Authority Terminal (terminal) on 40th Street. An old Italian lady waiting on line in front of him. Her black eyes dolorous, vexed—she kept asking everyone in the vicinity whether this bus went to "Joisey." It did, but where in Jersey? The same look, inconsolable: "Go to Joisey? Joisey?" Just as she was about to board, she pulled away, rapidly shuffled to the back of an adjoining line waiting for another bus . . .

At a younger time Mole might have gone after her. And if she had switched to a third line, so would he . . .

Walter. Meter-reader. Ledger. Cellar.

The assassin

misses . . . not having left his cellar. His flashlight. The oil heater when it's blazing sounds like birds. He said that once. Just that way.

Baron Hirsch Cemetery. Odd name / so

what? Customary grey stone. Words though from *Lear*. "Ripeness is all" is a lie. Green is. "More sinned against then sinning" is there. Mole is

there. No. Marya will (weeping) have his body fired. Broadcast. On his people. Also off: Mole gone)

His father in the hospital not conscious, moaned. Whimpered. He looked like a shrivelled monkey. Whimpered. Mole no help.

Mole left finally the hospital bought a pack of Camels: talk about taking it: there's a creature. And in India traipsing dreamily through the congested streets. Camels. Llamas. Burros. Hinnies. Mole is something other—goes after   it. Though Mole has a camel in him. A camel would be a zen fool if they let it. Mole too . . .

Selah.

A boy with broken-out skin sitting next to Mole on the bus. Liveried. A Catholic high school cadet. Doing mathema-

tics with a slide-rule. He will go to Holy Cross, major in
Chemical Engineering, serve in the army for two years as a
Second Lieutenant in the Quartermaster Corps, marry immediately upon exiting a young woman with straight light
brown hair, get a job with Dix Chemical, sire four children,
one a *petit mal* epileptic, watch TV, not listen to H-E-L-P . . .
    My father whimpered
    He would have liked Marya. Gentle. Left behind.
    His father would have like Marya.
    How old was Mole? Maybe eight, when with his father at
the Polo Grounds, his father spit (had to) on the cement
beneath his seat, when the man sitting not next but two seats
away, made a sound, offended stood, called my father a
"pig." My father astonished stood, trembling. Angled, long
bony wrists, embittered bone-dry white-grey eyes—against
Mole's father. Nothing happened. Abaddon moved—
changed, huffily, his seat. Mole didn't know what to say. To
his father.
    Death)
    We're near Hoboken. South, south to the cemetery.
    Had Abaddon moved to strike—Mole would have
lunged to protect . . . his father.
    Protect? Was that the start of it? No, it was in me.
    (Madness: "a refuge from unbelief")
    From parasite to paraclete.
    The boy sitting next to Mole has finished his math
homework, furled his slide-rule, closed his books. He is
smoking a Kent, looking straight ahead. Something surging
up through Mole's chest. When it is near his throat he
recognizes it: aloneness, his birthright.
    Marya . . .
    Mole who would like a cigarette doesn't really want to
ask the boy next to him. Doesn't know how to phrase it. But
finally does . . .
    Scarcely responding, the boy removes the pack from his
breast pocket, shakes one out. Lights it for Mole with his
lighter.
    Mole who doesn't know how to inhale sucks deep not
letting himself cough.

(Where is the old Italian lady who wanted to go to
"Joisey"? Standing on line. She'll be standing on line when
she gets there.)

Mole chose the coffin, resisting the hard-sell of the coffin-
seller.

Mole; his father's two living sisters; an old friend from the
company: an old Irish bachelor meter-reader; a pariah dog
with dried-out teats, yet wanting to caper near my father's
hole.

And the hearse-driver, who heard of Mole, wanted to
know about the weirdoes who called at H-E-L-P. Particularly
the girls. "Any nymphos?"

Selah.

Camus reminds: "From the mass of evils in Pandora's
box, the Greeks brought out hope as the very last, as the most
terrible of all."

Which, however, is but one version. Camus himself, at
his most plangent, labors, labors to   hope . . .

Is the Greek's "hope" essentially the Buddhist's "desire"?

Hope gone then: man is still and forever present. A white
stain. A bubble in the river. Hell or light. As the zen clown's
wound catches light.

Each (barefoot dervish) day . . .

As Mole was once a camel nearly / until "seeing" what I
had to do.

It has begun to rain, lightly. Mole puts his cigarette out.
He is feeling cold. (Where is his roof?)

What has Dix to do with the water coursing in the
hydrocephalic child's skull?

With the sound of the furnace blazing which Walter
called "birds"?

If Dix must, must birds not?

Heyerdahl said the Atlantic, weeks away from shore, was
strewn with oil. With plastic waste. "A sick sky over a
decomposing sea."

Soon though: outer space, where the entire "ecology"
will be radically unlike. Will it? There is in fact nothing the
polluted Giant can't suck up—then expel: altered, cut with

cola and sani-flush. In color (uranium). To expire by.
What's lambent dying from minute to minute yet stuck)

Light rain. Near sunset. Mole, who has laid grass and
dandelions on his father's grave, sits, his back straight against
the stone. Chilled. Facing south . . .

Oct. 13: Bitterness and dejection in the Dix camp. The
Senator's stepson, Raleigh Pat, killed him a nigger. Saturday
evening it was, in Columbia, South Carolina (young Dix's
military academy located therein), and Raleigh Pat was racing
his brand new Corvette. Or, according to the revised "official" version, it was the Negro who was racing in his head and
crazy on his feet from too much wine. Name of Willie Greene,
twenty something years old, common-law married, whelped
in Georgia, imprisoned there twice for "vagrancy," not
presently employed, a wino when he wrangled a few dollars
from his woman who was on "State welfare" . . .
Raleigh Pat, known to load up on weekends, was on this
occasion, according to the official version, "stone sober," as
were the three other cadets in his white two-seater, bought for
him by his new father.
It's already cost Dix nearly ten thousand dollars, including a few to the Negro's relatives—or putative relatives:
they materialized like "flies to shit" (Rebus). But the thing
couldn't be hushed up. First the Louisville *Courier-Journal,*
then the New York *Post* got on to it, accused young Dix of
special treatment and the rest of it. The customary "Liberal
spleen-venting, which here serves the double dubious purpose
of giving the potential losers something to rave about; another
phony 'issue' to take the edge off their inevitable defeat"
(Nubile to newsmen).
In fact the Dix team was worried. At a special "skull-
session," called a day after the thing was settled, the Senator's
staff tensely brainstormed on the theme of "output": positive
Dix news to offset the Democratic ugliness and rumor-
mongering.

DuVal Stett, who was invited to assess the effects of the incident on the South in the coming election, assured his friend that there was little to worry about, that he ought to be grateful it was "ony a nigra and not a white man was kealed." The team, who had come to the very same conclusion independently, could only nod their heads in agreement.

As to output, there were several suggestions. Smegma said "Apple": by which he meant "putting more and fatter input into the 'America's Peace and Prosperity Lead Everything' campaign."

However, no one on the team, besides Rebus (who invented the term), reckoned it would supply the needed smoke-screen effect.

Jock Zurco proffered his wife: more and frequent reports about her recent surgery to elicit sympathy from the voters, and "especially from the gals who have always been real sensitive to civil rights, and maybe were a little upset at that Negro dying down there."

Holstein scratched his head. "The problem there, Jock—and I'm speaking frankly—is that the thing—the surgery has already taken place. I don't think we can sqeeze any more blood out of that stone, so to speak. Or at least not enough to make a difference. What about Castro? Eventually they're gonna be recognized—the Cuban reds, I mean. There might still be time for the Senator to make a quick trip down there—say two, three days. That way we can grab the initiative from the Liberals without really sticking our neck out. Say a few more or less moderate things about the potential between our two countries—here the Senator can use his knowledge of the language, and of Latin America in general. All we want to do here is win back whatever voters we may have lost by what happened down there. To the Negro."

Rebus objected: "Cuba's explosive, Hank. You gotta remember we've got them here—Cubans, Puerto Ricans, Chicanos. And particularly in the big cities which are going to matter come November. What I'm saying is most of these Latins are against the reds down there, so that even if the Senator comes back with something that is only moderately favorable—to use your words—it will outrage them, these

Latins in the big cities. In my opinion it would make things a lot harder than they are now. Because I agree with Senator Stett right here, that we were way ahead before this thing happened, and we're still way ahead, no matter what the Democrats try to make out of it."

"What would you say then, Rebus?" Dix questioned.

"I'd say crime, Senator. It's been our bread-and-butter before, and, in my opinion, it still is. More than ever, in fact. You ask the average big city voter what's most on his mind, and he won't say Cuba, or the Soviet Union, or civil rights. What's on his mind is, number one, his pocketbook, and number two, getting mugged in the streets, or having his daughter raped in the corridor of his building. Well, let's face it, there's not too much more we can say about his pocketbook than what we've already put out. We've repeated, and we ought to continue to repeat, that Liberal-inspired federal bail-out programs and deficit spending have gotten us into this mess, and that these things can and ought to be rectified. We're in a gosh-damn predicament about this thing, you know, because we can't come down on what Gerry Ford has been trying to do—not if we expect him in our corner. Besides, what his team has been putting out is pretty much what we have in mind. So that leaves the old bread-and-butter: crime in the streets. I mean wasn't that the real problem down there in Columbia: this Negro crocked to the gills, an ex-con looking for a new mark so that he could get himself another jug of wine? Let's hit it head-on, is what I say; come out with a white paper full of specifics: how much we expect to beef up the police forces in each high-crime area; how we plan to increase vigilance of dope-users; and so on. We could make it an extension of that broadside on Women in Cities that we put out last winter. That really got to people—and so will this. In my opinion."

Smegma was nodding his head.

"You think Rebus is on target, do you, Harry?" Dix asked.

"Yes, sir, I do. It sounds like our best direction, Pat."

Dochmeier, two fingers in the air.

"Go ahead, Lance."

"Thank you, Senator. I think Rebe is on target also. Generally speaking. I would put forth this addendum: that since our anti-crime campaign would of necessity focus on the Negro—it's an unfortunate fact, but is just so happens that they are responsible for most of our street crimes—we ought to enlist a well-known Negro to front for us, so to speak."

"Who would you have in mind, Lance?"

"Somebody big, Senator. Someone who carries a lot of clout in the colored community. How about Abraham McKinley?"

"Yeah, but do you think McKinley really has a grasp of the issues?" Holstein wanted to know.

Zurco, who had dealings with black athletes, was shaking his head no. "I frankly don't think he has," Jock said.

"Well, what about Ricky?" Dochmeier came back. "Mayor Ricky of Davenport?"

"Well, how's he been doing in Nebraska? What's his record like there?" Dix questioned.

After a pause, Dochmeier said, "With respect, Senator, Davenport is in Iowa. From what I hear Ricky's been doing real well there. He's a loyal Republican."

"If he wasn't he wouldn't have gotten in," Smegma, who knew Iowa, said with authority.

"One thing, though," Holstein said, "Darnell Ricky is not all Negro. He's a mulatto."

This minor revelation silenced the team—for a moment.

"How in hell did he git such a moniker if he ain't all nigra?" DuVal Stett exploded.

There was laughter . . .

Lance Dochmeier, who was well-bred and originally from Massachusetts, wanted to say something to the effect that it was the white overseers who were responsible for their slaves' names—but didn't. He said: "Robinson. Piers Robinson, freshman Representative, California. He lives in Woodland Hills, has a stable background, soft-spoken. He was a big jock at USC, played with O.J. Simpson. He's a good-looking fellow, very light-skinned."

"He's a Republican?"

"Yes, he is, Senator."

"Do you know of him, Val?"

"I thought I did. At first. But the one I'm thankin of ain't light. Not by a long shot. He's also a Republican from in California some place. I cain't say his name. It'll come to me."

"This Robinson played ball with Simpson, you say? Did you ever see him play, Jock?"

"I was just thinking, Pat. I must've. He was a middle linebacker, wasn't he?"

"Tailback," Dochmeier said. "You're probably thinking of Puce. Hennerly Puce. He played middle and outside linebacker. Was an honorable mention All-America, I think. He's a freshman Representative from Oakland. A Democrat."

"Ain't the same House we used to know, is it Pat? Sounds like Reconstruction."

"We've got to live with it, Val. All right, we've got McKinley and Puce—"

"No. Robinson, Senator," Rebus corrected. "Piers Robinson."

"Okay, Robinson then. Anyone else you can think of, Rebus?"

"Well, there's that Chicano in Texas. Also a freshman in the House. Ramirez."

"He's in his second term, Rebe. Besides he's an Independent," Dochmeier clarified.

"Yeah, I know that, Lance. But he's closer to us than to the Liberals. Particularly on the crime thing, from what I understand."

"I wonder," Dochmeier said.

"Well, we'll sure as hell find out," Dix said. "You've got his name, Gwen?"

"Yes," Gwendolyn looked up from her pad. "Ramirez. What was his first name?"

Nobody seemed to know.

"Never mind, we'll get to him," Dix said.

Oct. 14: This evening "Kuznetsov" phoned the station. He was, in his own words, a "hunchback lawyer"—and quite successful. "In taxes."

It began, Kuznetsov informed me, in high school, with Geometry, a subject which, after a slow start, he excelled in. It was at this time that a characteristic nightmare he had been having regularly for several years was altered significantly. In the dream a young bent boy—"bent to ice," as Kuznetsov put it, was menaced by two erect figures, a male and a female, each lethally, though ambiguously, armed. Originally, the figures would make for the boy and he would frantically claw at the ice. But always they would get to him before he made much headway, and he, bent, with his back to them, would fearfully await punishment.

But coincident with his mastery of Geometry, his dream took a strange turn. The setting was the same, but when the figures attacked, instead of clawing at the ice, Kuznetsov turned, extracted a compass and struck back, penetrating them "in the vicinity of the eyes, though cleanly, almost like an incision. Very satisfying."

"Satisfying" too became Kuznetsov's life outside dream: "tailored, classical. Pope, Haydn, Poussin. I married a slim, healthy young woman out of Mt. Holyoke. Our child, blond, unbent, now three . . . when it happened again! After more than four years it happened again." The familiar dream, the murderous figures, armed, coming at him; he, bent, extracting (though apprehensively) his compass—but being easily overpowered . . . The dream ends.

As a result—"not the other way around"—Kuznetsov's marriage deteriorated, his practice suffered, his colitis erupted.

What he wants to know is, "Why now after I conquered this terror has it come back to savage me? If what I've done and tried to do is still not enough, I *can't* . . ."

Neither Mikhail nor Alexsei, old as they are, pant as they climb the steep flights to their three room apartment on the 6th floor: in 6b, directly beneath the pigeon-coop. Both men are in their middle sixties. Both fled Byelorussia in the thirties, during the purge, leaving their wives and, in the case of Alexsei, young child behind. Both work as "loaders" for the Lion Match

Company in Long Island City, a firm owned by Americans and staffed largely by White Russians.

Misha-Alyosha (as they are known), have been living together in the same flat for sixteen years, Misha sleeping in the bedroom, Alyosha on a convertible sofa in the living room. And all this time they have been travelling to work together, rising at 4:30, purchasing the Russian newspaper, riding the subway (changing trains three times), for an hour and ten minutes, breakfasting at a small Ukrainian luncheonette near the job, smoking after breakfast (Misha: butts, one of which is always behind his ear; Alyosha: Pall Malls, which he transfers from their original packet to his own black boar-leather container, and which as a consequence always taste stale).

Punching in at 6:00 A.M., joining the eight or nine other Russians in the warehouse, arranging the large cardboard boxes for pick-up, then loading them onto the trucks and trailer vans which come hard and often, backing up to any of the three loading platforms, the Irish or Italian drivers kibbutzing with the loaders, none of whom has more than a smattering of English. Laverty, for example, who drives for a Flushing distributor, backing his truck to Misha-Alyosha's platform, his grinning ferret's head out of his window, cigarette in his mouth, repeating: "Muhammad Ali, Muhammad Ali . . ." Gaunt Misha, a small smile behind the butt in his mouth, directing the truck, echoing: "Mu-hammad Ali, Mu-hammad Ali . . ."

For lunch, half an hour, beginning at noon, Misha runs to the corner, buys two hot dogs and a can of Rheingold from an old Puerto Rican with a pushcart—then runs back to eat and smoke in a corner of the warehouse. Alyosha dines again at the Ukrainian luncheonette on "soup of the day," followed by Spam or stew . . .

Often as not the roommates do not ride home together at 5:30. Alyosha's "woman," Mary, lives in another direction. She is a handsome middle-aged black prostitute whom Alyosha has been visiting three or four times a week for the last seven years. His family on his father's side had been Cossacks, and Alyosha still behaved like one with his shaven head, powerful chest and proud virility. He is partial (he will tirelessly repeat) to "smoked-meat"—that is, to black women, because they are (licking his lips, grinning) "sveet." His description of what passes between him and Mary never varies: "She: vun foot must ceiling holt" (Mole assumed this meant either her bed was unusually elevated, or the ceiling was broken)—"then this vun": here Alyosha makes an unambiguous gesture with his hand, thrusting it smoothly forward, back, forward . . . as if between her "smoky" legs: "Ah, so sveet . . ."

The other Russians nod and smoke and smile a little, and one of them, usually the other Alexsei, a small, wry man, holding up one crooked index finger, says: "Ah, you old men. No goot no more." To which Alyosha, feigning anger, thrusting out his chest responds: "Vat you say? You vant see?" one thick hand on the zipper of his pants . . .

Oct. 15: Mole on his roof removes a copy of Emerson, turns to the essay "Compensation"—but several of the pages are stuck together from the dampness. Rather than unstick them, Mole replaces the volume. Finesses his body into *Sirshasana.*

Who was it (one of Pound's people?) defined Romanticism as "spilt religion"?

Mole in Babylon was changing into his firing pants in the cramped locker area, when Loggin came in.

"You heah already?"

"Yeah, I'm a little early today."

"Hey, you got a nigger dick. I dint know that."

Mole looked up at him. "What do you mean?"

"I mean your dick's three shades darker than the rest of you. How'd that ever happen?"

Mole pulled up his jock, then slipped on an old pair of Army fatigues.

"You rubes with the thick glasses always surprise me by the size of your dicks. I seen it a hunnerd times: the most unlikely ones always got the biggest ones. But this is the first time I seen one that got the size *and* color of a nigger."

Loggin walked to the fountain.

Mole closed his locker and went into the toilet. When he heard Loggin leave he came out again, pulled down his pants and examined himself in the mirror. It was extraordinary: his penis was darker—much darker—than before. Mole held it in his hands—it was pendulous, heavy. Otherwise it looked the same: the larger than usual head, the thick red vein on the underside of the shaft . . . What could it be?

Sri Sen had often urged Mole away from questions like "what" or "why." The point was to accept the given— whatever it might be, however suddenly it might take hold: thence to extend "it" to its utmost natural limits (never beyond). As in the *Bhagavad Gita*. A *bodhisattva* might only become what he *is*. Mole was working on a headache . . .

Orpheus' disembodied head wreathed with weeds and cactus-flowers, off-center, slightly tilted, elevated in space, surrounded by tall boxes—so tall the frame can't contain them. These boxes contain windows, the windows contain faces . . .

Marya has in the last month or so completed four remarkable woodcuts. Not merely impeccable in technique— her work is nearly always that—but with a sudden knowledge. Between herself and her unconscious conception of Orpheus the shadow has contracted to that sliver of light that belongs to him, is unerringly his.

Oct. 16: "The teleologic instinct of the unconscious is unerring; pursue it—if you are able." (Richthofen)

Mole's penis didn't revert to the way it was, but remained pendent, black, heavy . . . I mentioned this to Sen in a letter I posted this morning.

Examining the rifle again: fitting the stock to his shoulder working the bolt, sighting the platform beneath him . . .

My hands weren't steady. I oiled the weapon and placed it back in its package.

Marya hasn't asked about the rifle again.

In bed this morning we spoke of children. If we were to have a girl child what would we name her.

Marya said "Faith."

I said "Kore."

She smiled.

Mole said: "We feel the same feeling. Both names are lovely equally."

"Faith and Kore?"

"Yes."

Oct. 17: Mole in the subway going uptown. Sitting next to an old, large-boned black woman wearing a kerchief on her head, with a shopping bag between her legs. Within the bag Mole can see a pair of shoes. Likely she is on her way to clean house for white folks.

Someone passing through the car. A wizened, though not really old, white man, his arms filled with cardboard boxes— four of them—each rudely fashioned with twine. He is walking slowly, though with certain steps, through the rocking car, as if looking for someone to talk to. He pauses before an unlikely prospect, a thirtyish, harassed-looking junior executive type; he says something to him (Mole can see his mouth move). The executive fidgets a little. The man says something further. The executive raises his attaché case to his knees, snaps it open, removes a copy of the *Times*, closes his case, places it between the glen plaid knees, unfurls his *Times* . . . but the man with the package is already moving on.

Next, he pauses in front of a teenaged boy, black, who looks like a rococo knight: resplendently dressed in azure velvet trousers, beige shoes with platform heels, a silken brown paisley blouse, his books on his lap, and, doubtless, a slender deadly rapier within his pants. His face is quiet, delicate, languid. Again Mole watches the package man's mouth work. The young fellow looks up quizzically, then himself says something—briefly. Instead of replying, the package man merely looks, benignly, it seems, at the young man's dusky gorgeousness, then passes on.

He pauses in front of me. I feel him staring at me, but when I look up I cannot catch his eyes which seem to be fixed on the dirtied window above my head.

"Wall Street. I'm going to Wall Street," the man utters without looking at me. The boxes, three of which he is holding by the twine, have bitten into his hands.

"This train is going uptown," Mole says. "Wall Street is downtown, isn't it?"

"Not right now. Later. I have to deliver these." With that, he drops the boxes, clanging, on the floor.

(The woman sitting next to Mole smiles.)

Now the man is looking directly at me with rheumy grey eyes. The left eye unlike the right: more recessive, the iris partially veiled by the lid. In fact the entire left side of his attenuated, unshaven face is deeply lined, afflicted. Including his left ear, swollen, covered with an eruption of some kind.

"Did you ever wonder why an animal attacks someone who's scared of him?" the man was asking Mole in a voice that was high-strung and abrasive, as if from sleeping in the cold.

"Why is that?"

"It's because the fear just pours out of him. Makes an odor."

"Ah."

"I've smelled it. What do you say to that?"

"I think I've smelled it also," Mole says.

"Not me," the package man says. "I'll give in ugly."

The train stops, a few people leave, including the woman who was sitting next to me. The man remains standing, his boxes spread on the floor.

"I'll give in ugly," he says again.

"Why not?"

"Have you ever been to Wall Street?"

"Yes."

"I gotta go there. Drop these off."

"What's in them?" Mole asks.

"But not now. Later."

(Several people in the subway car are observing fitfully with neither especial interest nor surprise . . .)

"Where are you going now?" Mole asks.

"I'll tell you something else. I was that way when I was on top. Ugly." He kicks one of the boxes for emphasis. "Do you know what I mean?"

"What do you mean by ugly?"

"Have you ever been there—Wall Street?"

"Yes."

"What do you think of it? I'm not going there just yet. You know what I think? They're a lot of swine. Ugly."

"I see."

"A lot of swine. Waal, I got to go there."

"Why?"

The man has already picked up his cartons, moved away from me . . .

Oct. 18: One of Blake's illuminations for his prophetic "Milton" is of a figure both Promethean and Orphic, wearily recumbent upon a narrow cliff that fronts the sea. He is being embraced by his anima who desperately tries to comfort him— yet cannot. Above, an enormous rapacious bird circles . . . Blake's caption is: "The Creative Act and the Eagle of Inspiration."

Mole in his hammock dreamt of it. Marya it was who tried to comfort him—but then he *became* Marya, while the recumbent figure merged with . . . Dix.

That morning I presented Marya with a poem:

ORPHEUS

> entered singing,
>> slid
>> then,
> singing fell
> plum-
>> meted
> for it was endless, be-
> coming as he singing

down
less a man: a

dolphin
coyote
lap-wing, bill working, goat-
sucker . . .

     by the time he
tumbled on his shins into
China he
was a katydid (Euridice
dead)

A shepherd found what
remained in black Japan: a
cricket's shell / he had
sung himself / away

utterly. Though Euridice without a
larynx
will not   smile)

After Marya read it, she embraced me. We made love without
words . . .
     Afterwards, Mole stood naked in front of her.
     "Look at me, Marya."
     "I am, you're lovely."
     "Look at my cock."
     "Yes."
     "It is black. Do you see that it is black?"
     "Yes . . . it is darker—"
     "Feel how heavy." Mole took her hand.
     "It *is* heavier, isn't it?"
     "Yes."
     "How—"
     "I don't know. I don't know, Marya."

Oct. 19: Orion, the Sister, Perseus, Cassiopeia . . . So clear, the late Fall sky. Mole before dawn on his head on his roof, buring. But as a bodhisattva might: naturally, matabolically . . .

> The sight of the stars always sets me dreaming just as naively as those black dots on a map set me dreaming of towns and villages. Why should these points of light in the firmament, I wonder, be less accessible than the dark ones on the map of France? We take a train to go to Tarascon or Rouen and we take death to go to a star. It is certainly true that as long as we're "alive" we can't visit a star any more than when we are dead we can take a train.
>
> Anyhow, I don't see why cholera, the stone, phthisis and cancer should not be heavenly modes of locomotion like ships, busses and trains here below, while if we die peacefully of old age we make the journey on foot . . .

Van Gogh in a letter to Theo. Mole on his head believes it. Even as Sri Sen believed something like it, using "it" (as he twice did when pressed) to justify Mole's impending and premature leave-taking.

If only Mole's flame had burned more coldly, more containedly, it might have ended otherwise, growing old with Marya, with H-E-L-P.

The irony was that people (Mole's people) viewed him as being precisely contained—needing to see him so, not wanting to witness his, uh, disfigurement. How could they *not* see him their way—having let Mole touch (with his star-nose) their broken places?

Though like the drowning, they scratch and tug at him, he must, like Antaeus, stay rooted to a firmer place.

Mole, flushed, rights himself, touches his weapon in its sheath, fingers his knife, approaches the edge.

Dix's platform, dais, microphones, cameras, staff, manikin souls, canned applause, the President-elect himself: all of it beneath me in the pseudo light, casting no shadow . . .

Oct. 20: What for several weeks had been discussed in veiled whispers by not more than a handful of the *cognoscenti* in certain key Republican "clubhouses"—is abruptly in the open. The NY *Post* headlined it thusly: "SMEGMA-ZURCO RIFT WIDENS."

To the more historically-minded observers of the Washington scene, it recalled the Kissinger-Schlesinger break in the Ford administration. Only here the potential ramifications of the feud (if in fact it was one), were much more unsettling, for the simple reason that Forrest Patrician Dix was not yet President. And though most of the recent polls favored him by as many as ten points, that might change radically should this very high-echelon rift be substantiated.

Some of the more panicky Dix team members suggested that the Senator confront the charge head-on by addressing the American people on network TV. Fortunately the calmer heads prevailed: such an address would only be an implicit admission that the cohesion of the Dix team was jeopardized.

It was decided instead that, first, an item detrimental to Lemming (the Democratic Vice President nominee) would be planted in Geoffrey Hyde's syndicated "Homely Protestant" column; then Nubile would call an ostensibly no-axe-to-grind news conference . . . The operative maxim here being, as Rebus reminded: "The best defense is an aggressive offense."

En route to H-E-L-P, Mole pauses at the park on Chrystie Street to watch the hookers. They are in several clusters: one outside on the street leaning against the iron fence, smoking, nodding, making remarks to the occasional male passer-by. Another group sitting or leaning on the broken stone benches beneath the juncture of two trees, a sick ginkgo and a dying sycamore.

A young woman detached herself from this group and slowly angled towards Mole.

I watched her move, the slow-motioned heroin lurch . . . She raised her head sideways to Mole, looking at him through one palled eye.

"You wanna go out, ba-by?"

(It was nearly always phrased like this.)

Instead of replying, Mole continued to look at her. She was pretty, with a trim Afro on a small, shapely head, kittenish features, slight build. She looked very tired, and not more than eighteen.

Now she was appraising me with both eyes.

"You wanna go out?"

Mole didn't answer.

"Or you jus a ass-hole bandit?"

"What is that?"

"I think you it—someone who get off jus watchin. An usually where he can't be seen. Is that whatchoo are?" Her look was one part anger to two parts playful irony.

"What is your name?" Mole asked, hoping—half expecting—she would answer: Butter.

She said "Bea."

"Beatrice?"

"Yeah, Beatrice. You writin a book?"

Mole looked at her closely. A raindrop fell on the back of his hand. "Yes, I am."

"All right, what's the name?" She placed her hands on her hips. "I mean the title. What's the title of this book?"

"Star-Nosed Mole," I said.

"Uh. What the fuck that mean—star-nosed mole?"

"It's starting to rain," Mole said.

"Thas right—and you afraid you gonna melt. Hey, you a big-ass book-writer. Ita ony cos you ten to get a piece of Bea. I got a lot more underneath"—she grabbed hold of her breasts with each hand—"than it look like in clothes. I give you a good time—don worry."

"I'm not worried—"

"Hey, you got a cigarette?"

Mole just happened to have one. He gave her an unopened pack of Gitanes.

"Where you get these at? I never seen them before."

"They're French."

Mole watched her thin trembling fingers tear the packet open, light one with a large monogrammed lighter she took out of her pocket. (He remembered his knife)

She coughed. "Sheat—what they put in this?"

Mole heard one of the other hookers say, loudly: "What the fuck Bea doin with that rube?"

Beatrice heard also; her manner became more business-like: "Hey, dig it. You like French shit? I can do it jus the way you like it. Because if you don wanna go out, I ain't got no more time to bullshit witchoo. Whatchoo wanna do?"

"Where's your place?"

"Around the corner. Ita cos you two more for the room. That twelve altogether."

Mole, who didn't have his watch, supposed he had about an hour before having to turn up at H-E-L-P.

"All right."

"It ain't far. Follow me."

Bea gestured to the other hookers near the benches, then turned briskly towards the park exit. Once outside, she veered right, towards Houston Street. It was raining harder, and Beatrice, who must have felt cold, had stuffed each hand in the other's sleeve.

Mole caught up to her.

"What's the matter with your leg?"

She looked at me out of one eye. She seemed sullen. "Nothing matter with my leg."

"You seemed to limp a little . . ."

Oct. 22: After a brief, painstakingly amiable introductory, Nubile was ready to accept questions.

Hank Reardon of the Salt Lake City *Sentinel* fed him the first one: "Mr. Nubile, I suppose you've seen the item in the 'Homely Protestant' to the effect that Senator Lemming has been accused of quote campaign irregularities unquote in his '74 win in Connecticut?"

"Yes, we have, Hank," Nubile responded demurely.

"Well, what does Senator Dix think about this? People have been saying that it's liable to knock out Sanderson-Lemming for the count even before November 3."

"Yes. Well, obviously the allegation, if substantiated, would have to prove irrepararably damaging to the Democrats, since we know full well that the American public is not only an alert, but a concerned, public, and they will not tolerate corruption among their highest elected officials. But at the moment it is *only* an allegation, and until it is substantiated, it should not, and it will not, figure in our campaign to elect Senator Patrician Dix to the Presidency.

"I want to emphasize this, Hank—and gentlemen, because Senator Dix wishes to make his position quite clear. It has always been the Senator's principle that a campaign should rely only on what is part of the public record. Now, until this allegation—this highly serious allegation—about Senator Lemming's conduct is verified, we on the Senator's team shall certainly ignore it as a matter of principle."

Nubile looked beyond a flailing Julia Saphire to Glick of the Boston *Globe*.

"Mr. Nubile, where did the 'Homely Protestant' get his information about Lemming?"

"I wouldn't know, Mr. Glick. You would have to ask Mr. Geoffrey Hyde himself for that."

"Because," Glick continued, "Hyde has been known to come up with a few clinkers in the past."

"That may be, Mr. Glick, though it seems to me that the 'Homely Protestant's' record has, on the whole, been a very good one."

Brafman of the Miami *Herald* was recognized.

"I'm sure you've seen the NY *Post*'s story—and it's been picked up elsewhere as well—about there being a major breach between Congressman Smegma and Coach Zurco. Can you comment on that, Mr. Nubile?"

Nubile removed his glasses and smiled superiorly. "That's interesting. That's a perfect example of what I just finished saying in reference to the allegations about Senator Lemming. It's really a doggone shame—and here I think the Democrats would agree—that while the Press pretends to maintain such a close scrutiny of its elected officials, there is not a single watchdog agency that can effectively legislate honesty among the Press. Consequently you, Mr. Brafman, can ask me in all seriousness to comment on the willfully provocative headline of a Democrat-toadying tabloid. And I

shall. Because though we find the NY *Post* and all it stands for
an unspeakable blot on the fabric of our free society, we have
absolutely nothing to hide.

"My comment, Mr. Brafman, is that Coach Zurco and
Congressman Smegma are not only eminently dedicated
colleagues, but good friends. We are all of us friends on the
Senator's team. Which doesn't mean that in the give and take
of brainstorming sessions which often precede policy deci-
sions, team members don't sometimes make a strong and
aggressive case for what they believe in, for what they believe
will most benefit the American people . . ."

Oct. 23: After making love this morning, Marya held on
to me when I made to move away . . .

The Madison Avenue gallery lady has asked Marya to
accompany her to San Francisco to meet a collector who
appears interested in purchasing several of the Orpheus
pieces.

Marya is reluctant to go.

"But why, love? You like San Francisco. It will be only
for—how long did you say? Three days?"

"Yes."

"And this collector, Atherton, could only be helpful to
you, with his museum connections, and the rest."

"Yes . . ."

"You don't want to leave old Mole?"

Marya was still holding on to me.

"I won't be gone when you get back," Mole smiled.

Marya looked up at me with frightened eyes.

Mole took her head in both hands and moved her closer
to me. "I want you to go, Marya."

When I got to H-E-L-P, I found a notice from Dingel, the
owner.

"Various factors, financial and otherwise"—Mole wondered about the "otherwise"—"have necessitated the termi-

nation of station H-E-L-P. The final broadcasting date will be 31, October. Salaried employees will receive payment both for October and November."

That was it.
When G.J. arrived a few minutes afterwards, Mole showed her the notice.
"Sklar was right," she said.
"Yes."
"But why? Dingel is a bloody millionaire, isn't he?"
"I think he is," Mole said.
"Do you think someone—someone with influence who found the station objectionable, might have pressured him?"
"That's possible."
"I guess it doesn't matter a damn that the station was helping some people who couldn't find help elsewhere."
"That's not often a primary consideration," Mole said. "Not even in enterprises like this one."
Sklar was coming up the stairs . . .

Oct. 24: I drove Marya to the airport. After she boarded her plane, Mole went into one of the airport everything-boutiques. At once his eyes were drawn to the Dix seal, in black, centered on the dust jacket of a volume prominently displayed. But when I looked at the book I saw that the seal, ingeniously modified, was actually a swastika within the letter D (𝔅). The title in gaudy mauve was "TYRANNUS DIX."
Mole examined the thin volume, written by a man called Ludwig Abner, under the imprint of "Omega," a scandal-mongering publisher from New Jersey. Just in time for the election. The dust jacket put its case without undue modesty:

—TYRANNUS DIX is *not* a back-patting campaign biography, because unlike nearly all of the books that preceded it, Ludwig Abner's appraisal is not indebted to his subject. Dr. Abner resisted all grants, gifts, subsidies, and special favors from Dix "affiliates." The result is a book of unadulterated honesty and conviction.

—In the corrosive pages of TYRANNUS DIX Dr. Abner traces the illicit origins of the family's first million and follows its growth and world-wide effects from Grandfather Sylvan P. Dix through today's Dixes.

—Here is the revolting spectacle of murderous uranium being bartered for dollars, and dollars—millions of dollars—callously buying Power. Here are the lamentable facts about how the American people have been sacrificed upon the Dix altar of greed and corruption.

—*In TYRANNUS DIX you will discover*

HOW penny-pinching Senator F. Patrician Dix dares to make speeches about the obligation of *every* American to "pay his fair share of taxes"—and then himself PAYS *NO* INCOME TAXES, while his "masseuse" pays hundreds of dollars every year.

HOW, through owning shares of hundreds of banks, industries and corporations, the Dix leverage permits the family to control them as if they were total possessions.

HOW Senator F. Patrician Dix (with the silent but deadly aid of his brother Leggett, and Leggett's financial empire) has connived and abused Americans' constitutional rights—in order, first, to PURCHASE HIS SENATORSHIP, AND NOW THE PRESIDENCY!

The book contained 159 pages between very wide margins and 28 pages of photographs . . . Mole placed it back in the rack.

Oct. 26: At H-E-L-P tonight Sklar, fulminating virtually without cease since Dingel's notice, has been jotting down his re-employment prospects on a long yellow pad. The one that seems to have a special claim on his affections is "opening an enema-supplies boutique." He was about to proclaim this possibility for the third time in the last half-hour—when the phone rang.

The man, in a halting voice, referred to himself as a "blind black news-seller." His kiosk, he said, was outside the

Delancey Street IRT, "on the south corner." He heard that our "program" was going off the air, which saddened him, "cause, you see, they took what I had in the Service. Korean war, you know? Man, they took my eyes away! Gave me a dog instead. Now this. You goin off the air. Terminated, right?"

"Yes," Mole said.

"I jus wanted to say I'm real sorry to hear it. Real sorry. Sellin these papers like I do, I'd listen to you in my stall, you know? It's a shame, man. It's like they strip you of every bit of what is yours. They strip your wildness from you . . ."

Oct. 27: Marya returned. Atherton, the collector, decided not to take any of her pieces. He liked, he said, her technical proficiency, but considered her vision of Orpheus "too predominantly sombre-hued." He suggested that Marya address herself to "something Indian, perhaps after the manner of Dubuffet," whom, in her way, she reminded him of. He would, he said, be interested in seeing something of this sort . . .

Marya felt dejected.

Oct. 28: . . . Tierra del Fuego . . . Tierra del Fuego . . .

Mole awoke with the southern ice of these syllables in his head, swelling his temples. A piece of him tugging at him, wanting to go back.

Mole hanging on;

The Lord Buddha, when he was nearly there, was confronted one last time by his demon Māra.

The uncanny Māra addressed him: "By what right does Gautama Siddhartha, the privileged aristocrat, seek enlightenment?"

Gautama's reply was to lower his right hand so that his fingertips touched the earth, in this wise indicating that it was not Gautama Siddhartha who was seeking the final goal, but his larger self, the same that resides within the earth and partakes of every living thing and is ancient and immortal as the universe.

This silent triumphant gesture has become known as the earth-touching *mudra*.

Thus Mole in *Padmasana* on his tar. Hanging on;

Middle-aged, she lives with her mother above the cellar of Mole's tenement. She is nameless. Four years ago, walking along Park Avenue in April, a carving knife fell from the seventeenth floor of a "landmark" building and lodged in her skull, damaging her spinal cord. Physicians agreed that any attempt to dislodge the knife would kill her . . .

Her husband divorced her and was given custody of their child. She moved in with her widowed mother. Paralyzed but lucid, seven inches of stainless steel protruding from her skull, she sleeps on her side . . .

Oct. 29: Falling away from Marya into something like sleep, Mole remembered that he had forgotten his books. Some 1500 of them lining the east side of the roof. Well shielded from the rain by the tar overhang. To begin with, it seemed necessary to reverse them, so that each spine faced the wall. This Mole proceeded to do, commencing sleepily (it was 3:20 A.M.) with Henry Adams' *Democracy*, its pages yellowed from much bad weather. Adams subsequently (wisely) retrogressed to Mariolatry, the esthetic womb of Medieval France.

Next, the bent black slave (here Mole "awoke"): Aesop, who denigrated the apocalyptic gesture. Had to.

Alchemy.

Two lives of Alexander.

The Areopagites.

Abaddon . . .

Mole's tenement began to awaken at about 6:30, yet Mole was not even half done, pausing as he was at this book or that with admiration or loathing. Studying Buber's face in the gloaming of the false dawn. Or the Haiku masters: Basho, Buson, Shiki, and Issa; the frontispiece of this volume a Hiroshige of two pilgrims blithely penetrating the unknown . . .

Or the life of Delius, who said: "I honour the man who can love life, / yet without base fear can die."

Or Mole's favorite Plato, the "Ion."

Also Tagore: "I slept and dreamt that life was joy; / I awoke and saw that life was duty; / I acted and behold: duty was joy."

Mole would have to work through the morning—yield less to temptation. Still it was necessary to know what would go to whom. My black Washington Bridge would-be suicide, for example, would get a Camus. Either *Sisyphus* or *The Rebel*. And the hunchback lawyer . . . Well, we'll see.

The sun, meanwhile, rose with rosy clubbed fingers behind Mole's left ear. Instinctively I felt my left trouser pocket. The knife was still there. Shiva still there, will be until the completion of some "yuga" in the dim planetoid future, when some wondrous other will arise from his ashes—dancing . . .

& on the dance-floor somewhere in the interior of Saturn, an American couple (Dallas stock) will tango . . . go . . .

The *mise en scène* alive in Mole's stomach. Another reason for his going.

At 8:45 Mole was joined by the Jewish cat who leaped onto the hammock and meowed for liver which Mole had for the first time in a long time forgotten. Which reminded me of Racine: I would present my copy of *Phaedra* to the hunchback lawyer.

But how will Mole distinguish one title from another if all he sees are pages? Easily. In the same way in which the Magus selects the card from a deck. If I should err it may well be salutary. Such as Li Po for Mencius—or the other way around.

Meanwhile the day went about its business: the Puerto Rican laborer feeding his pigeons, women hanging or removing their clothes, a repairman adjusting a TV aerial, a boy exercising with dumb-bells . . . No matter. Mole, unobserved, continued doing what had to be done. Once only pausing to retrace his circle—for no good reason, but that the palimpsest might take root.

At ten past four he was finally done. Stefan Zweig's *The World of Yesterday*. A gift from a friend of many years ago. A nice sentiment. An unmemorable book.

Oct. 30: Hoss Loggin was looking ornery. It might have been his recent haircut which left the back of his neck chicken skinny and quite pink. Or perhaps it was Mole whose last firing day this was.

"You done good," Hoss was saying in his carrel a few minutes before Mole was due to fire. "Pretty good anyways. A whole lot better than I expected, I don't mind tellin you."

"Thanks," Mole said. "It feels a lot better now. Than it had."

"You bet your butt. You know what it's like?"

"What's that—shooting? No."

"That ain't it. I'm talkin about firin. We got different names for things in the Service. You ought to know that being you was an officer. You know what it's like—firin?"

"No."

"Fuckin—pardon my Greek. It's the same shit. Fuckin and firin."

"How so?"

"That's right. I don't mean exakly the same. Rather what they call a symbol. Lookit, when you was a kid you thought the whole thing was stickin it in. Am I right?"

"Yeah."

"Right. Stickin it in. And likely that's what you did them first coupla pieces. Am I right? In, out, off—that's it! Hell, that ain't dick. Ony you don know it. Till later. Till you bucked around some. You follow me?"

"Yeah, Hoss."

"Shit, you ain't done *nothin*. You might as well be fuckin your fist. Finesse, buddy. That's the word. You push, you pull. You play with your piece. Which means lettin her play back with it too. You want the best gook, not the first one you see, but that pesky critter way up inside her there. When you pick *him* off you know it cause it feels good. And for her too.

But it don't come right away. You got to finesse."

"Uh-huh."

"Well, ain't it the same thing firin? You got your piece on your shoulder. You pull the friggin trigger quick like. You ain't done shit but maybe got the fat outside white of the target. Like that other joker I told you about that dropped his fetus. Now he dint even get the fat white. You got to finesse, aim it, gentle it. Respeck it too cause it jus like a woman who she ain't treated right gonna be the goddamnest lay you ever had. You follow what I'm sayin?"

"Yeah, I am."

"I kinda thought you was. So I'm gonna tell you something else."

"What's that?"

"Life, buddy. It's rightchere. Because it ain't no different from firin a piece . . ."

Nov. 1: H-E-L-P finished.

Mole there alone at dusk collecting his few belongings . . .

The phones already disconnected.

Mole can hear the wind. He walks to the wide sooty window. With effort opens it, pushing it up from the bottom. He stands in front of it, looking out at the grimy window of the old foundry (now closed) across the narrow gutter.

Mole undoes his belt, removes his trousers and under-pants. Steps outside onto the window-sill . . . then extends his left leg so that it is planted on the foundry window-ledge opposite.

He straightens, three stories above the trash cans, straddling the narrow gutter, the wind stirring his thighs, the ripe black of his loins.

Winter's closing in. He can smell the garbage . . .

ALL SOULS' DAY: . . . Pushing up out of his hole he emerged into someone's TV room, the thick carpeting like black soil—suddenly a beam of white light sliced through the

false dawn hitting him full in the face. Someone shouted:
"Get the Negro!"

Crouching instinctively he plunged back into his hole,
thorns hooking his flesh. The descent was steep, the city thicker
now. No odor. He didn't know where he was. His bare feet
struck against stones. He heard them behind him . . .

Exhausted (having lain so long), needing to rest, breathing heavily, leaning against a pay phone, he heard one behind
him shout: "Negro, get ready! We're going to cut you in
pieces."

Trembling, he pushed forward into the center where light
must be. Passing faces, none of whom saw him, he heard their
machetes behind him. It had begun to hail . . .

Somehow he made it. To the center. Yet the trees were
gone. Glass, potted-plants, light without heat. He didn't
know it. He heard the machetes . . .

He veered into a building, through the doorman, down
into the cellar. On his hands and knees he scraped at the vinyl
soil with his fingers, needing to get back . . .

They found him that way, took him.

*"From antiquity certain days were devoted to intercession
for particular groups of the dead. Having previously celebrated
the feast of all the members of the church who are believed to
be in heaven, the church on earth turns to the next day,
November 2, to commemorate the deceased members whose
souls are believed to be suffering in purgatory . . ."*

Time to dole. Mole at 3 A.M. on his head on his roof. The
Jewish cat off somewhere brawling . . . In spite of Gandhi,
who was very wrong at least once, when, during the Holo-
caust, he cautioned the Jews to lay down what few weapons
they possessed, and bravely look their assassins in the eyes as
they were being led to the ovens. *Ahimsa.*

Recollections of the *"Mahatma"* decorating the pages
of the Indian dailies—except when they are at war with

Pakistan. And the blowzy bourgeois members of Congress, clownish in their Gandhi cloth, their fingers filthy with curd, belching after water buffalo steak . . .

And the untouchables, whom Gandhi named *Harijans*: children of God, barefoot, squatting, sweeping beneath the knees of their betters—sweeping . . .

Mole was sliding. Sri Sen must have felt it, for in his most recent letter he laid lots of *Bhagavad Gita* on me: Lord Krishna counseling the worrier Arjuna to do what he had to do irrespective of result. Disinterestedly. Which for Mole meant murdering a piece of himself.

Beneath his signature, Sen had drawn the Om sign—but within it was the Dix logo which Sen had symbolically canceled with crossed black lines. Very nice. But why in black? Isn't Dix's evil precisely un-black, so much a part of what it has fed on as to be scarcely visible; denuded of real passion, devoid of dream; of a piece with the virulent manicheanism that governs us here? Not black; white. White in spite of Sen, whose very *Tantra* aspires to white.

But time to dole:

The boy could scarcely walk for the weight of his head which inclined to and partially rested on his left shoulder. Mole looked closely at his eyes which were blue but blank as ocean. No force. I reached among my books to withdraw what I hoped would be a copy of Issa. It was. Large-hearted philosopher-child. Mole handed the copy to the hydrocephalic, who accepted it listlessly, glanced briefly at the title, and cumbrously sat himself down near the hammock, but against the wall.

The blind black news-seller was preceded by his dog, a Doberman, who must have smelled the Jewish cat on Mole— he growled viciously, the blind man had difficulty restraining him. Not wasting time, I chose a folio Aesop in braille. The blind black news-seller and dog moved to the farthermost side of the roof, to the north, beyond the pigeons.

Though at one period in his life he had worked hard at it, Mole was never able to get on at all well with dogs.

Kuznetsov in dark grey pinstripes, with his large Russian-boned, not unhandsome face, was, Mole immediately saw, doubly-humped like a camel. His shoes, though badly scuffed, were obviously well-made. Mole handed him Racine: French and an elegant rendering in English on verso / recto.

Kuznetsov handed it back without even glancing at it.

"Not this."

"What then, Kuznetsov?"

"Plotinus."

"Plotinus?"

"Yes," said Kuznetsov. "Or Gogol. One of the nose things."

"Plotinus," Mole said—but came away with Pater. No. The next volume he extracted was in fact the *Enneads* (largely unreadable) of Plotinus.

"A graffito here and there in the margin. Please ignore them," Mole said.

"Don't matter," Kuznetsov said. "I'm goddamn through with what has to be clean. Can I use your hammock?"

"Yes, of course."

Have you ever seen a double-humped hunchback in pin-stripes climb into a hammock, and once there, recline? It is a sad picture.

(Sen, who was always, in his way, eloquent, outdid himself in his most recent letter to Mole. "Go," he exhorted, "love without the help of anything on earth.")

Mole's young Roman Catholic would-be had lovely legs, especially between the knee and ankle. When she extended an exceptionally small hand, Mole saw the red nail-polish and the slit wrist.

"You did it," I said.

"Yes."

"I have a good many books here. What is your pleasure?" Mole tried not to sound rueful.

"I don't know."

I removed a copy of Saint Teresa. A small edition of her selected writings.

"What's this? It's religious, right?"

"Only in the truest sense," Mole said. "Religion need not have anything to do with what you were taught in school. The word really means to join, or connect. Saint—"

"No. I don't want it."

"All right." Mole thought a minute before removing a paperback of Keats. "Beauty," he explained. "And a little sexy too."

She took it and withdrew, settling herself on a page of old newspaper by the pigeon-coop.

I had Camus' *Sisyphus* ready for the George Washington Bridge black . . .

Slender, tensely alert, quite dark, with an engaging combination of despair and energetic wit about his eyes, rather resembling Cleavon Little, the actor—he held out his hand.

"You Mole, right?"

"Right."

"All-reeet! Hey, wuzzat?"

"Camus. On suicide," Mole said.

"I'm hip. I read it."

"You did?"

"Yeah. It deep shit. An essay, right?"

"Yes. Kind of—"

"Yeah, I read it. Dug it too. What else you got?"

Mole turned his head to the smoggy heavens, then reached for DuBois. Came away with *Souls of Black Folks.* "You know this?"

The black man took the slim volume. Fingered it with long, large-jointed fingers. "Far-out fucking name. He's a blood, right?"

"Yes."

"Thought so. It ain't no long-winded shit, is it?"

"No, I wouldn't say so."

"Yeah, I'll give it a goin'-over, since my man Mole recommend it. Hey, you know I did it?"

"The George Washington Bridge? You went over?"

"Naw. I punked out. Too fucking high, man. Looka here." He pointed to a quarter-size grayish discoloration near his left temple. "Rusky roulette. You remember Johnny Ace? Soul-brother? Real soft soul sound? Bluesy shit? That's the way he done it. Rusky roulette. Big-ass 38. Took me three turns at the cylinder. Man, Mole, I couldn't wait on it no more—this peace and shit. Cause you wanna know the truth—I don believe it gonna come. Not for black folks. Big dick or no."

"I think I understand," Mole said. "Why don't you sit down now."

"Yeah. Where the brothers at?" He spotted the blind black news-seller and his dog near the north edge of the roof. Stuffing DuBois in his rear pocket, he went that way.

(Sen also said: "Humanity is less the living than the dead." He didn't mean "dead" so much as *samadhi*. Which means what? Maybe a hundred and twenty-five people since Gautama Buddha know what *samadhi* means.)

Mole's transvestite with the strawberry birthmark on his face approached wearing mufti—except for the four-inch heels on his shoes, and a hint of rouge about his cheeks. He asked for a copy of *Auntie Mame,* which I didn't have. I suggested Genet's *Our Lady of the Flowers*—though reluctantly, suspecting that he had less than a high tolerance for the lurid. Yet it was the only volume that came to mind. As I handed it to him I asked him whether he was still with Dix Chemical.

"You must be kidding. That schlock house! I'm with Pan Interiors. Are you familiar with us?"

"No, I don't think so."

"We decorate. Mostly uptown. Park Avenue. Fifth. You know Peter Max?"

"I've seen some of his work, yes."

"What do you think of it?"

"Interesting."

"It's interesting, isn't it? He's been a major influence on us."

"So you're happier there than at Dix Chemical?"

"Lord! there's no comparison. At Pan I do my thing. But 'happy'—that's something else again. Can you honestly say *you're* happy?"

"Hmm. That's a tricky question," Mole said. "I'll have to think about it."

"Is this—how do you pronounce his name?"

"Genet."

"Is this Genet"—the young man tilted his head ironically—"a fag?"

"Yes."

"Is that what you think I am?"

"It's not what I think you are principally," Mole said.

"Principally." The tone was defensive, mocking. "I'll have to think about that one."

For Moishe the peddler, Mole had not made up his mind between Nellie Sachs and Isaac Singer. The old peddler, his "shoes" contrived out of old newspapers, quietly shuffled over to Mole. He was a few minutes early. Mole touched him on the shoulder affectionately, and with his other hand offered him a copy of Singer's *Gimpel the Fool.* In translation.

The peddler accepted the book, but appeared embarrassed. Mole glanced at the newspapers on Moishe's feet.

"You read only in Yiddish?"

"Yeh," Moishe replied with mournful eyes.

Mole didn't own a single book in Yiddish. The few things he had in German didn't seem appropriate.

"Keep it anyway," Mole said, motioning to Singer as he gently led the old Jew to a place near the chimney.

Preacher McGee, the pig-killer out of Missouri, was drunk. Mole was saddened to see it. Prepared to give him R.M. Bucke's *Cosmic Consciousness*, I removed Burton's *Anatomy of Melancholy* instead. Mole decided to let it stand.

The red-faced preacher of Jesus didn't even glance at the title of the volume which he accepted with a strained politeness. When they shook hands Mole attempted to draw him closer—but couldn't.

. "Whut now?"

"Sit someplace, Preacher."

(Mole was feeling increasingly less certain. Marya must have sensed it, because though asleep, she folded a slender arm about my waist. If she were awake Mole would have read to her from Sen. It wouldn't have mattered. Marya previously had indicated something less than complete confidence in my teacher's wisdom. Though she conceded—Mole had shown her photos—that Sri Sen looked uncommonly wise.)

Mole's dwarf, though dead, was grateful for *The Sea Wolf*.

"Gusto. Lots of anger, right?"

"Lots," Mole said.

"But you know I like poems. I wrote one that time when I called you. Remember?"

"I do. 'For the Dwarf,' right?"

"Yeah, right. That's what I like best, poems. You got any? I don't mean the 'Sky—Oh, my!' stuff."

"Let's see." Mole reached for a copy of Ted Hughes's *Crow*—but came away with a selected Kipling, which would do as well.

The dwarf seemed pleased. With his Kipling open in his hands, he ambulated to the hammock. Only after he tugged at it did he see that it was occupied by the ensconced—and evidently asleep—hunchback. The dwarf must have had his mind set on the hammock, because he seemed distinctly irritated as he waddled from it to the clothesline, beneath which he lay, minuscule, on his side. Reading.

Mole himself was on his side in the corpse *Asana*. On his left side. With his back to Marya. Not snoring. Dreaming:

Black-eyed, her bat-wings vibrating, she is straddling him, her genitals hammered gold-on-gold, a reliquary: the flesh of Mole's flesh contained therein.

ELECTION DAY: My Dear Marya:

Knowing something of who I am, you must know now that it could not have been any other way. I would like you to remember Mole's love for you, for his people.

Burn what remains, my sister. On a cold clear winter morning, broadcast his ashes over the broken streets outside what used to be H-E-L-P. That I might remain with them.

Mole)

Dix? He made it. I took him. They got Mole back—fast. After which we closed our bright eyes   slept . . .

At last.

"Return, O Love in peace / into your place, the place of seed, / Not in the brain or heart."

FICTION COLLECTIVE
Books in Print:

Fiction Collective books, catalogues, and subscription information
may be obtained directly by mail from: Coda Press, Inc., 700 West
Badger Road, Suite 101, Madison, WI 53713. Bookstores: Order through
George Braziller, Inc., One Park Avenue, New York, NY 10016.